T0169437

THE HIDDEN ICON

BOOK OF ICONS
VOLUME ONE

JILLIAN KUHLMANN

DIVERSIONBOOKS

ALSO BY JILLIAN KUHLMANN

Book of Icons
The Dread Goddess

Diversion Books
A Division of Diversion Publishing Corp.
443 Park Avenue South, Suite 1008
New York, New York 10016
www.DiversionBooks.com

For more information, email info@diversionbooks.com

Second Diversion Books edition May 2017.
Print ISBN: 978-1-68230-718-2
eBook ISBN: 978-1-68230-110-4-

For Kelsi

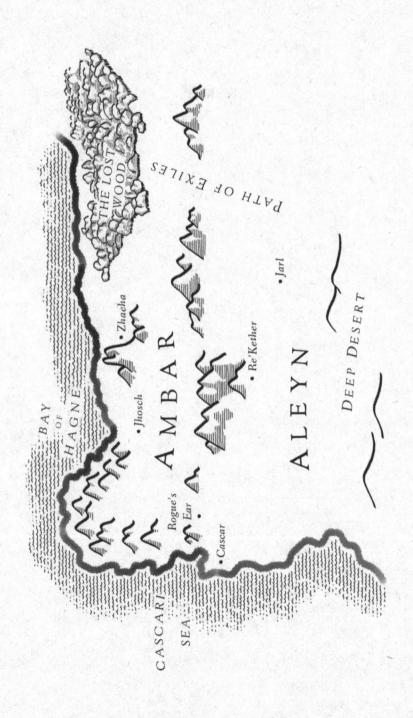

CHAPTER ONE

When I was nervous, I cycled through the seven histories of Shran in my head. And when I was very, very nervous, they tripped their way off of my tongue like tumbled stones, growing brighter with every telling.

My favorite is the story of Shran's youngest son, Salarahan, who was interred alive without his heart. The organ was held instead for many blood-won years by brother after brother as a powerful totem. Salarahan rose from his living grave after his brothers had slain each other and all but destroyed their father's kingdom, reclaiming his heart and the hearts of his people.

As Salarahan did, I preferred the keeping of stories and animals and children reared not to fight but to tend to children and animals and stories after them. It was in my blood, his gentleness, though my brother and sisters were more like bulls than the tiny, cautious bird I was named after, Eiren. It fled my mother's lips no sooner than she'd kissed my birth-slicked head, her last daughter, and the last in a long diluted line beginning with that gentle prince.

But even as I opened my mouth to begin his story, a look from my mother silenced me, her dark eyes full of meaning. They were outside the bolted door listening, our captors. And they were no more worthy of a tale from me than they were the kingdom they had snatched from us.

It was not the work of war time to prefer words to action, but I was no warrior for all we'd been at war most of my life. My father liked to say that the conflict began when my fingernails needed their first clippings, and after fifteen bloody years, I had bitten mine to the quick as we waited to surrender, prisoners in the palace that had once been our home. Ours was a story I didn't want to tell, but even as I sweated and shook with worry over our fate, already the details of the narrative collected in my mind. I looked at my mother, her heart breaking over and over again on her face and bleeding deep in the lines newly etched there, at my father and brother, my sisters, and knew they were no more ready to hear it than I was to tell it. But some stories are like hearts falling heavily into love: they cannot be stopped once they have been started.

Bolted or not, I felt sure the reliquary door would buckle in the oppressive humidity of sorrow. We were all hot and nervous and trying to hide it, my mother and father from each other, my brother from my sisters, my sisters from each other. Nobody bothered trying to hide anything from me. I stirred a thick layer of sand with my bare feet, evidence of the years of neglect since we had been forced to abandon our capital for the deep deserts.

"It hardly feels like home."

My middle sister's voice was as plain as her face. Her paints and perfumed oils were with everything else we had been forced to abandon when we were captured, her gilded bracelets exchanged for bangles of red flesh, rubbed and raw. It had been a long ride.

"That's because we kept our beasts out of doors, where they belonged."

My brother, Jurnus, glowered at the closed door. He wrinkled his nose as though he could smell the men, the livestock stink that clung to their skin and too-thick beards, some of them with hands furry as mitts on the spears they bore. My brother's swords had been taken, too, for all the steel had never tasted blood, cast into the sand like discarded toys. A drift had kicked up and over them within minutes, burying them along with his hopes of someday wielding them. Lashed already to horses, our skin crisping after so many months in hiding underground, his had not been the only dreams to die.

No one answered Jurnus' insult. My father's gaze was inscrutable, but it was my mother's attention I sought again, following her sable eyes as they swept over her children and into the corners of the empty reliquary. Where green and yellow glass had hung in the stone-worked windows there was nothing now but the relentless indifference of the sun that passed over and over, day after day, thoughtless, as one would look upon a room too often frequented. We had taken this place for granted. There were shadows in the room the light could not touch, and in them I saw the ghosts of the treasures we had once kept here, treasured memories of my girlhood. What I remembered about being a child in the palace was a latticework of shadow and light, my bare feet padding from study desk to prayer bench, practice room to bed and over again. It had been a pleasant life, for a little while.

But my mother's expression haunted me more than my memories. I studied the vault of bones beneath her skin, like mine the color of the honeyed beer she and my father enjoyed, the taste of which had always paled considerably when compared to the thrill of pilfering some from their reserve. Like my face, too, hers bore the ugly stain of resignation. Our captors might not have had the power to change our eyes and lips, but they had all the rest and gave us both the expressions of helplessness that we wore.

"Do you remember the story of the world's edge?"

My mother's voice broke my gloomy reverie. I looked at her, into eyes pitted with weariness. Hardship made many women lean and ugly but my mother had been made more beautiful, thin with struggle but shining with a will to best it.

"I remember that sacrificial maidens were thrown into its boiling abyss," I answered roughly, which wasn't, I knew, the answer she was looking for. This was the oldest of games that I had played with my mother, trading bits of story back and forth between us. She'd told me many times how she had whispered stories to me when I had been in her womb, how I had beat back my answers against her belly and breast. This game had always cheered me, but not now. I didn't want to be drawn out of my sadness. What was the point?

She wasn't giving up.

"But if they had opened their arms and eyes they would not

have sunk, but flown to another world." My mother held my gaze, and I couldn't have looked away even if I'd wanted to. She often knew just the right story to tell, but I wasn't willing to listen.

"You want me to open my arms to *them*?" I bristled, waving at the door. "They're more likely to cut them off than return the gesture."

"We can't know what they intend to do now," she insisted. If my mother had addressed any of my other siblings I might've believed her. But me?

"I can."

If the reliquary was full to bursting with our regret, a greater force of bald aggression waited just outside. It was as tangible to me as the sand in my teeth, the press of stone against my skin where my skirts had torn.

"Eiren," my father began, a cautionary note in his voice, but Jurnus raised his own in my defense.

"This isn't the time for stories. It isn't over yet; there must still be some who are loyal to us in the city, or—"

"There's no one left I'll allow to give their lives for us."

There was nothing gentle in my father's voice now. We had lost countless thousands in the years we had been at war, the bravest among them at our last stand in the desert. My eyes slid from my father's face to the stains on his pale tunic: soil, sweat, the rust-dark smudges of blood. The contingent of the guard who had been with us in exile had served him the whole of his life. I did not need to look at his face again to know that it was as hard for him to have lost these friends as it was the entirety of our kingdom. My temper cooled, but my dark thoughts could not be curbed. Were we waiting here to die, or worse?

My mother bowed her head in prayer. There were no benches here, no idols, but hers was a faith that did not demand such things. My sisters joined her, whispering, clutching at tangles in their hair. I made no utterances myself, listening only to my mother's fevered words when her low voice joined theirs. The meaning was unimportant to me. I was interested most in their steadiness, the current that ran beneath my mother's tongue as she spoke, the moisture pearling on her lips. Sweat and spittle were her offerings, her devotion a shore against which I could anchor myself. It had always been this way, but how much longer would we be allowed to worship as we wished, to grieve together? I thought of the dogs Jurnus had kept when we were children, how he had to foster the pups apart once they'd weaned from the bitch, how the sire had wandered once he'd bred. We would not remain a pack. It didn't matter what father said. If we were together, we were a heart around which the blood of our people would pool and flow.

And the monsters beyond the reliquary door knew it as well as I did.

As if on cue, the bolts creaked, the door tugged open by several of the soldiers who had waited without. My feet whipped under my skirt, shoulders shrinking. I was slight enough as it was and didn't need to try to hide, but when my father turned and stood I found myself peering around his legs like a child.

A lone guard strode into the reliquary, planting his feet in the mosaic mouth of a serpent that coiled in once-glittering blue; I noted his height, his heavy dress, the beard he no doubt cursed in the arid heat. His gloved hand clutched a spear, and there would be a whole host of others at his back if our postures proved anything more than defensive.

"Which one of you is Eiren?"

If I'd held a spear I would've snapped the shaft in surprise. My mother rose, too, blocking me completely from the guard's view. I could see him still between them, a sliver of nose, mouth, and armored muscle.

"Why do you want my daughter?"

The indomitable will conveyed in my father's stance was echoed in her tone, and the guard's face hardened. I was proud of my mother, of her strength. Even if I didn't feel like I had any of it.

"Your daughter," he began, a pause as cold as the words that followed as he counted us, even me, little more than a scrap of cloth and skin between my parents, "is one of only six people left in this gods-forsaken land who will do as you tell them. I encourage you to insist she do as *I* tell her to."

My mother and father were joined by my sisters and Jurnus, who leapt to his feet with such vigor he might have had in his hands again the weapons that had been taken from him. I swallowed, hard. The guard did not need the soldiers waiting in the corridor to cut my family down. I could no longer see his face through the living barrier of their bodies, but I wouldn't feed his thirsty spear.

I rose, ankles weak as water, and touched my mother on the shoulder, and then my father.

"I'll go," I said, whisper-stiff. Their looks were as knife-edged as their parting bodies as I passed between them, hips and elbows thin from many hungry months in the desert. My sisters' expressions were curious and Jurnus' nostrils flared in indignation when I ignored the short, sharp shake of his head. They were all wondering the same thing and I was, too: Why did he want me when he could've had one of them?

I crossed the stone serpent's belly, following the design with my eyes to keep from looking at the guard. The serpent was fat with swallowed prey, a warning to intruders that crossing the royal family would cost them their lives. But not anymore. Our resistance might cost us ours, and it appeared I would be the first to go.

Before they bolted the door again behind me I caught my mother's eyes, saw in their depths a prescient gloom. She raised a hand as though to shield tears, but I knew better. I knew her thoughts, that she believed she would never see me again. She didn't want to remember me this way, the defeated sink of my shoulders, the shallow, surrendering scrape of my sandal.

But it was too late. For all of us.

CHAPTER TWO

The guard didn't look at me as we passed through the corridor from the reliquary, didn't speak. The soldiers barred and locked the door again behind us, but I heard instead the sounds of shattering wood and the terrible scream of steel against stone. In the caves where we had been captured we had waited hours in the dark, tasked to hear the death of each man and woman who had sworn to preserve our lives at the cost of their own. I saw again the first soldier I had seen up close, her grim lips and bared teeth in the torchlight, bloodied spear brandished as one of my servants twitched his last on the cave floor between us. I'd been so afraid I could have trembled out of the ropes she'd used to bind me. I felt the ghosts of those ropes tighten around my wrist and ankles now, fighting to follow the man who stalked before me.

I feared him, too, giving him no reason to touch me, no reason to raise his voice in anger. We took a winding stair that opened on to a wide, brushed stone landing: a bright place where we had played as children. I didn't recognize the broad-leafed, flowering plants growing there now or the imported heavy wooden furniture. The somber faces carved into the arms of chairs told me all that I needed to know: you are not welcome to sit here, you do not belong.

The guard took a position at the top of the stair, like a block of stone or wood himself barring the exit. Two figures stood opposite me behind a narrow table, a woman and a man standing nearly the same height. They regarded me with a grave curiosity that chilled me more than the guard's callous attentions. I couldn't help but stare, my lips parting in the witless expression one of my sisters was like to take with a handsome man. These two were not soldiers. The man wore a half-mask roughed of some metal fitted to his features, riding the bridge of his nose and curving back to his ears. It was the mask I saw and little else, registering but barely the sandy hair, the thin, blank line of his lips. His eyes were fixed on me, and I fought the urge to squirm under the cool, measured notice I received.

The woman's expression was intelligent, stirring uncommon beauty in an otherwise common face. She drew her dark curls severely back from her face, and a sliver of glinting metal marked her brow above soft, too-kind eyes. I didn't want them to be kind. It had taken all my nerve to follow the guard this far, and now I felt even more alone, more vulnerable. I opened and closed my mouth once, twice, dumb as a grazing animal when there is nothing left to eat. Their unwavering attention could have galvanized even the slowest of beasts, however, and I found words where there had been none.

"I don't know what you hope to gain from me."

The woman's expression was shrewd, but not cruel. She looked away from me for a moment, catching the man's eyes. I sensed the stir of something between them, the unspoken understanding that can pass between two people who know each other well. After a moment, he turned and walked out onto the high walled balcony that circled much of the room. His dark clothing seemed to gather and repel light in the same instant, and I didn't like not having them both in the room where I could see them. But when he was gone she spoke, her voice husky like that of a much older woman, pleasant and deep, and I had to look at her.

"Don't be alarmed. We wanted to meet with you alone. I am *Dresha* Morainn, daughter of—"

"I know whose daughter you are."

She didn't need to wear the circlet for me to know. Morainn was their princess, soon to succeed her father, no doubt. Of course we were meeting alone. If she hoped to negotiate, she was wise to keep her distance from my brother and sisters.

"Eiren," I answered, though I knew she didn't need my name. I was stalling, unsure of what to say to her, to this kind-eyed princess of monsters. "Are you going to interrogate my brother and sisters, too?"

"No."

She moved around the table, hands skirting papers, implements for writing and measuring distance, inks in tinted glass bottles. This was a familiar place for her but not for me, not anymore. I bristled, and as she drew nearer her full frame and considerable height made me feel weak as a foundling child. Morainn had eaten well and stretched her legs in the flower of her youth, and I'd spent the last five years living like a rodent in a cave.

"I'm not going to hurt you," she continued, casting her eyes out to the veranda where the man stood, his head tilted slightly, listening. Morainn's voice was calm, cool, as though she were attempting to subdue me. "So you needn't act like I'm going to."

Had she spoken with my sisters in this fashion, they would have been at her throat already, if not with a knife than with words, at least. One of them would at least have insulted her height.

"That is difficult for me to accept," I countered, baring blistered wrists, ragged nails, bruises yellowing with age from where I had been dragged across the cavern floor.

Morainn looked away, exposing a profile that was as commanding as her height. For a moment I thought she might shout, the jut of her lip petulant, like a child. I chewed my own in a moment's hesitation. A lifetime of war had taught me little about our enemy, but I'd seen more than murders. My hands hooked against my bare arms, feeling again the bite of other hands, the soldier that had taken hold of me and bound me to a pack animal to be driven back to the capital. A flood of hatred had accompanied his touch, for I needed even less than his sneer to know the depth of his feelings. He could not have known that in his face, when he had touched me, I had seen the face of every one of my people he had killed to reach me.

Just as Morainn could not know what I saw in her, next.

"I know," she said, her voice soft and hard at the same time, features as still as the horizon bleached white in the morning. "If we'd known, you would have been spared."

Something slipped between us and it was like a colored lens passed over my eyes, some thought of hers that I could no more snatch from the air than I could a mote of dust. I resisted the moon-pull of her thoughts as I always did the thoughts of strangers, not because I was afraid of her, as I had been with the soldiers, but because I was afraid of what I might see. I held my breath. The man outside turned toward us, no more bothering with even the pretense of our privacy, his face without distinction in the strong sunlight.

There was no stopping it. I was flooded with her impression of me, a figure of myth who didn't resemble me in the least. I wasn't a person to her, but a means to something I did not understand. I was a tool.

And she feared me.

I was spared scrambling for a response by the man, who abandoned the terrace to rejoin Morainn.

"What she means is that you are not what we expected, *Han'dra* Eiren," he said, his tone empty and the formal address putting distance between us. Where Morainn had felt curious and sorrowful and *alive*, this man didn't seem to feel anything. "You've changed things."

I stood motionless, ferreting out the heart sounds of my family elsewhere in the palace to ground me. Their thoughts were clouded, anxious, distant. A storm of confusion and fear tumbled thunder in my gut, and I thought I might be sick, empty what meager breakfast they'd given us in one of the foolish potted plants they'd imported. He addressed me as though he had all of the answers and I none, like I was an ignorant child. What I had seen in Morainn retreated, and what I was left with, just myself, didn't seem like enough. I could do things no one else could, knew things I had no business knowing. But I had still been surprised to be singled out, as my brother and sisters had been, my mother and father, too. Perhaps they had been even more surprised.

"What do you want? Tell me." I managed, quiet but firm. Morainn softened, features falling as easily as the drape of her skirt, though the man seemed as unaffected as before.

"No," he said simply. There was a subtle change in his temper, like an offering of water after a hot day's fasting. I read a promise in his shaded eyes and tight mouth: he wouldn't tell me *yet*.

He was less formidable in proximity than he had been at a distance. I could not keep from studying his face as the moment lengthened to discomfort, the rough lip of the mask below his cheekbones, splitting his brow above. His hair strayed from where it had been smoothed back, softening his unnaturally muted expression. Morainn interrupted what might have become a battle of wills between the man and I, each of us silent and stubborn as stones.

"You're afraid for your family. I can offer you their protection."

Morainn had the power to promise me what she offered. I didn't need to look into her mind to know it but I did anyway, because I could. She was far easier to read than her brother, for the man was her brother, the blood bond between them as fierce as the sun's blaze on the terrace. Only my nerves had kept me from seeing it before. Whatever her motives, she meant what she said.

"Why would you do that?"

"Because I want you to return with us. Without a fight."

I gaped. I couldn't help it. Morainn didn't understand the full scope of what she asked of me, but her brother did, and it was his attention to my response I was more shaken by than the request itself. I looked at him, but couldn't hold his eyes for more than a moment. He wanted me to answer, and I didn't want to.

"I don't have a choice, do I?" I asked at last, my stomach hardening as though I had swallowed stones enough to fill it.

"No." Even as her brother spoke Morainn laid a hand upon his arm, softening his blunt answer with another question.

"Would you really choose not to go?" She was trying to tempt me with what she had promised in return, my family's freedom in exchange for mine, but in that moment I was only painfully aware of the tenderness between Morainn and her brother. It was nothing like the little rivalries and competitions between my siblings and I. If they'd been here, their opinions and actions would all have been wildly different, though they would all have felt their choices worthier than mine, too. Wasn't I the youngest, the quietest, the coward? I wasn't a leader. Blood or grain spilled, a man's head cut from his neck or a flower torn from its stem, I could and had only ever sat idle. Because only I could see what acting rashly might bring. I could see into the hearts and minds of others and it stilled my hands, and my sisters and brother, my mother and father, they couldn't understand. Nobody else could.

But Morainn and her brother wanted me. I didn't know why, but did it matter? She was right. I wouldn't say no.

"If I go with you, they'll live? A proper life. Not one in chains." The Eiren that had been content to wait out the war in exile would never have made such a demand without the support of her family, but she'd never been asked, either, how she might've changed things. She had never been alone.

I watched Morainn until I was satisfied that her nod of consent was truthful. My parents would never rule again, but they would be safe. That was enough. Though I felt again the strange impression Morainn had of me, that I was not a person but a tool, I had made my choice. Morainn raised her hand and the guard that had been my escort made room for me to pass back down the stair.

But her brother wasn't ready for me to leave. His eyes caught mine as I made to turn, arresting.

"You are more than a tool, *Han'dra* Eiren."

CHAPTER THREE

I followed the guard without a thought for where he might be taking me, my heart and all of my senses hanging still in the air before Morainn and her brother. I had barely recovered myself when I shuffled into the reliquary, eyes sweeping empty as cold lanterns over the anxious faces of my mother and father, my sisters, my brother. I couldn't rouse my voice. There wasn't room in me for answering questions when I suddenly had so many of my own.

How had he known what I was thinking? I had never met anyone who could do as I did, and my shock at Morainn's offer was eclipsed by the revelation of what he and I alone shared. Was this why they wanted me? A shudder and a thrill jangled up my spine, stopped from spreading by Jurnus' hand on my shoulder.

"Eiren, what happened?"

"What did they want?"

"Have they cut out your tongue? Tell us, Eiren!"

"They haven't," I said at last, wondering how much time I had left with my family, what I could say or do before we were parted. The thought of telling them about my bargain with the Ambarians made me wish I *had* lost my tongue.

I sat down, many beginnings wetting my lips but none of them the right one for telling something so big. My family stood around me, quiet now, anticipating terrible things in the silence that began to pound between our bodies, strong as a pulse.

"I have to go. They've asked me to go with them."

"Demanded, you mean," said Jurnus hotly, but the others agreed with him. I didn't need their nods of assent to see it. "You won't go."

"Of course she won't," said my father, more calmly than his son but with no less fervor. "We heard the guards talking; we know that a member of the royal family is here. There must be something else that they want."

They can't possibly want just you. It was a thought without malice, but it stung all the same.

"There isn't," I insisted, raising my voice to rival Jurnus' as he opened his mouth to interrupt me. "But if I go, they'll spare your lives. They didn't tell me why but I believe them and I have to go."

It sounded even more absurd coming from me than it had from Morainn, and as I looked from one sibling's face to the next, from my mother to my father again, I knew they were thinking the same thing.

"I have to go," I repeated. I could hear their protests even before they voiced them, and I could feel, too, the hurry of bodies making ready throughout the palace. I would be gone soon. "And I don't want to spend my last moments with you arguing about why I shouldn't."

It was my mother who sat down first, unclasping her hands to take both of mine into her lap. Father moved to stand behind her, laying a hand upon her shoulder.

"They didn't say why," she observed quietly. "But did they say for how long? Did they say if you'll be coming back?"

I shook my head, confidence slipping as I realized how little I had to offer my family, how little Morainn had offered me. Jurnus sat down at my other side, my sisters on the floor before me. My father was the only one who remained standing, and when he laid his hand upon my head, just for a moment combing dark hair back from my brow, I couldn't regret what I'd done. He was worried for me and confused, too, but a thread of confidence shone in the tangles of his concern. Under my father's hand I knew I'd done the right thing, I'd done the only thing. Still my eyes grew hot and damp, because we'd always been afraid that war would part us, and now the ending of it had.

"Well, since you haven't got any answers, why don't you tell us a story, Eiren," my mother continued, not unkindly. I would much rather have had a story from her, but talking gave me something to do besides crying, and she knew it.

"Tell us the story of the sandal maker's daughters, Ren." My eldest sister's voice trembled like a bell, but still somehow managed to sound composed. She would have made a fine queen someday, I thought bitterly. At least she'd live to see another day.

"Each of the sandal maker's daughters was more beautiful than the last, though he refused them everything they asked for and demanded that they sit everyday in the broad window of his shop, their shapely feet displaying his finest creations. The first daughter, who was as slender and dark as a smudge of oil smoke, kept her legs tightly crossed because she was convinced the patrons of her father's shop came to peep at her and not to buy. The second daughter covered her olive smooth face with her hair, closing her eyes beneath a curtain of curls and sleeping. She snored occasionally, and it was the duty of the youngest to prod the middle sister awake if she should become too noisome, and to warn the eldest of traffic on the road. The youngest sister sat nearest the window's edge, when she sat at all. Her name was A'isah, and she had a heart and a head larger than even an entire street of shop windows could contain."

Despite their lack of physical similarity, for myself and my sisters all had the same milk-tea complexion, the same dark hair, the sisters of this story had always reminded me of my own, and did now so keenly I almost could not continue. I persisted, however, thinking that if I didn't have the strength to bid them goodbye, I had no strength at all.

"One afternoon, a curtained litter approached the sandal maker's shop, supported on the shoulders of several men. As it drew near A'isah could see that there was room enough in the litter for two, but when the curtain was drawn aside there was only one occupant. The man inside was dressed richly, but neither his face nor his body bore the physical marks of labor that might've earned such splendor.

"'I have come to see my bride fitted for her wedding shoes, and there is no sandal maker finer than the one within to do the job,' he told A'isah. 'Will you go and get him?'

"'I cannot leave the window. Not until sunset,' A'isah explained. Her sisters, awoken by his arrival, nodding a silent chorus. They were not even to speak to customers, and many who came by this way knew better than to try to talk with the girls. But not this one.

"'Then I shall wait here until then, and we may go in together.'

"And though it was but ten steps beyond the door to their father's workshop, the young man sat himself down in the window and tempted even the eldest sister to come and sit near. All three sisters enjoyed a merry reprieve from heat and boredom in his company."

One of the first times that I could remember my mother telling this story, my next eldest sister, Lista, had asked why it was that A'isah's father did not come out straightaway at the sounds of their talking and laughter, or why the sisters did not think it strange that the young man would sit and wait with them instead of going inside. My mother had explained that this was the way of stories, and of young men and women in stories. But not, she'd stressed, of scheming princesses who hoped to stay in their parents' good graces. A shred of a smile crossed my lips at the memory.

"The young man and the three sisters spent hours in the window, teasing stories from the sisters as a thirsty man draws water from a well. Only when the sun had set did the three sisters lead him within the shop to speak with their father. He did not dally with the older man as he had with his daughters.

"'I am to marry in three days and my bride must take her first married steps in shoes of the finest make,' the young man explained. 'I am told your work is unrivaled, and judging by your daughters, I am sure it must be so.'

"His flattery was not lost on their father, nor the sisters either. Whether he spoke of their faces, figures, or shoes, it did not matter to them."

I paused, chilled by a presence I felt outside the door. This was someone who could hear and feel what passed within just as I could sense what happened without, a man who didn't need a spear at his back to intrude upon us. Morainn's brother had joined the ranks of the guard, and though I couldn't see his face, I knew that he could hear me. But I would not let him intimidate me, so I continued the story.

"A'isah fought to keep her heart from running away with her as the young man spoke of his bride. When her father asked for measurements, it was not lengths and particulars that he gave, but poetry.

'Her heel is curved as a bud on the vine; the ankle delicate as a reed. Toes like precious gems she has, tucked one against the other like pearls in the mouth of an oyster. Like A'isah's here.' The young man bent and brushed his fingers against A'isah's foot, her toes showcased in a pair of her father's fine jeweled sandals. She thought then that his bride was a very lucky girl, indeed.

"But he did not stop there, describing the arch of his bride's foot like an arc of light in water, her bones as fine as feathers, gesturing to the feet of A'isah's sisters as he spoke. Soon they were all sitting, and A'isah's father was hard at work measuring and shaping, holding soft leathers of many colors for the young man's approval.

"The work could not be done all in one night. The young man promised that they would all come to the wedding, and that he would return tomorrow to check on the sandal maker's progress.

"Because the sandal maker had no template but the feet of his own daughters to compare, he kept them all awake very late and fed them honeyed meats stuffed in pastry, bid them drink spiced wine to keep them still. When A'isah woke the next morning she was sore-headed and stiff, but when she took her place in the window, only her middle sister was there, snoring. Their eldest sister was not abed and their father explained that she had gone.

"'She's not here,' he said, the shapely heel of a tawny bridal shoe sparkling with embroidery before him. 'She has been taken to be fitted for a fine dress for the wedding. She will join their party tonight.'

"Jealous of her sister's good fortune, A'isah took her place in the window and dreamed of such luck for herself, of an afternoon on the arm of a fine and generous young man.

"That evening their father dipped again into their stores of wine, the two sisters drinking perhaps more heavily than the night before to keep from thinking of what revelries their eldest sister might be enjoying. In the morning A'isah thought her skull might split in two, but when she rose to brew tea for herself and her sister both, she was alone. Her father emerged from the shop's storeroom, holding the beginnings of a second shoe. When A'isah asked after her sister, her father explained that she had gone to have her hair dressed, and would be joining the wedding party that evening. A'isah could not sulk, thinking that if her father finished the shoes tonight, she could join her sisters and the wedding party in the morning."

I felt my mother's eyes on me and when I met them, they were shining with tears and not because she knew the ending to this story already. The pressure of the man's presence outside the door grew more heavy, almost like a stranger were laying a hand upon me. I had the strangest feeling that he, too, knew what awaited A'isah. I did not relish the way this tale turned his heart as his presence in our capital turned mine. It was not my way for such cruelty, but once begun, a story must be finished.

Perhaps for wars it was the same.

"That night A'isah consumed only a little wine, not wanting to be sick again. Her father worked until she saw the first light of morning on the work bench, at which point he let go his tools and stepped away from her. The young man had appeared behind A'isah but when she turned to see him, she saw instead the mad god Ro'khar, a monster who delighted best in the tortures and troubles that beset young women. The beast smiled the young man's smile, and in the shadows behind it she saw her sisters, leashed together like animals on the floor. They could not rise, the hems of their dresses bloodied from the wounds on their feet.

"'My bride waits for me,' Ro'khar said in a cold, terrible voice.

'And her shoes are not yet finished.' A'isah howled as his hands and her father's pushed her back into the chair and her father set the knife upon her feet. Her fine toes, from smallest to largest, were culled like berries into Ro'khar's waiting palms. When they had finished their grim work, A'isah was tossed to the floor with her sisters.

"The door to their father's shop grew wide as a greedy maw and the curtained litter passed through. Ro'khar presented the slippers on his knees, and the curtain rustled as though by a breeze. Through bleary eyes A'isah watched as the bridal shoes were lifted, suspended in air as though worn by invisible feet, and saw her own toes wiggle upon them. Ro'khar tossed A'isah's father's fee behind him before climbing into the litter, his last words cold, calculated to hurt them more, if he could.

"'Be grateful your faces were not finer, nor your breasts full.'

"They were alone then, the three sisters and their father. If they had been different girls their tale might have ended with his death, but they were not. Neither would they seek revenge, for the sisters heard well the warning in Ro'khar's last words, and knew better still the meddling of gods in the mortal world.

"A'isah pulled herself to her feet and her sisters, too. The door the litter had forced wide was now only wide enough for three daughters to pass through to the window where they worked. As it had always been. But A'isah did not take them there. One hand each upon the body of the other, they walked stronger together than they had ever have managed apart. The dust of the road that wound away from their father's shop filled their wounds and closed their hearts to the cruelty of men and gods."

My last word trailed into a breath that I held, not wanting it to hiccup into a sob. I felt the arms and hands of my family upon me like the weave of a burial shroud. What life I'd had with them was over, and it felt the same as dying. I heard the door to the reliquary open, but not the heavy footfall of booted soldiers. Morainn's brother stood there, and he would not be kept waiting.

I couldn't say goodbye. Hot tears streamed down my cheeks

and when my mother brushed them away her cool thumbs seemed years distant. I was a child again and crying over a skinned knee or the sharp teeth of a comb pulled through tangled hair.

"Eiren, Eiren," the hushed voice of my mother in my ear, a note of panic like an insect buzzing. Her hands were shackles, but I had to be free. I wouldn't give this man, or the soldiers at his back, the opportunity to pull me away.

"I have to." Quiet. So quiet that when I rose my skirts rustling seemed like a shout. "I have to."

And I was up, I was parting from them, not looking but at one trembling foot placed before the next until I was standing in the corridor beside Morainn's brother. Someone closed the door behind me. And I followed him with the soldier's spears clinking at my back and before us, too, threatening anyone who might try to stop what was happening.

But there was no one left to stop this. To stop me.

CHAPTER FOUR

"My name is Gannet."

He wasted little time, addressing me when we had only just turned the corner out of sight of the reliquary. My curiosity about him distracted me from my grief, but I didn't respond. He already knew my name, and who knew what else besides.

Undaunted, Gannet continued.

"Tell me, your stories. Are they meant to frighten, or inspire?"

I was surprised. It certainly wasn't a question I could have anticipated.

"It's the listener who decides," I answered after a moment's consideration, feeling curious and sad and confused. I didn't like not knowing how much Gannet could read from me, what he took that I did not offer.

"So they have no meaning if there is no one to listen to them?" He was trying to antagonize me, his blend of interest and indifference exactly like what he had shown before.

"There are always ready listeners," I said, though I was sure I was talking myself into a trap. "A tale doesn't exist until it's been told."

Gannet's slight breath could have been a laugh, and I wished that I could see more of his face. Even the conventional means of reading someone were barred to me with this man, with his masked eyes and brow unreadable.

"Then it's not a very good tale."

I couldn't think of anything to say to that, and he seemed so sure of himself. Irritatingly so. The nearer we drew to the grounds the more anxious I became, the reality of what I had agreed to threatening to overwhelm me. A few days ago I imagined that death would be the worst thing to befall us, but we could've hoped to be reunited beyond the veil.

But something told me the request Morainn had made of me was not a request at all, and I knew it was better to leave of my own accord than to depart my city in chains, or worse.

Canopies of bright silks were hung as though in celebration on the grounds, filtering what little light remained in the day. There were many people busy plying rations and supplies on pack animals, into carts, fortifying tented caravans against the heat. In the center of the bustle was an enormous barge whose size defied travel, but it was toward that vehicle we moved. The soldiers before us dispersed to ready themselves, but did not go far. Three remained still at my back, drawing even closer as though I might, like some wild animal, bolt in the open.

Gannet made no motion to depart as a bearded man approached, plucking in turn at the hairs on his cheeks and the tunic that stuck to his skin beneath his armor.

"Antares," Gannet murmured. "Captain of the Guard."

Skin ruddy with heat, I could smell the heavy odor of the Captain's sweat as he drew near. His linen blue eyes pierced as cleanly as any spear.

"It is a mighty escort for one woman." Antares spoke as he approached, waving a hand at the busy soldiers. His expression sharpened. "But you're more than just a woman, aren't you?"

I didn't answer. As I had with Morainn, I felt he knew something I didn't, but the images in his mind were formless and strange.

"May we board?" asked Gannet, a tightness to his words that hadn't been there a moment before. Was it what Antares had said? With anyone else I would have been able to dig a little deeper, see more than they wanted me to, but I could see no more into Gannet than I could a stone. From Antares there was only the curt confidence of a military man.

"With haste."

I followed Gannet within the barge without being beckoned

or spoken to. He seemed more than willing enough to make me aware of what it was he wanted without using words. I felt the compulsion first as though it was my own; the realization that it wasn't creeping over me like the unexpected chill that comes with passing underground. I couldn't fight it, not with the soldiers now barring the exit.

The barge, with its many curtained partitions and willowy poles driven into the light planks below our feet, seemed like another world. Hardy little plants vined above our heads, fed from pouches of water that I saw a servant draw from, as well. While I gawked at such a useless luxury she filled a cup hardly larger than a thimble, draining it in one swallow. Shielded from the sun, it might be possible to believe you were in the comfort of some gardened pavilion. But then the barge would rock from some little movement, or a whispered conversation would pass through many layers of curtains. There would be little privacy here.

Gannet nudged me, again without words and certainly without touching me, and I followed anxiously. I wasn't prepared for any more surprises today, but my curiosity was like a hunger, growing and growing, demanding to be fed. The dark plane of Gannet's shoulders angled before me, and my question tumbled out, clumsy.

"Are you the only one?"

He knew what I meant. Yesterday I couldn't have imagined anyone being able to do what I could do, but his cool temper, his surety, made me suspect that he was not alone. He was too little like me to be alone.

"Not like you have been," he replied, his expression shrouded by the mask he wore. "But the others aren't like me. Their gifts are not the same as mine."

But they had gifts. They knew things, or could do things, which meant I wouldn't seem so strange. Not as different among my enemies, as I had been among my kin.

The thought soured in me, but I wasn't given time to sulk. Gannet stopped and parted a light curtain that divided a compartment near the steady center of the barge. It was little more than a cupboard, furnished only with a bare cot and lidded basin.

"You want me to stay here," I assumed, and Gannet nodded. But he didn't leave, stepping closer when behind him came two servants bearing a wicker trunk. I stiffened. He had no smell even as near as he was. I could have lifted a finger to brush the sleeve of his shirt, but I did not think I would feel human warmth. This was madness. No matter what they had offered, I feared what was ahead of me more than what was behind.

When the servants departed, Gannet looked at me again, retreating the few steps he had drawn closer.

"You have many questions. I will have answers when you begin asking the right ones."

"Will you?" I asked, skeptical. I would have known if my brother were telling the truth, or if my mother were lying to protect me. But with him, nothing. I swept past, seating myself with as much composure as I could manage on the lip of the cot. "You will not find me so agreeable if I am not soon given cause to be. Not to you, and not to your sister."

Though I could not see his brow behind the mask, I hoped that I had surprised Gannet, that he would not underestimate me. I knew I should've waited to show that I knew something about him he hadn't shared, but I was irritable and scared. And I just didn't like him much.

"Keep your voice down." His was low and sharp, like a knife hidden under a cloak. I thought he might grab me, but I didn't flinch, and neither did he move. His eyes were on the floor. "You must never refer to *Dresha* Morainn…in that way."

"Why?"

"You can ask her."

"I'm asking you."

"Do as he says."

I started. The last had come from Morainn, appearing behind her brother like a shadow. How long had she been in the narrow corridor?

"I thought I was," I said, waving my arm to encompass the tiny, curtained chamber. I'd come, as they had wanted. Did I have to be quiet, too?

Morainn's features darkened, her thoughts complicated. Fear, regret, anger. But not with me.

"You possess one of our secrets. No doubt you'll collect more. But believe me when I say that sharing them is not worth the price you will pay for it."

She could make promises, and she could break them. My family would be safe only if I cooperated.

I turned away from the pair, face hot with feeling. I heard Morainn go, but Gannet lingered. I felt the wheels beneath the barge groan and begin to turn, and I wished there were a window so I could see what I left behind. Already in the barge the smells were unfamiliar, the murmured words accented differently than I was used.

I was not alone, but I felt it.

"Why me?" I asked softly. I knew he wouldn't answer, but I couldn't stop myself asking.

"I'm surprised you don't know."

"How can anything about me be a surprise to you?" I snorted, not caring if he felt the depth of my contempt. "I must seem so simple."

"You are not simple. You are ignorant," Gannet said, though this was no compliment, either. "And a liar, I think."

He crossed to me then, the sway of the barge seeming to still as his weight joined mine. I tensed as he drew near. Though he was not a particularly tall man, I was small even for a woman, and for me he was as formidable as a mountain. He opened his mouth as though he might say more on the subject, so deliberate he could've been raising a hand to strike me. But when he did speak, his tone had quieted.

"You should sleep."

It didn't feel like a command, but the weight of his words hit me like one. I sat down on the cot. Gannet left without saying anything else, but he didn't need to. Where I was and what was happening to me were my own doing, among the first things in my life that were. Gannet had called me a liar because I openly scorned circumstances that deep, deep down, thrilled me. I feared my captors, but I feared more the ugly independence my choice had wrought, how already it was changing me.

Sleep was laughably beyond my reach. I lay on the cot, eyes roaming the darkness. The sun had set, and I could have mistaken the sudden movement then for the shifting of one of the curtains that divided my chamber from the rest of the barge. But it was too slight even for the wind. I looked down and saw a scorpion, his body like so many links of dark chain, skittering across the coarse blanket but a finger's width from my hand. I leapt from the bunk, fell, crashed with the creature racing after me. My scream was breathless, strangled, fear mummified in my lungs as the scorpion's tail, bright as an onyx bead, whipped like a lash above his back.

And a blade swept him from his mark, leaving a gouge in the floor like the beginnings of a ritual sign.

"*Han'dra* Eiren." The captain of the guard, Antares, stood there, offering a hand in the same instant that the other pinned the scorpion to the floor with his spear. The squirms of the creature's dying were brief and soundless. "Let me help you."

But I didn't, rising shakily without his assistance and backing as far away as I could. If he was slighted, he didn't show it.

"We have seen many of these pests in the desert," Antares continued, though we shared a look that proved to me he was wondering exactly the same as I was.

How had it come to be *here*?

Antares gestured for me to move to the center of the chamber, and after a moment, I complied, my loose skirt drawn up in fists without needing to be asked. He swept the room with his eyes and his spear, stripped the cot, his limbs and armor near enough that I could smell him, the day's exertions on him, feel his tension without the need of my talents. My discomfort had as much to do with his proximity as that of the dead scorpion. But he was thorough, and I knew that he had finished when he exhaled, for he had held something in his mind as ugly and as hard as the breath in his lungs.

"There are baskets of fruit and root vegetables in a nearby compartment, dark places full of sweet things I am told these creatures like to eat," Antares lied. Someone had put the scorpion here, or it was not so unbelievable to him that someone would. I didn't know why he would try to deceive me, but I knew that he didn't want me to worry. That worried me more. "But that one was alone. You're safe."

He retreated to the chamber's entrance, pulling the curtain closed without a word, his look full of more meaning than I could process.

I would never be safe again.

CHAPTER FIVE

I couldn't chart the exact moment we traveled far enough from my home that I no longer recognized the landscape. It wasn't that sloping sand and rock had much to distinguish themselves, only that it became impossible for me to deny that what I had admired at a distance now troubled and slowed the sprawling caravan. We were stopped in the highest hours of the heat nearly every day to replace a wheel or tend to a split beam, to bury a beast or see to rations reduced for the soldiers who marched all around us. I didn't know what to think of my being fed at all, especially now, when they made the choice to keep me in comfort over their own.

Though burdened with the barges and pack animals and carts heavy with rations, we were moving with surprising speed over the desert, closer every day to Morainn's kingdom, to Ambar. Even riding hard I imagined it would take twelve days to reach home, maybe more, and I did not like to dwell on the distance, increasing with every hour.

At night it was easier to imagine myself somewhere more familiar, and the quiet gatherings by fireside were not unlike those I remembered in the caverns deep in the desert. My presence was compulsory, but I tried to ignore that fact. We stopped only for a few hours, to wash and eat and rest, but it was enough.

As it was during the day, when I wasn't confined to my chamber I was with Morainn. Why she kept me close I didn't know, not when there were armed guard enough to ensure I wasn't going anywhere. She had two maidservants, Imke and Triss, who didn't seem to do much but complain of the sand in her clothes and her food, the flies as plump as her littlest finger alighting on everything. But they were a distraction, and she couldn't have enough of those. I wanted deeply to dislike Morainn, but she was not unkind. She wasn't even terribly spoiled, though I wasn't surprised to learn after our first encounter that she couldn't, or wouldn't, take no for an answer.

"You Aleynians are very fond of your stories," she observed one evening. I didn't like the sound of our name on her lips, though I supposed my people weren't Aleynians, not anymore. "Tell me one."

My desire to comfort myself in the telling of a tale warred with not wanting to share with her, with her servants, the guards, and Gannet. Especially Gannet, who I knew already couldn't appreciate them.

"I don't think I know any that would be to your liking."

"I think you might be surprised by what I like."

"Let me entertain you, *Dresha*," Imke began when still I hesitated, shooting me a hard look for all her soft address of her mistress. She was the more martial of Morainn's servants, and I didn't need to see the wicked little knife hanging from her belt to know it. "I can do better than Aleynian poison."

"There is no harm in her stories," Gannet interrupted, looking down on Imke and away, into the darkness. He surprised me. His were the only pair of eyes that weren't on me now, a strange mix of curiosity and trepidation plain on the faces of those who thought their expressions guarded by shadow. If they wanted a story I would give them one.

"Even the cruelest story is a balm, not a poison," I said, holding Imke's gaze until she looked away. "But I will let you be the judge, for this is the cruelest story that I know.

"Shran had four sons. They were united only in their hatred of their youngest brother, Salarahan, who was small for his age and tricksome. When he wanted to hide, no amount of shouting could draw him out again. The elder brothers were lashed by their tutors for letting Salarahan come to harm through their neglect, and only when the whistle of the beating with whip or switch or palm had stopped would the littlest brother appear, whole and safe and looking quite perplexed about what had passed in his absence.

"The brothers hated him, though, not because they were beaten but because they had no mother to coddle them after their beating. It was Salarahan's doing that their mother was dead, for Jemae had given her life for his. This, above all of his crimes, they could not forgive.

"What the brothers did not know was that their mother's had not been the first womb to shelter Salarahan. The goddess Theba had lain with Shran in the guise of his wife because she had desired him, but so great had her shame been to carry the child of a mortal that Theba came to Jemae at the time of her blood and thrust into her the bundle of life that was Salarahan. Because Theba was a fearsome goddess and the fiercest, and because these were times where the rule and forecast of the world was not questioned, Jemae accepted what she had been told and said nothing so that her youngest son would not be feared as his true mother was."

My attention drifted away from the physical concerns of the moment, reveling as a good storyteller does in the details, in the pleasure of a captive audience. And they were captive. As I spoke the dread goddess' name I heard not even a breath escape my listeners.

"As their mother's death had given the elder brothers cause to hate Salarahan, so their father's drove their hands at last. Shran would not divide his kingdom, but neither could he will it to one of his sons without first having proof of their love for him. Though it is rarely fair to lay the same task before one's children, whose strengths often flourish in the shadow of another's weakness, Shran asked them each to bring him a likeness of their mother. Whoever gave him the finest would be king after him.

"While his brothers raced to do as their father asked, Salarahan hesitated. He had always suspected that his mother was not the same as his brothers. They shared every feature with their father, but there were many things, little things, that caused Salarahan to doubt. These were troubles he did not wish to lay at the feet of a dying man, however. He was determined to please his father not to have the kingdom for his own, but to ease the passing of a beloved parent."

With a polite sweep of my eyes I could look from Morainn to Gannet, wondering if they thought of their mother and father as I did now, as I always did at this part of the story. My father, a diplomat with little to resolve in exile but the careless jealousies of his daughters, would never meet with theirs.

But how much did they know their own father? Morainn had been sent into the desert to lead a bloody campaign, and Gannet could not even claim her openly as his sibling. His dark expression I took to mean he knew his father as I did, in rumor and whisper.

I felt sorry for him, and was quick to bury those feelings in the sorrow of the tale.

"The brothers met again the next morning in Shran's bed-chamber. His middle sons each presented a crude portrait, sketched from the relief that hung in their mother's untouched bedchamber. They fell to fighting over whose idea it had been first, not looking at their father. Shran only shook his head before inviting his eldest son to step forward. Behind him came a young woman clad in one of Jemae's shifts, her hair dressed in a fashion that had gone out of style many years ago. Shran's eldest son opened his arms greedily to her, and if he understood the horror of what he did, he did not show it. Shran looked from his eldest son to his youngest with tears in his eyes.

"Salarahan had fashioned a bust from the soft clay of the river where he had been told Jemae liked to go most often to wash her feet with her maids. The features of the sculpture were modest, a fair likeness ornamented with flowers taken but moments before from the terrace gardens. Salarahan's work was not to be rewarded, though, for even in the moment that Shran raised his hands to embrace his youngest son, Salarahan's true mother exerted her influence over the family one last and devastating time."

The fire had wasted without anyone to attend to it, though it didn't seem that anyone attended much to my story, either. Their eyes were looking everywhere else, and I noted that Morainn was shredding the hem of a fine shawl in her hands. I couldn't hear or feel what they were thinking. Gannet had stepped nearer to me, revealing in a glance that he was somehow responsible for whatever shielded me now. If he spared me from knowing their true feelings or barred them from me I didn't know.

Perhaps this story was not so harmless.

"Theba didn't need to appear herself to stir in them the jealousy she felt at Salarahan's work. It didn't matter to the dread goddess that she had abandoned the child. She expected his allegiance all the same. The brothers' rage was her rage, and they tackled him, shattering the bust. Salarahan did not shout or struggle but watched his father as though he knew what was about to happen. Perhaps he did. Shran's last breaths were spent in an attempt to right what was so obviously wrong in his family, but his gasps were ignored by the elder brothers. Theba drowned their minds with whispers, plots for how they might have the kingdom for themselves, and their father died.

"Still in the thrall of the dread goddess, the brothers restrained Salarahan and dragged him to the dungeons. But Theba's plan was a more sinister one even than this. It was not enough for her that Salarahan should suffer his father's loss and the loss of the kingdom. He had disappointed her, and showed himself now to be the son of the woman she had forced him upon and not her own. For Theba, all faults were mortal ones, and what half of Salarahan was mortal would suffer sorely for his ignorance.

"Salarahan was shown no more mercy than a slaughtering animal when his brothers lashed him to a rack and carved out his heart. Theba told them that the possessor of Salarahan's heart would live in health well beyond his own years so long as Salarahan was restrained, for he could neither die nor live a full life without it. His howls fell on ears that were filled already with Theba's cruel promises."

"When their work was finished, the brothers claimed to their people that Salarahan was dead. He was buried in a state befitting a king's son. His tomb was sealed, for the brothers feared mightily what Salarahan might do if freed.

"But Salarahan would not for many years yet walk again the roads of men. Other, higher roads he sought, plagued all the while by the poisonous tongue of Theba. She came to him in his tomb when he could neither defend himself nor deny her. Though he looked a man gone to his last sleep, Salarahan was tormented by the truths she revealed to him about his own nature and her part in it. Perhaps this is why he was so many generations lost to the living world while his brothers slayed each other in turn so they might possess Salarahan's heart, extend their lives and their rule."

The hour was not so late that I would not have been permitted the remainder of Salarahan's tale, but there were shouts coming from the edges of the camp and growing nearer. Gannet, who had not seated himself throughout the telling, stood alert and was joined soon by several of the guard, eyes turned all towards the approaching commotion.

I could not have been more surprised if it had been the specter of Salarahan descending on us than I was to see my brother, Jurnus, restrained by Antares and fighting still. I got to my feet. I knew as soon as I laid eyes upon him that he had meant to deliver no message and had come instead to rescue me, no doubt against my parents' wishes and his own limited good sense. His head was ringing with his thoughts, and they sounded like raucous bells to me: his desire to fight, his unexpected terror, the knowledge that more of our people waited outside the camp, idiots all.

Morainn rose and had only to narrow her eyes before he was released. Antares, however, did not stand away from him.

"What are you doing here?" Morainn bristled so it seemed her curls stood on end, and even Gannet shifted his weight from one booted foot to the other, shoulders thrust forward as though preparing to strike. In that stance he appeared taller, but Jurnus was taller still. Whether bravado or bold stupidity drove my brother's next words, I did not know.

"What is *she* doing here?" Jurnus' eyes flashed, gesturing at me. His voice was sharp, slashing against the silence as surely as his words created it. "Is she your slave? A trophy? A whore?"

Antares proved himself a man where my brother remained a boy and stayed his blade at this insult. Before he could do anything else, and before Morainn's temper commanded he do something else, I crossed quickly to Jurnus.

"You need to leave here," I hissed. Everyone could hear but I whispered all the same. "It isn't safe."

"It isn't safe for you!"

Jurnus didn't bother keeping his voice low. He was wounded by the desire to prove himself against a man such as Antares, a desire he had harbored for years and never indulged. He wanted a fight. As for the captain, he responded only to a threat. Jurnus wasn't one, but he would do his duty if pressed by my reckless brother.

With every moment now Jurnus' fevered thoughts crowded out my own, his single-minded impressions of me, his imagined glories of war. I was little more than a stone in his path. It was like being home again. And I realized with the heated hammering of my heart that I was angry, too.

"Go, Jurnus. You won't find your pride here, and you know already that I can't go with you."

Even as he opened his mouth to speak again, Morainn silenced him with a look that brought Antares' spear to his back. She assumed a posture that reduced even the tall guard captain to a mere shadow. I wasn't sure he needed his weapon, for Morainn's attention was like a knife point held against my brother's throat. I saw him before her as a boy, startled in some misdeed by one of our sisters or our mother, blanching in anticipation of his punishment, and I felt for him despite my own hurts.

"Your sister made a sacrifice for you, and you throw it in her face? Go now, or you'll leave here in pieces."

Her threat was as real as the point of Antares' spear, but there was a part in it that was outraged on *my* account, which I could not have anticipated. Jurnus only heard what he wanted to, and responded in kind.

"I won't follow your orders as blindly as my sister has."

His words stung. But I was not surprised by them. My brother was neither a patient nor a temperate man, and not a fool, either, for all he was acting like one.

Morainn drew level with him. She did not have to look up to look him in the eyes. She leaned even closer, her mouth hardly a hand span from his ear. What she said she said for Jurnus, and for me, as well. We were the only two that could hear her now.

"It is not Eiren who follows us, but we who have followed all of our lives the road to her."

I did not understand Morainn's words for all I knew she believed them utterly, and in Gannet's mind there seemed to be colors whose names I did not yet know, fruits spilling alien seeds in strange furrows. What he believed of me could not be given form, and he was quick to disguise it. There was a tremor on his lips and in his eyes, what looked like anger but was something more dangerous still.

"Enough, *Dresha*," Gannet said lightly, his restraint as obvious as the mask upon his face. He leveled his gaze on Jurnus next, as though dealing with unruly siblings in turn. Morainn seemed to recover herself in the moment it took for him to speak and turn from her, and she removed herself a pace from my brother before continuing in formal, icy tones.

"You know the way," she said with stony finality, her tone humming dangerously as she finished, as though in warning. "Hurry along, child."

I did not doubt that Morainn would kill Jurnus herself before ordering him killed by another, and what little comfort I had taken in her company would be all but diminished now. She turned her back on him, and in so doing on Gannet and Antares and I, as well. Imke and Triss were on her heels like a hem as they marched towards the barge and to bed.

Jurnus gaped, a confusion of fury and intrigue stirred in him and spilled too easily into me. I could not move or think for myself, consumed by the strength of my brother's feelings, of his spirit. Gannet put a hand on my elbow, but two fingers, even, and urged my return to the fireside. I resisted him. In the touch I felt none of what I had seen a moment ago, and Morainn's words sang in my blood a mystery. Would she spill it as easily, shared as it was with that of my brother? I did not think so.

Perhaps Antares and the others sensed that my brother had been undone, or they themselves suffered senselessness at Morainn's vigor, but they stood away from us, and Jurnus seized the moment to speak hurriedly to me while he could still. His whisper was thin as paper.

"This is not well at all, Eiren," he managed, as shaken by Morainn's fervor as I was. Gannet could hear him as easily as I, but neither man seemed eager to engage the other. "You are a hare among vipers. It is not well."

I held his eyes. Flaws or faults, I had been given a chance to see my brother again, and likely never again.

"It is the course of things, Jurn," I said softly, laying a hand on his arm. I could feel the charge of his feeling, the heat of his heart, through the thin cloth of his shirt. The blood and breath we shared would divide us now. "Go home."

Yet I had never known before and nor had Jurnus, not really. We were children of this war, and I was not surprised that he could not give it up. He did not know how to be a man, let alone a man of peace.

More time we were not given. Antares' spear and those of his command lowered on Jurnus, indicating that he had better be on his way. He squeezed my hand and I felt the weight of his, sturdy and covered in a fine veil of sand. When he let go, it was with a reluctance I had not read in his words or face, and I wanted to cry for the mysteries of my family that I would never know.

Gannet acknowledged Jurnus' departure only in removing himself to speak with Morainn, and I burned in renewed frustration with the thought that I knew what he intended to do only because he allowed me to, that he abandoned language so often for a particular suggestion of his choice. I could not speculate or assume, I was not given the privilege. I was maddened further when he returned to my side, when every angle of him convinced me that it was time for me to retire. I allowed myself to be led as a mule might, casting begrudging glances over my shoulder to the path my brother had taken out of the camp.

"It is fortunate that he interrupted your telling," Gannet observed, though I had said nothing. If he meant to goad me, I would not give in.

"And why is that?" My tone was airy, though it was difficult to convince him of my ill concern, cramped as we were on the narrow planks of the barge as we moved toward my compartment. Gannet did not answer until we were within the little chamber, the full dark dominant all but for a halo of weak light given off by a lamp that had been lit there. If my face was garish in the shadows, Gannet's was an eyeless haunt.

"Our kind do not speak so idly of Theba, *Han'dra* Eiren."

He wanted me to ask why, but I resisted. There was no privacy even in the dark, but I did not have to acknowledge him, and I sat down on my cot as though to signal he ought to leave, and I to bed.

"Salarahan is a symbol to your people, is he not?" Gannet continued, oblivious, a strange inflection in his voice when he spoke the name, as though I had heard it wrong all of my life and now knew better.

"His stories shape and change us, as do those of his father, Shran," I replied, as near to an answer as I could offer.

"Stories have power," Gannet agreed, which surprised me. With some hesitance overcome, he strode the length of my little chamber and stood beside my cot. I stood again, too, for the discomfort of having Gannet in my room was doubled by his proximity. That I should be dwarfed by him was unbearable.

He studied my face, and the direct questions I had wanted to ask, and what few I had managed to, burned up my throat like bile.

"You appear in our stories, *Han'dra* Eiren, and our futures, as well. As you have studied Salarahan, we have studied and waited for you."

As he spoke I felt as though the moon beyond the canvas and cloud above us became as a great eye and focused upon me. My breath was drawn from my lungs and pinned there, neither exiting from nor entering my lips.

"You have been alone among your people. No one in Aleyn shares your gifts, and even those like me, who do, do not manifest them in the same way you do. In every life you have been as you are, but this is the last life, for you and for everyone." His voice hummed with certainty and sadness, and I was afraid then, in the dark, next to this man who was not like any other I had met or would ever meet.

"Gannet," I began slowly, as though addressing one of my sisters when we had exhausted discord and sought understanding. I did not want him to know my fear, if he did not already. And I was frightened: by his fervor, by my ignorance, by the little, ugly thrill that had seemed to stir in me when he spoke of my gifts. "I don't know what you are talking about."

I was surprised by the patience in his voice and his face, his lips softened by the shadows the mask cast upon them.

"We are made in the guises of our makers and in rare cases, we are their full likenesses, the essence of what they are. These we call icons, and no icon leads a full and ignorant life. We are born to some purpose, and that purpose is the only reason we have been allowed to exist."

Our kind. We. I wanted to snatch the words from his mouth, an impulse so violent it seemed an alien thing in my heart. I managed speech instead, my heart crowding my throat against eloquence.

"Tell me."

"I call you *Han'dra* Eiren, but that is not your true name. You are an icon, as I am. You chose a cruel tale, but what is cruel is your ignorance. It is your tale. You are Theba."

Behind my fluttering eyelids the moon flared and broke into pieces so many they could double the sands we skirted. Though I was standing still next to Gannet, I imagined my body breaking up in the same fashion. That he should tell me with her ugliness so near to me in story, as I so recently championed the son she scorned, I could not believe it. Not of him, and not of me.

I opened my eyes.

"How do you know?"

Though Gannet had not allowed me entrance into his mind, I was for the moment laid open as though I were a set table, a living feast. He knew these words were but a fraction of the tumult I felt.

"I knew as soon as I saw you brought into the city. *Dresha* Morainn has no cause to doubt me. I recognize my own kind."

His kind. If they were like him, how could they be anything like me?

"And if I tell you that I am not Theba?" It was a question he expected, and even as I asked it I searched myself for truth. Did the reading of dreams and hearts make me a creature of vanity and destruction? By what measure was I this icon and not another, if any at all?

"It doesn't matter what you say. Believe or disbelieve, choose action or inaction, the world will change around you. You are Theba."

It was no easier to hear his proclamation a second time than it was the first. Even knowing now what Gannet had kept from me brought me no closer to understanding why, or what was expected of me. I turned away from him, but there was nowhere that I could go. I felt as though I were unraveling. I had been so sure that what I had done to protect my family was right, but Theba had no understanding of what was right or wrong. She was a monster.

Gannet seemed to sense my distress, for he removed himself a pace or two, returning to the opening of my little chamber. I was not ready to let him go, though. Not yet.

"Why did you wait to tell me?"

I could not imagine that he had needed to confirm my identity if I was to claim it. There had been something between he and Morainn on the terrace, a strangeness I had felt and had been feeling since our departure. Things would continue to be strange; this secret had changed nothing.

For a moment Gannet seemed uncertain, as though his reasons were not part of the telling.

"I wanted you to know before we reached Re'Kether," he admitted finally, catching my eyes. "You gave me more than reason enough to tell you tonight, with your story."

"What is Re'Kether?"

"An ancient place. We will pass through its heart, where the ruins have…memories. Theba walked there once."

I was chilled by his words, and by the numb look on his face as he spoke. It was too much, all of this at once, and I fought the urge to slump against my bed in exhaustion and fear. Theba had walked there once, he claimed. But what he didn't say, he thought: she would walk there again. In me.

Curiosity was easier then than the horrors that fought to overwhelm me. Though my voice was far from steady, it signaled that the last question would be mine, and his a willing answer.

"If I'm Theba, what does that make you?"

His face could betray far less than it had, it seemed, turning stony, almost inward. To what cold place did he go when he looked like that? Gannet's answer came quick and quiet, his retreat after just the same.

"That is not my secret to give, *Han'dra* Eiren."

CHAPTER SIX

It was eight days more before we reached the first ruined village. I only knew it was a village by the foundations half buried in the sand, bricked in a pattern that revealed hearth and pit stones, the cellar lain in the east to cool during the hottest hours of the day. As the road we took narrowed between the growing number of ruins, we were forced to slow down. I could walk beside the barge in the sun, and sweat and breathe freely and feel human again. But I wasn't free, not with a trio of guards near me at all times. And I wasn't human, if I chose to believe what Gannet had told me.

Even though I didn't believe him, I had begun to question every impulse, every thought, wondering if the things that I felt and wanted and willed weren't actually mine. Gannet had said that for his kind, there was no distinction between icon and deity. Eiren was Theba. Theba was me. But I couldn't accept it.

"There's nothing in your heart that isn't hers," Gannet insisted after one particularly heated argument.

"The dread goddess doesn't have a heart."

His look had been cold, unknowable.

"Then neither do you."

There was more he wasn't telling me, like who he was, and what he and his sister wanted with Theba. But like his first secret, these were guarded as closely as his masked features. I turned a grim eye on the outlying buildings that grew more numerous and nearer together until they were clearly recognizable as the little sprawl that tumbled naturally outside of a city. The soldiers whose job it was to clear a path for the barge grew anxious, as though some gloom hung over them, as well. They gathered gingerly, almost with fear, those stones that threatened our path. As I peered down what I could only imagine as alleys and wasteways, scrubbed by sand and the hard glare of the sun over many hundreds of years, I felt a darkness touch me, too. Had it spilled over from the soldiers, or as we approached the decadent center of these ruins did I simply begin to feel it, too? I did not need to know what they knew about this place. Shadows sprang from where there were no stones to cast them, and when I looked again they were gone.

At twilight Gannet descended from the barge in search of me.

"We won't be able to navigate a safe course by night," he explained, and as he spoke the barge slowed.

"We'll have to stay?" We had moved sluggish as candle fat rolling down a taper in the ruins, and though I wanted to be away, I was as drawn to the ruins as I was inexplicably repulsed by them.

Gannet's eyes were hooded in the growing dark and the thin shadows created by his mask.

"Just one night. You'll need to remain with *Dresha* Morainn. Re'Kether breeds foul dreams by night, and I won't leave you alone."

Though he had shared with me far stranger things, I sensed that Gannet spoke from his own discomfort, and that he valued solitude as highly as I did. I had the feeling, too, that he would consider a bad dream here a far greater threat to me than the scorpion had been.

I followed him aboard the barge without being beckoned, but goaded him with my words.

"Are they foul because they're true?" For all the ugliness I felt in this place, I knew there were secrets I would fare better knowing than not knowing. Gannet didn't even look at me before speaking again.

"Why are you interested in the truth now? You've denied it at every offering."

I scowled, rubbing dry hands together between sleeves that were growing tattered from being worried between my fingers. Would I dream of Theba if I slept, rending the world, her spittle a lava flow down shattering mountains, her voice like a thunderclap? That was not truth, only madness.

In the front of the barge, Morainn reclined among cushions and oil lamps, numbered more than they had been on evening visits I had made before.

"I am sure Gannet doesn't need to tell you that I hate this place," Morainn said, lips quirked almost in a smile. She had been far more candid with me of late. I wondered if perhaps Gannet had spoken with her, if there were greater secrets between brother and sister than they kept even from everyone else. I knew she knew who he believed me to be, now, though I did not see how that could be cause for friendly overtures.

When her servants offered us food and wine, I accepted my share with a polite nod, hungry from my walk. Triss was in wild spirits over the evening we were to spend in Re'Kether, though not enough that she was distracted from her duties.

"I won't shut but one eye," she insisted, piling pillows stuffed with light, breathable fibers upon Morainn's couch, too many, almost, for her to lay back without being toppled by their volume. Triss moved on to pour tea for the assembly, myself and Gannet included. I watched him carefully for some indication that Triss was overreacting, but he gave away nothing. Even if there was something truly to fear in the growing dark, I didn't think he would seek his cues from such an empty headed woman.

Imke remained silent, and I studied her, curious. Triss could not be anything but what her little rituals and services made her, but I was sure for Imke there was something more. She had a hand in every mundane chore and vain request just as Triss did, but her carriage and her little knife suggested to me that there was more to her duties than shaking out the bedding and serving meals.

"We will be gone from here in another day and you will tell stories of it for weeks and tire me brainless with them," Morainn sighed, ignoring her tea in favor of rising and pulling aside the curtains Imke had only a moment ago closed. Morainn's willfulness seemed born in part from her station, and she reminded me of my sisters at moments like this one, petulant because she could be. Still, I sensed that Morainn was not all happy with her lot, however many others might've traded her for it. She was as much a mystery as her brother.

"What do you see?" I asked, trying not to sound as desperately curious as I felt. Morainn cut her eyes to me, narrow but soft.

"I don't see anything. The moon hides her face, and offers no light tonight."

Triss brightened.

"They say the moon is always new here! There's never any light to see by."

"My father's brother captained an infiltration force that came through and back through Re'Kether twelve times in all," Imke offered in support, not caring how her words would sound to me, the infiltrated. "There was never any moonlight to guide or comfort them."

Triss did not seem to take much notice of Imke's words, but Morainn and Gannet attended to them, as did I. Morainn closed the curtain, but not completely. The shred of inky black that remained visible shivered and I shivered, too. Did something wait there for us, for me? Gannet looked at me sharply, and the look I gave him in that bold moment urged him to give me reason to stave my curiosity, or suffer it forever.

When we settled to a meal, our bodies were tense, our mouths opening more in half-formed fears than they were to talk to eat. We had hardly eaten a thing when Antares interrupted us, appearing at the curtained threshold with a curt incline of his head.

"Those who have not bedded down for the night patrol the perimeter, *Dresha*," he reported. "Even those who presume to sleep will be on their guard."

Morainn nodded, and she seemed about to invite him to sit and share our meal when our tenuous company was interrupted by a howling I could not describe. It sounded like neither man nor beast, and no sooner had we upset our rice and tea onto laps and sitting cushions Antares swept out, spear at the ready. Gannet was on his feet, as well, and I felt a startling openness in his mind, as though he were searching for something. There was fear there, but also a bold curiosity that feared nothing, not even for his own life.

And this, this frightened me.

The howl came again, sharp like the call before a murderous lunge. I backed away from the table, shaken, wary. Morainn did not cower, but looked boldly from window to window, to the doorway for the return of Antares or worse. I felt the urge to break from them, all of them, when they had so much to occupy them that was not caging this particular bird. I knew in an instant that this howling was not a call for me, but for them, to distract them so I might escape.

The soles of my feet felt as though they were moving already, twitching and burning to go. As the howl rang out again and everyone remained distracted, I took the few, quiet steps backward that remained between me and the wide, curtained window, brushed the silk aside, and leapt to the sandy road below.

Fires had guttered low without their keepers, but there was light enough to see by. I wove quickly through abandoned kindling and packs tumbled over in their owner's haste to assess the threat, rations heated and growing cold. I ran into the ruins. I didn't feel the dread and darkness I had sensed before, growing more sure with every passing moment that what I had felt had been colored by the weakness of the company I had been forced to keep. Re'Kether would shelter me where they could not.

Though I passed out of the firelight, I could not mistake the low, crumbling foundations, the shattered artifices that littered sand-strewn paths. No doubt these had once been paved, the jeweled feet of some ancient people wearing memory into stone. I could almost see their fine sandals and trailing robes tracing patterns in the sand, characters I was sure I could recognize were they not shadow and distant history. My heart hammered at the thought and for a moment I was seized with the terror of losing myself in the darkness, that the howling was nothing more than a siren song. The fear passed as quickly as it had come, replaced with a renewed desire to escape. I had been in chains, and soon here I would be free.

By touch alone I was sure I traveled nearer the city proper, and with every stroke of my hand in the air I felt for the high wall I had seen as the caravan approached. Gannet had said the wall kept as much in as it did out, but like hands cupped with water, it was not as solid as it looked.

I felt something pass across my cheek, like a stray hair, but not mine. I faltered again, breath catching in my throat. Gannet had not wanted me to be alone in my chamber, and now I stood alone in the ruins. The caravan lights were distant, and I could hear nothing, not even the howling, not any more. Had they captured the creature, or had it followed my lone scent into the ruins? I shivered and my hands brushed against the stone of the perimeter wall. What beast dared to hunt in so ancient and empty a place? What had it to feed on but spirits? I had more to fear from the folk of the caravan than here.

Taking another step forward, I opened both hands out in front of me as though I were reaching for a prayer statue. My mother's idols were nearly always depicted in this way, all but one, who offered neither salvation nor steady confession. I did not want to think of her, not now, but her hard face had been behind my eyes since Gannet had given me her name: Theba.

The howling began again, or so it seemed at first. What I heard now was more like a chorus, individual voices picked out of the dark. What could have been the wail of an infant, an old man, a grieving mother, all were woven together in a cry of centuries of dormant misery suddenly and violently roused. With each footstep the voices in the choir grew more numerous, but I could not stop myself, kept moving, feeling, reaching into the dark. Tears sprang to my eyes but across my lips stole something like an expression of glee, a celebration of their pain. It wasn't mine.

I gasped and stumbled over a broken cobble. Strange energy shot from my skin like cracks of lighting striking, again and again, the square illuminated and my body, too. There was a heat like I had drawn dangerously near a fire trapped under my thin clothes, and the smell of something burning, like hair, filled my nose. Indistinct forms were visible for an instant and no more, and nothing moved in the darkness that dropped heavy as hands clapped over my eyes. The cries were silenced and suddenly I heard movement, like many pairs of feet moving swiftly towards me. I saw no one now, but the shadows were furtive, alive.

"Eiren!"

I heard Gannet's voice and then recognized his form, outlined in my mind as though in a reverse silhouette: a lone, bright figure where all else was dark. The lightning sprang from me again, a brilliant, deadly arc that flared between us. He dropped reflexively, the wild crackle dissipating after having missed its mark.

Had I meant to kill him?

Had something within me meant to?

But his fear wasn't for himself. For the first time, I could sense his urgency and his need to find me, his worry that he might not. I felt as though I were rousing from a deep sleep, that my escape had lured me to a trap of another kind. The cries and howling had stopped, and I heard nothing but the huff of his breath and my own. I was aware of how far I had come, how dark it was. The alien lightning had originated in my heart, my bones, my blood, and it had attracted or repelled stranger things still. Unsure of him though I was, he was the only familiar thing. I scrambled to my feet in an instant, and Gannet didn't hesitate, taking my hands and racing the both of us away from that place.

CHAPTER SEVEN

Only the threat of being stranded in Re'Kether with a broken wheel or a lame beast kept the caravan from moving the instant Gannet had secured me aboard the barge. Delirious, bones chattering with fear, I couldn't focus, didn't recognize Morainn's face hovering over mine. I had moved a sandaled foot in time with each of Gannet's booted ones, but now I stalled, my senses still not wholly mine.

"What happened?" Morainn hissed, looking between Gannet and I. "Was she taken?"

"She was tempted," Gannet said, removing one of his hands from my shoulders to gesture that I have a seat. I felt as weak as I had during childhood fevers, but it was my spirit that was shaken, not my body. I sat down despite not wanting to.

"If she tries to run again I recommend we restrain her, *Dresha*."

This was from Imke, who received sharp looks from Gannet and Morainn both for saying so. Words sprang to my lips: that I would run if I wished to, that I would go home to Re'Kether...but Re'Kether was not my home.

"Triss, food and drink," Morainn ordered, the light colors of her skirts distracting as she settled beside me. My sisters had worn such things. I had, too, when we had been meant to rule. But not now. I picked at the stitches in the hem of my tunic, loose folds hanging unbelted, stray threads like the hair's light touches I had felt in the ruins. Gannet had come for me, but I had not been alone. Or had I imagined the others, briefly shining in the light that sprang from my body?

"Eiren, will you eat?" Gannet's eyes were the least guarded I had seen them, shades of the worry I had felt in him still visible in their depths. They were all sitting around me now as though it were I who held court here and not them, Gannet and Imke joining Morainn, Triss perching on a cushion only after she had brought warm tea and bread.

I lifted a cup, and it was filled for me.

"What happened?"

The answers I wanted were not the same as those Morainn sought. She wanted to know how I had come to leave the caravan and why. I wanted to know what I had met in the ruins, where the cries had come from and how I had silenced them, if indeed I had.

"There are unhappy spirits in Re'Kether, among other things." Gannet's tone was factual, as if we were discussing the weather or we were bent together over a map, plotting an obvious course. "Re'Kether is in ruin because of Theba's wrath, the dead buried without the comforts of visits from their descendants, without offerings. We shouldn't have come this way."

I laughed. Perhaps I was scared still or perhaps I had been driven mad, but Gannet's words seemed to me a weak interpretation of what had happened in the ruins. I wanted to believe that it had been my imagination, but just as I knew he was telling the truth as he saw it when he told me that I was Theba, I knew that he was just as adamant now.

"That Theba can laugh while a man is dying is the reason you are not welcome here," Imke said, her words snatching the air from my lungs. Being a little less in control of my mind made it easier to pierce hers, like fingers of torchlight in the dark. The howling we had heard had come from a man, one of the guard, and he would be dead soon, if he wasn't already. But what of the other cries? Could one man hold the sorrow of hundreds?

"I want to see him."

Triss only just caught the cup of tea I discarded as I rose, Gannet and Morainn quick to follow even if their posture told me they meant to dissuade me. They shared a look whose depths I knew, that everything that had happened since we had been forced to camp in the ruins was exactly what Gannet had hoped to avoid.

"And why shouldn't you?" Antares stood in the entrance to Morainn's chamber, sweat and ash a grim veneer on his features. He strode forward, cutting through Gannet's resistance like a sharpened stone through sand. Antares was a soldier, but not a fool, inclining his head in a gesture that encompassed Gannet and Morainn both. "You should see him, as well."

We were not a merry party that descended from the barge. Though steadier than I had been a few moments before, my footing was lost as we approached a low fire where several armed guard stood watch over a prone figure, his own spear driven into the sand out of his reach. Triss had elected to remain on the barge, but Imke had walked with us, and was first into the circle of light to see the howling man. There was a flicker of something familiar in her, and I wondered if someone among her father's party had suffered a similar fate on their passage through Re'Kether. That would not have been worthy of boasting.

What thoughts I had for Imke were dismissed in confronting the sickness of the man on the ground. A blanket was tangled in his legs, though I suspected his shivering had nothing to do with the evening's chill.

"He stopped screaming less than an hour ago," Antares explained. It was as though he were giving her some tactical update, an appraisal on how we might proceed forward from such tragedy. "I found this among his things."

Antares produced a cloth pouch, but when Morainn lifted it to peer inside, Antares lowered it gently away from her face. "Not too close. It's poison."

The word seemed to have as much power over the man as the substance, and he writhed in the sand, coiling like a snake that had gorged itself. Gannet knelt beside him and eased one of the man's hands away from his chest. I could tell he did not want to be touched, but whether it was because of his sickness or because it was Gannet, I didn't know.

"He administered it to himself," Gannet observed, a note of

grim surprise in his tone as he uncurled the man's fingers, displaying an ochre stain on his fingertips.

"It is well known that many lose their minds so near to Re'Kether," Imke said, shooting me a look which I caught and wanted desperately to crush, as though I were within the ruins again and in the thrall of something outside of myself. I had more questions instead of answers, and reason to trust my company even less. The howling man had been a distraction, but I did not know if he had meant to free or condemn me by allowing me to escape into the ruins so near the ancient city.

"What is his name?" I asked, the question one a child might ask, the gravity of death too much to consider. Before Antares could answer, the man raised his eyes to me, his hand raking from Gannet's grasp.

"The dead have many names for *you*," he managed, his voice the rasp of a broken instrument. He did not need to say her name for me to feel the shot of it through me: *Theba*. The man's head was thrown back in violent convulsions, pounding like a drum. Gannet and Morainn shot each other a look, observed with more than a little interest by Imke and Antares. I thought the man might scream again, his mouth dragging open as though a hook pulled at his lips. But he didn't. He spoke his last in the same stringy tenor.

"One war ends. Another begins."

I turned away when two of the guard bent to lift his body. I knew I couldn't watch as they took him to be buried or burned, couldn't bear to see the tracks his dragging boots would leave in the sand. But it was his words that frightened me more, not his death.

Without looking at Morainn for fear I would bowl her over with a glance, nor at Gannet for fear of what he would tell me without speaking, I returned to the barge. I was not surprised that Gannet followed, only that no one else did.

"He knew me," I observed, making an assumption that Gannet confirmed with a nod. He'd never said as much, but the look he'd shared with Morainn hadn't been one of surprise over what the man had said, only that it had been him who had said it.

"Only myself, *Dresha* Morainn, and the Captain know who you are."

"Obviously not."

I didn't have the strength to argue with him over who I *wasn't*, not now.

"The ravings of a dying madman are not my concern," Gannet said dismissively, watching me. He was lying, and that surprised me almost as much as my being able to read that he was lying. I sat down on my cot with a sigh.

"There was lightning in Re'Kether." My words fell flat, the air heavy with things we hadn't said. I didn't protest when Gannet sat down beside me, as far removed as the narrow space would allow. "That's never happened before."

We looked at each other in the dark. I was growing more adept in the little alterations of his expressions despite the mask, but his eyes were still shielded, inscrutable. I didn't need to tell him that I knew the lightning hadn't come from the sky.

"By tomorrow's end we will be far enough from Re'Kether that it will be safe to explore your talents. More will surface, and stronger, but it's too dangerous now to test them. You should try and rest," he said at last. It wasn't much of an explanation. All nerves and irritation, I rose, tangling my hands together in my skirt. How could I rest? Gannet's eyes cut to me, narrowing in study.

"You're going to argue with me," he observed. The corners of my mouth quirked without my consent, and I pressed them down again, thinking that a man had died, that I had nearly died.

"You don't have to argue back," I returned. I didn't want to say that something in me had changed towards him, but as I looked at him now I could see again his features illuminated as they had been in Re'Kether: lit by some inner fire, his or mine, or ours. The moments between when he had rescued me and we had returned to the barge came back to me, more clear even than the last few moments had been. He hadn't spoken to me as we had raced from the ruins, but dazed though I was I had sensed his warmth, his steadiness, his ferocity.

"I cannot always give you the answers you want, *Han'dra* Eiren. Some I do not know. Many are not mine to give."

I sat down beside him again. Closer, this time.

"Even your speculations are more informed than mine," I pleaded. What had happened in the ruins, and what had happened after, haunted me. I needed answers, and I needed Gannet to give them to me. "You understand the things that I can do, the things that I may do."

He looked off, eyes unfocused. I wondered if he saw something in the shadows that I could not, as Jurnus had often claimed he could when feeling particularly put out about my intuition. Monsters he had seen, most often, and here at least that would be true.

"You are untrained now, which means you will be strongest when your feelings get the better of you. Stronger still when you are in a place Theba has touched."

Gannet seemed to regret sharing this information, though I had stories enough for explanation. Theba had divided Shran's sons and so his kingdom, and it was only after many hundreds of years of war that Salarahan returned and with him, peace. It was just one of many stories of the destructive force that was the dread goddess.

I shuddered again at what I had risked in the ruins, at not knowing what had drawn me there. I wanted to escape the caravan; I wanted to be home. But the compulsion I had felt to flee had not been all mine. Something had been waiting for me there. And if I was indeed the icon of Theba, I would not be welcome any place.

I did not like the thought, either, that if these powers were hers, they had been with me all of my life.

"What happens when I'm trained?"

"You will be strong all the time."

It was my turn to look away, the two of us staring into distances much greater even than the ruins that stretched beyond the barge. The urge to go into the ruins, the lightning, had not been mine. But they had come from something inside of me. It seemed to me that the stronger I became the less control I would have, but the desire to test my own boundaries was too great a temptation.

"Will you train me?"

At this Gannet shook his head and quickly, as though to ensure that I had no delusions. Or, and I started as I read his thoughts, that he did not.

"You will be trained by many hands, least of all mine. I have other duties."

So I would be again among people I did not know and who did not know me, even in the ways that Morainn and Gannet and the others did. When I spoke next, my voice was shielded, and I extended what cover I could to my mind, as well.

"I'll be trained for a purpose. Like you were."

It was the first time I had allowed my own tongue to accept that I belonged in some way to whatever it was Gannet was, what I reluctantly accepted myself to be. It felt like I had swallowed something thick, slow to go down and slower to settle in my stomach.

Gannet nodded, but didn't speak. The heel of his hand brushed his lips, and in the dark it seemed like a pale stone matched against the muted iron of his mask. In that moment he was more artifice than man. As bullheaded as any of my siblings, I continued.

"And you can't tell me why."

Gannet rose, his heavy sleeve brushing against my bare shoulder as the cot shifted underneath of him. I was reminded again of the sensations in the ruins, the feeling of being brushed past, of people just out of reach.

"I won't go far," Gannet said, ignoring my last. "I know you value the distance you keep from us, and I will let you keep it now."

He parted the curtain and crossed into the narrow corridor. They would be rough on the animals tomorrow in their haste to be far from Re'Kether, and though I felt for the beasts, I longed that we should go even faster, even if it meant putting greater distance between me and my home. What would they think of me now, should I ever return? A man had died because of me.

If I were Theba, he had not been the first, and neither could I hope that he would be the last.

CHAPTER EIGHT

We were twenty-eight days from my home and four out from Re'Kether when I began to dream of mountains, their summits split in the smiles of long-dormant volcanoes, rivers and rambling, forested slopes. While I had stories for such things, I had never seen their like. But now I could see the white-capped mountains where the Ambarians made their homes, and they were a wonder to me every time I laid eyes upon the horizon.

In the dreams, though, I ravaged the mountains and rivers and forests. I was a devastating wind made of lightning and stone, the waves of a merciless ocean; I was a fire that tore down from the sky and laid everything to waste. When I woke I swore that I could feel the charred soil on my feet and my hands, as though I walked in the dread places I dreamed, but my body and blankets were damp only with sweat.

Gannet told me that we would travel by sea, by way of Cascar. The city-state was another conquest, and I couldn't help but think of how different my life would have been were it not for the war: I would have met these sea-dwelling folk, would have facilitated exchanges of material and culture if we had been at peace. But I couldn't remember peace. It would take us longer to travel by sea to the north, but Gannet had assured me the shorter road through the mountains was treacherous. I hadn't fought him, but after Re'Kether, there wasn't anything that could frighten me more than what I feared I harbored within.

"You are lucky to be alive."

Imke startled me, coming upon me as I sat in the shade of the barge while the animals were rested. If Morainn had sent her to spy on me, or if Imke had intentions of her own, I didn't know. I certainly didn't need an additional guard. The three I had grown used to were always nearby.

"I am," I said, curling patience under my tongue like the pit of a sweet fruit, sure that she would make some point and leave me be. Since the man had died in Re'Kether, Imke had been colder towards me, warier even than before. I assumed they had been friends, or lovers. Though I blamed myself for his death, it didn't make me feel any better to have Imke blame me, too.

My words obviously did not satisfy her, for Imke's gaze narrowed.

"Why did you go in to the ruins that night?" she hissed, her voice the tell-tale rattle of an adder. Her next took on an uncharacteristic harshness, even for her. "You can't have hoped to have escaped. Only death will give you your freedom now."

My own fears having frayed my nerves to shreds, I imagined Imke responsible for some of the ill that had befallen me, the scorpion, the night in the ruins. But Imke was sworn to Morainn's service, and she wasn't a fool. But I was, confusing dislike with an intent to harm.

Still.

"If you're going to threaten me, perhaps you could use your little knife. I am not afraid of words."

Imke's cheeks flared, though just as she seemed ready to rebuke me she cooled again. One of the soldiers walked past, and it was enough to send Imke scurrying back onto the barge. I followed once I was sure I wouldn't run into her. I might not have been afraid of Imke's words, but I was in no hurry to receive any more of them.

I was surprised to find Gannet at the entrance to my chamber, alarm rising briefly in wonder whether he were coming or going. But he'd been waiting for me. He gestured that I move within, holding aside the thin curtain, and I did so with a question on my face.

Once within, Gannet strode several paces across the room

and back, and I, wondering if perhaps some stranger malady had followed us from Re'Kether than what we had suffered while there, remained silent, watching him. Had everyone gone mad?

"Antares told me about the attempt on your life," he said in hushed tones. Given how dire circumstances had become, I had to consider a moment which attempt he meant.

"The scorpion, yes," I explained. I knew that had been a lie at the time and repeated it only because I didn't have the patience for Gannet's conversation, not now. The few sentences I had traded with Imke had exhausted my reserves.

I held my hands out as though I had better answers for him in my palms.

"I've seen him near here at night, and others. I am as well guarded as any prisoner could hope to be."

True to what I had observed of him thus far, Gannet did not rise to my attempt to bait him.

"It's not enough. It's not my place to teach you, but things have changed. We don't have the luxury of waiting."

I backed against the edge of the cot, sitting down in a slump of surprise.

"And that's all it took to change your mind?" I asked, thrilling at the thought of what secrets he might share, but surprised, too. He'd been so resolute against educating me. If danger alone was the catalyst, surely he would have taught me something before we reached Re'Kether?

"The world and my mind change every day," Gannet replied, the hint of a smile on his lips. I knew less of what to make of that than I did his change of heart.

Gannet stopped pacing. It was ridiculous, really, when one could only take three steps in any direction.

"You have no control over your thoughts, not in what you share or in what is shared with you," he explained. "I would like to help you learn some measure of control."

I didn't attempt to hide my surprise, because, as he said, he'd have known it anyway. He took a seat next to me, and I wondered at the attachment we had forged in the desert. Gannet was more like me than any of the others with whom we traveled, but there was so much that I didn't know about him, so much that I was sure I would never know. In his company more than anyone else's did I want for the comfort and closeness of my family, because I had been most intimate with him and it was such a sparse feeling I could hardly call it intimacy. He reminded me of everything I had lost, and even on occasions such as this one, how little I had gained in return.

I dragged myself out of my thoughts at his words.

"I want you to imagine that your mind is like a chain of mountains on the horizon," he said, his voice still and hard. I read his eyes, black as a new moon and just as distant. I could see that he didn't think that he would be a patient teacher, and I endeavored to do just as he asked.

"The night and day come and go and are beneath your notice, neither rain nor snow nor wind can change you. On one side of you the sea is churning and crashing, and this is the world. On the other is a deep vale where you dwell, your thoughts, your wants, the things that you fear."

I gasped as a feeling like he had his hand on the pumping organ of my heart traveled through me, nothing at all like the little readings of me I knew Gannet had done in the time we had spent together. As invasive as the feeling was, I was keenly aware of just how gentle he was being with me, and this twisted in me, turning discomfort to a pleasure I could not understand. "You don't possess the ability to keep me from your mind, not yet, anyway. But I do believe you can drive me away."

I had the strangest sensation of being in two places at once; I was sitting with Gannet on my cot, but I was also in an internal world, the one that Gannet had described. He was there with me. His presence was not threatening, but I knew that he did not belong there and I should drive him out. Strengthened by the context Gannet had given me, I imagined myself at the foot of a great mountain, but this was one of my own making: cragged and cliffed, a terrible wind stirring the sands into dunes at its base. Behind me there was an oasis with water and shelter enough for only one, and he was not welcome. I willed the wind at his back, my dream come to life, sweeping his feet out from underneath of him and hurling him like a seed on the air back over the mountain.

My eyes snapped open and met Gannet's, which flashed an emotion I could not read behind his mask before he looked away. I felt myself again, singular, my worries and wonders shapeless without his hand to guide them. I had to catch my breath, for I had been holding it, and my hands had tightened white in the cot's coverlet.

"It worked," I managed, and knew the answer to my next question before I even I asked. "Have I always been able to do this?"

"Yes," Gannet admitted, the tenor of his voice departed some from that of a teacher. "It's from that power, too, that you will learn to shield yourself all of the time, as I do."

"And until then?"

He seemed strangely discomfited by my question, raising and dropping both of his heels against the barge floor as though to firmly anchor himself.

"You will go on as you have, blazing like a safe house in a storm. I'm the only one that will know any better, for now," he answered finally, not looking up from where he had turned away. Uncertain, I knitted my hands together in my lap. From what storm would he look to an enemy for sanctuary?

"You know everything I'm thinking, then?"

"It's not that simple," he insisted, meeting my eyes again. His were blank, careful. "Your mind, our minds, are not the same as everyone else's. Most people sound to me like the chatter of animals, but you, you're like the language of moving water or wind."

My cheeks filled with color at this unexpected compliment, though I was more surprised by what he said next.

"What I sense from you is never explicit, never clear. You do have secrets from me. I heard you better," and here he paused, as though this was what he had not wanted at first to say and I had urged him to it. "I heard you better before I even met you, when you were brought out of the desert. That was how I knew who you were, not seeing you, as I said before. But hearing you."

"And what did you hear?" I asked, finding it difficult to speak around the curious lump in my throat.

"Many things. Your hopes. Stories. Remembered days with your siblings when you lived in the palace." Gannet passed a hand over his brow, as though he perspired. He didn't. I thought back to our return from exile, the stories I had told aloud to distract my parents and siblings from the hard road, the heat, and the barbarians who drove us on without a care for either.

And another, apparently, who'd spied on our despair from the comforts of our former home.

"I don't suppose you heard anything you liked. You haven't since."

My words were hard, but I didn't care. It was easier to be angry, and I was grateful for something that wasn't the strange tenderness I'd felt moments before.

Gannet's eyes were cautious slits.

"Now wouldn't be a terrible time to practice some of what I've just taught you, unless you enjoy being uncharitable."

"You're hardly the picture of charity." I was seething now, refusing to break the eye contact he had made. "So you've attempted to enlighten me. I'm still a prisoner. What use do I have for your pity?"

We stared at each other, and I took his advice, for all I wouldn't want him to know it: I walled up everything that wasn't disdain, including the hope that my temper wouldn't keep him from teaching me more. Especially that. Gannet didn't look away, though it wasn't brazen pride that filled his eyes. They were fired with something else, swallowing up much of my anger in their stillness.

"I'm not foolish enough to pity the icon of Theba."

Before I could respond, there was a light cough at the curtained entrance to my little chamber. We both looked up, away from each other. Surprised though I had been by Gannet's earlier claim to teach me, Morainn standing at the entrance to my chamber was wilder. She didn't often leave her cloistered luxury, and I had never been able to tell if this was by choice or design.

"Imke and Triss are asleep," she offered by way of explanation, as my surprise was no doubt evident on my face. Morainn looked less formidable in the half-dark. Her circlet was absent, also, revealing a weary brow. "I escaped."

Gannet rose as she entered, though there was no sense of urgency in his movements. With so few places to sit, he remained standing while Morainn elected to take his place next to me on the cot. He lit an oil lamp next, as though the three of us were old friends, gathered for an evening drink. And we weren't.

But as Gannet relaxed idle on his feet, as Morainn settled beside me as one of my sisters might, I realized we weren't entirely enemies, either. And I wasn't sure when or how that had happened.

I considered again the stories Gannet might have heard in whole or part from his distant observations of me on the road into our capital. The best of them had been my father's favorite. I took a deep breath, like one might take to fan the flames of a dying fire, and delivered myself the evening's greatest surprise.

"Gannet was just about to tell me a story," I said carefully, looking at Morainn. Her eyes widened in surprise, but I saw, too, the hint of amusement in the way her eyelids crinkled nearest her nose. "I hope you've not yet heard the tale of Charrum and the key of hearts."

"I haven't," Morainn answered, tilting her head questioningly towards her brother. Now we were each poised as listeners, though I was far more interested in how Gannet would respond than the tale. He didn't disappoint. Eyes hooded, he opened and closed his mouth once, wetting his lips, before answering.

"The one with," and he paused, sharing a muted flash of what was obviously his impression of the young rogue Charrum challenging the bandit king. It was surprisingly like what I had always imagined, though I supposed that was to be expected.

"That's the one." I couldn't help but smile, both because of what Gannet had shared, and because he hadn't refused my dare outright. It made me a little forgiving. "I can begin, if you like."

And he did, a light nod confirming for me how little experience Gannet had telling stories.

"Charrum was a seeker of treasures, and the greatest treasure of his heart was Felea, the daughter of the wealthiest merchant in his village. Her hand in marriage was promised to the man who could deliver to her father the most unique, most priceless, most coveted object in the world. The trouble was that Felea's father's wants changed with the rising and setting of the sun. He didn't know what it was he most wanted, and so it didn't matter what Felea wanted most, which was to wed Charrum and leave her father's house forever.

"In his twentieth year, Charrum rose to a challenge laid by the local bandit king for a great treasure, perhaps the very greatest of treasures, and one that he felt would please even Felea's father. To enter the bandit king's service Charrum had first to pass a test of spirit, and he made his camp that night in a circle of standing stones that were said to be haunted. Charrum laid himself down beneath the stars without a fire, shivering in the cold glare of the night as he waited for whatever was supposed to appear to appear."

I paused to give Gannet a window, watching his face carefully to see if he remembered this portion of the story. I had rehearsed it several times over in my mind before I told it aloud on that difficult journey, to steady my own nerves before trying to steady those of my family. I chose it now for both purposes, because he might know it, and because in telling it, I felt closer to them.

He didn't interject, so I continued, grateful for the rapt attentions of Morainn, reclined in the narrative as much as she was on the sparse coverings of my bed.

"As Charrum slept, three ghosts set upon him, pinning his arms and legs to the earth with their rotting limbs. The first ghost pried open his eyes, the second tugged at his ears, and the third caught hold of his tongue.

"'What is like a man but is not a man, has room enough for

one but one is sometimes too many, and is desired by men and babes alike?'

"The ghost with his hand in Charrum's mouth only let go for a split second, and the young man uttered his reply.

"'A woman,' Charrum said, his tongue released like a clapper in a bell. The ghosts vanished as quickly as they had come, and when Charrum looked about him now he saw not standing stones but many doors, each carved with a sigil. This frightened him no more than the ghosts had, and when he stood to examine them he recognized the symbols for water and blood, earth and flesh, screaming and song."

There was no question then that Gannet intended to continue, for I felt the slightest touch of his mind upon mine, as polite as a hand upon the shoulder to avoid startling someone in a room alone. Like Morainn, I turned my energies then to listening. It had been ages since I had gotten to hear a story, and a pleasure I had greatly missed. I tried not to think too much about the fact that it was Gannet who told it.

"Drawing his knife, Charrum stalked out of the circle to a nearby wood and trapped there a rodent foraging. He returned with it to the circle, crooning before the sigil for singing before turning his knife upon the creature. Only when it had cried out did he deliver death swiftly, his whispered apology to the animal abrupt and tuneless compared with his song.

"Before another sigil he spit, and another he mixed the blood of the creature with his own when he cut into his palm, dripping the mingled blood upon the door that had been a stone. For flesh he bit into his cheek, and put his hands into mud to print on the door of earth."

While not a terribly skillful storyteller, there was something about Gannet's measured voice, his quiet confidence, that seduced me. He told the tale just as I would have, but it was different because it was coming from him, colored by the things inside him. I listened, hardly breathing, as he teased new life from a story I thought I knew completely.

"When Charrum had done all of this all six of the doors opened, each seeming to lead to rooms of greater treasure than the last. He knew even as he looked upon rubies and emeralds, gold and silver, upon a banquet table sagging with dishes of his favorite foods, that the bandit king would take only the man who would take for himself what was of greatest value. And so, when faced with unimaginable riches, Charrum settled himself down again and built a fire, roasting over it the thin carcass of the animal he had killed. He did not even take from one of the rooms a jeweled chalice for water to wash down his sparse meal, but cupped his hands together in a nearby stream.

"Charrum laid down to sleep after his meal. He dreamed and in his dream the bandit king visited him with a fourth and final challenge. He was pleased with Charrum's performance, and he promised him that the treasure would be his. It was, however, in the possession of another, and if Charrum wished to claim it, he would have to steal it. Because it was often the way of challenges such as these, Charrum was not surprised to learn that the treasure belonged to Felea's father. That he should take it only to trade it back again for the hand of his bride seemed fitting."

Gannet paused, looking at me strangely. My breath had returned, but it was short, steaming on my lips. I had been going through the telling in my mind, our two versions like hands rubbed together for warmth, a pleasant friction. With that look, he asked me if I wanted to continue. And I did.

"Charrum waited until very late the next night to go to Felea's father's house. He was stealthy as the shadows themselves, slipping from garden to cold hearth to halls that were lit well in daylight but were dark as pitch on a cloudless night. Many tools he had to avoid detection: stones that would erupt in smoke if thrown, mirrors to reflect the light should he be surprised. At every door he paused and pressed a little horn against the wood, listening for occupants awake and moving.

"Charrum dispatched several guards in near silence, clapping a hand over a mouth here, a sharp strike to the neck there, but he didn't kill. The morning sun would wake them with throbbing heads, bruised egos, and nothing else.

"There were traps and snares, too, that he could not have anticipated, set cleverly in the stones of the floor and into the walls. With keen eyes and quick feet, Charrum avoided them all. Because he knew where he would keep so great a treasure if it were his, Charrum stole quietly into Felea's father's chamber, grateful for the man's bear-loud while he searched. The bandit king had not even told Charrum what to expect, only that he would know the treasure when he saw it. He picked the locks on several chests before finding the one that he wanted, empty but for a plain, ornate key. Taking it without thinking, for he did indeed know without knowing, Charrum left Felea's father's room."

"Charrum decided to risk looking in upon Felea as she slept," Gannet interrupted, not looking at me as he made for a more commanding telling. I closed my mouth against the tale that he now picked up, heart tangled up with my breath now, too.

"The lock on Felea's door was no barrier to him, though he was challenged by her curtained bed. He could make out only a little the figure that slumbered within, but he knew it was his love. With hands more deft even than those that could make a man sleep without killing him, that could bind a woman to him with only a promise, he parted the curtain."

I found that I was as still as the stones that Charrum had slept among, for in Gannet's telling I heard things that I had never told. He seemed at once to feel envy and disdain for Charrum, for Gannet was not like a man from a tale whose purpose was clear.

"Where there had been no moonlight now moonlight fell upon her cheek, her gold-lashed eyes, lips parted in dreaming. Charrum made to brush his fingers across her cheek, but in that moment shouts were heard, and Charrum knew he had been found out. In the same instant Felea woke and began to shriek, her cries fading to puzzlement when she recognized Charrum. There was no time to explain or to touch, for in an instant there were guards upon him, and Felea's father himself to confront."

Gannet caught my eyes again, but his was not the look of a teller who wishes to pass a tale, but something else. Was it regret? He knew the ending to this story, and I understood his hesitation. Morainn waited, more ignorant of what passed between us than I was. I looked away, but listened hard.

"Despite the guards that restrained him, Charrum thrust the key forward. 'I have stolen this, and you shall not have it back again unless you promise me your daughter.' Before the guards could act, he put the key in his mouth and swallowed it. At this, Felea's father fell to his knees, but it was gratitude that he expressed, not anger or shock.

"'You have taken a great burden from me, and for this I will allow you to choose. I think you will find you no longer want my daughter, if indeed you ever did.'

"For when Charrum had swallowed the key, he had relieved Felea's father of wanting for anything, because the key itself was a thing of want. It drove men and women to desire what they could not have, what could not be, what had never been and would never be. Felea's father had acquired great riches while driven by the key, but he had never been satisfied. It was he who had lain the task before Charrum, had pretended to be the bandit king. The key was a powerful object and could not be given away, only taken. And now Charrum had taken it.

"As the young thief looked upon his would-be bride, he was consumed with desire, though not for her. He would have to be a man as wealthy as her father, wealthier, before he could deserve such a woman."

Morainn's little gasp was just what a storyteller wants at such a moment, and when Gannet allowed an appreciative silence to stretch to an invitation, I laid my hands together in my lap and finished the story.

"In Felea's room that night Charrum might have joined her in her bed, but now he could only say goodbye. The key had seen into his heart, and showed him for what he was," I concluded, looking at Gannet. His eyes were on the floor.

"A selfish man," Morainn said, her judgment plain. She was hurt by the story's end. I had been, too, years ago. Now I shrugged, neither in Charrum's defense nor against him.

"A man, only. Did Felea deserve him?"

"What is deserved doesn't seem the object of this tale," Gannet spoke coolly, but there was no time for a rebuttal. Bells sounded, faint and distant as a thunderclap. I thought maybe I imagined them. My gaze narrowed in question on Gannet.

"The bells of Cascar," he announced, straightening from where he had relaxed slightly against a supporting beam. "We will be there in the morning."

Morainn seemed more stirred by his pronouncement than I was, though I thrilled at this news.

"We won't linger. A day at most," she said. The woman who had reveled in a tale was a leader again. She surprised me with a light hand on mine, her look unreadable but calm and contentedness there for me to see with other senses.

Gannet lingered a moment after his sister, and when I thought to ask him to go so I might rest, he spoke.

"There was more to your choice of that story than your confidence that I would know it," he insisted, causing my mouth to drop open slightly at this sentiment, undoing all of his earlier assurances that I was not as easy for him to see as the naked sky.

"If you're so sure," I dodged, not certain that even I could articulate my reasons. Charrum was not a sympathetic character, but there was a comfort in his flaws that I was beginning to realize our lives would not allow for.

Something darkened Gannet's expression, and it could have as easily been a true shadow as one sprung from a sour thought.

"When we are done with traveling, I will tell you of Karatan," he said quietly, his words stiff. "He sought treasures of the spirit, not of the material or the flesh, and found them better."

I shifted uncomfortably, not in the least displeased with the tale I had chosen, but feeling a faint sting at Gannet's words. I couldn't help but rebuke him.

"One must be undone by want to understand it, spiritual or otherwise." All of the strange heat I had felt while he told Charrum's tale was gone, forgotten in my irritation.

Instead of giving me the argument I wanted, Gannet said nothing, parting the curtain and leaving me. I'd never felt more alone. I deflated into myself, head and shoulders rolling forward in defeat. How was it that I had lost, or felt that I had, when he refused to engage me? There was a desire in me to make some impact on him, on everyone.

In Cascar, I would have my opportunity.

CHAPTER NINE

Not more than a wheel of the great barge rolled into Cascar before I could feel that these people weren't anything like me, or anything like Morainn's people, either. In the streets men and women mixed paints that changed color with the heat and temperament of the person upon whom they were applied, children bore torches as spindly as their forearms that gave off a green and gold light courtesy of the oils they burned, and strange fruits and spiced meats piled carts on every corner. I was hungry for things I had never known existed.

They extended nothing more than the resigned welcome of the conquered when Morainn's force entered their city, and it was Antares who negotiated our passage on two vessels. As it had happened in my home, so would a contingent of the guard remain here, as well. But I knew they weren't needed. I did not sense the murderous drive for revenge among them, nothing like the high heat of the recently subdued, like my brother. Even if they had known, there was no spirit of rebellion here.

I could not see the open water, not yet, for all I could hear it, a great humming, churning thing that nearly caused me to lose my feet for trembling. We walked to the harbor now, Gannet and a veiled Morainn as well as her handmaids, and soldiers enough to guard me and the others, too. In the faces of the Cascari I saw now a wary curiosity. Even in the children I saw it, an uncanny criticism that was not cold, but steady.

A high wall surrounded the harbor, and here was for me the first of many miracles. Visitors who traveled by sea were welcomed by a lush garden, flowering trees and plants of such broad, waxy leaves I felt sure they must be something mocked from cloth. As we walked I brushed against them, and they felt as solid as if I had met with a body in passing. I shied from touching them directly, however, as though their spell might be broken.

Look up, Han'dra Eiren.

I stiffened at the increasingly familiar and yet still so unnatural feeling of being not quite alone in my own mind. Gannet's presence, however slight, was like a shadow cast, but a shadow with such depth and dimension that it seemed a hole I might fall into.

But I did as he asked, and was rewarded for it.

I did not at first realize what it was that I was looking at. Here was an expanse that seemed at first glance to be like the sands at deep dusk, still and tinged with blue, but this color was so deep. As I looked it seemed to shift in depth and in shade. Such a vastness of water I had never before seen, not even when I had visited one of the great well caches beneath our capital. It was as boundless as the sky, and I approached the window gravely, as though before me were some altar at which I was meant to pray.

I let out a breath. I hadn't even realized I was holding it.

Some authority must have emptied the harbor, for when I tore my eyes away from the sea I didn't note anyone at work or commerce but a few folks near two stout vessels where a man waited for us. His face split in a suspicious smile.

"We expected you two days ago." His measured gaze passed between us, narrowing further. "And I see the rumors are true. Is the princess your prisoner or should I treat her as a guest?"

It did not surprise me that news of my curious departure from our capital had reached this place, but I wasn't sure how to manage this man's candor. There was a pause so potent it almost stilled the splash of the waves against the dock, and Morainn was quick to fill the space given for someone to speak.

"We won't be needing chains, if that's what you're asking."

I couldn't see her face behind the veil, but I felt her agitation.

"Of course, *dresha*," the man said, but there was nothing

deferential about his address. Perhaps these people were not as resigned as I had thought.

As he turned to ready what I now took to be the vessels that would carry us, I edged toward Gannet, hesitant.

"It's not what I expected," I said. Gannet followed my gaze and we stood together, both looking out as though this edge of the world was beyond our scope of understanding. What Gannet's life had been like, where he had traveled, and the idea that anything was as much a mystery to him as he was to me was an amusing one.

"It wasn't enough for my father," he said quietly, eyes behind the mask darting from the view to my face. The others had drifted away, leaving the pair of us relatively alone on the pier. "Nor will Aleyn be. Though I can't fault his nature, not when it brought us to you."

The way he said it sounded almost as though he meant to say brought *me* to you, which surprised and alarmed me in the same instant.

"I find it hard to believe that anyone could be so ready to welcome Theba into their home."

"I wouldn't use the word 'welcome,' exactly," Gannet mused. If he had been any other man, I would not have been surprised by the slight tugging of his lips into a smile. But with Gannet, I was sure I imagined it. "For your protection, it is best if you're known only as *Han'dra* Eiren until we reach Jhosch."

He named their capital and deflated my spirit in one breath. I looked down and could see the water churning underneath the warped planks.

"Should I worry?" I was sure that if I could see them, Gannet would have quirked a brow.

"You should exercise caution. If you must make yourself anxious to do so, then by all means, worry."

The response I felt his was owed died in my throat when Antares came striding down the dock, behind him the last of the soldiers who would be accompanying us and several Cascari servants. I couldn't brood over Gannet's words for they began to load our provisions onto the ship, and the soldiers urged us to follow. I couldn't keep my eyes on their spears when the blue unfolding before me demanded two, and both of them wide open. In the waters that lapped at the boat's sides there was a delicacy and a play of light and foam that belied the great expanse beyond the capability of my eye to focus. I thought of the stories of sirens who lived in the deep, whose eyes bounded upon the waves to the shore and bewitched those foolish enough to gaze too longingly out to sea.

"I should go with *Han'dra* Eiren."

"I won't have an icon on my vessel."

"You won't have a choice."

Gannet was arguing with the man who had greeted us, his passage to the deck where I now stood with Morainn and Triss blocked by the man's bulk. The heat wavered over his dark clothing, but Gannet would not be dissuaded. Neither, it seemed, would the man be. If I'd felt Gannet's will even moderately oppressive, it was nothing compared to the battle that was brewing before me.

"I will go with *Han'dra* Eiren, if you are concerned for her safety." Antares strode forward, dodging expertly between the two without seeming to slight either of them. An impressive feat, for an armored man. I could see in Gannet's face that this would not satisfy him, but now it was Morainn who interceded.

"We'll be but one night and one day out, Gannet. We can manage without you."

Her words were cold, but I didn't need to see her face to know that she didn't mean them to be. Morainn's station demanded such a response. Whatever Gannet had been about to say, he swallowed it, his face taking on the sour look of having eaten something spoilt. He turned his back on all of us and walked to the second craft to quarter with the greater portion of the soldiers. They were even less happy with this arrangement than he was, their discomfort a wave to rival those that pounded the far shore. I was surprised by the little anxiety I felt at the thought of not seeing him for a night and a day, and told myself it was because as irritating as he could be, he was the only one like me.

Even if I didn't like who that was.

The vessel that carried us settled low in the water, but not so low that I did not have to stretch to plunge a finger's depth into the waves we created as we sped forward, the sail blown back like a belly fat with feasting. The water was cold, and a chill raced from my hand down the whole length of my body. I wondered why Aleynians kept to the dry vapors of the desert when there was so much shore to house us. Did we not have tales of fishermen? Had they come from the Cascari?

"Would you like me to take you to your quarters now, *dresha*?"

Antares hovered at Morainn's elbow, and she waved him off, just as she had so many sand flies from her lounge on the barge.

"Not yet. I want to see Aleyn behind us before I go below."

She caught my eyes when she said it, and I was sure I imagined the apology I saw there. Her mind was a tangle, or perhaps I was too distracted to see.

There were men and women crawling over the deck, tugging at ropes and turning great gears that I could only assume contributed to the speed we gathered as we moved into deeper waters. The man who had greeted us, who must have been the captain, gestured for Morainn to come forward, and as though I were another one of her shadows, I followed Triss and Imke as they trailed in her wake. But my eyes were fixed on the water, at least until he started to speak.

"Beautiful but mighty," he shouted over the sound of the spray, grinning. His next he aimed at me. "No sandstorm can rival the fury of the sea, not even in the deepest desert."

His tone irritated me, as though he were speaking to a child shying from a strange animal.

"When you have lived to see the deepest desert, then I'll believe you," I shouted over the crash of the waves. "And only then."

Morainn laughed, clearly enjoying our banter, and she hooked her arm in mine before leading us both to lean against the strong ribs of the boat. I let her. There was an ease and a swell to this sort of travel that I could prefer easily to that of traveling by foot or barge. It was almost as though I didn't know how far or how fast I traveled, as though we were steered by powers far greater than could be contained in the captain's limited guidance. I could see the ship that carried Gannet and the soldiers at a greater and greater distance from us, but I didn't waste thoughts on Gannet. It was exhilarating to lean into the growing wind and I tossed my head back, feeling that more than my hair was buoyed on the air that rushed off of the sea. I wanted it to be fuller, faster, and I felt an answering wish, echoed from the depths beneath us.

A little gasp, part in fear and part in excitement, issued from Morainn's lips, and she grinned at me.

"It's almost as though it's alive," she trilled, her giddy expression turned on the captain now, who was looking straight at me. In his face there was the Cascari distrust, an ugly mark upon otherwise handsome features. I didn't like it, and I didn't think I liked him, either.

I inhaled deeply, spray and salt filling my lungs, and when I exhaled the boat rocked. I was surprised: did this power come from the waters or me? It didn't feel as it had in Re'Kether, that I was the tool and some distant force the master. I was in control. I knew that what I did was dangerous, if I was indeed doing anything, but when I saw the weak look on Triss' face, pale and tinged with green, there was in me such an absence of compassion that I was divided from the self that I knew. Eiren would have a care for Triss, selfish though she was, and Eiren wouldn't have gone on to do what I did then.

But I wasn't Eiren, not completely.

I breathed again as though my body housed a great well that I couldn't fill. The sky darkened and the wind spun like a song, pitching the vessel this way and that. I plunged myself into the middle of my power as one might whisk a raw egg, feeling with every sense the brewing storm, the sea. Morainn's voice came to me faintly, and when I felt the captain's rough hands in restraint on my bare shoulders, I brushed him aside as easily as one might a little stone. He was to me even smaller still, nothing but a grain of sand.

I thrilled, I thrilled, my hands like cresting waves themselves as my mind dipped beneath the water's surface. I was more than diving, I was within the sea and I would possess it. The boat rocked violently and I could feel the beams splitting beneath my feet, but all of these things were so distant from the desire that consumed me, the desire so much bigger than my body that it must expand and consume the ship, too. I knew that what happened was my doing, but I was powerless to stop it. I didn't know how. I didn't even want to.

My struggle was a tempest, flooding first my heart and then the rest of me, the ship. The cold water shocked me, and though I had raged but a moment before with alien strength I was driven now back to my body. My ankles swam in the sinking ship, needling rain and the screams of my companions pounded against my face and ears. Too swiftly the power fled me, all of my want replaced with horror as Antares and Morainn came suddenly into focus, Morainn dragging Triss to the bow and Antares firing off a crude explosive that flared and stank of minerals. The captain and Imke were lost among the tangle of struggling crew.

I deserved to be abandoned for what I had done, but Morainn was not as cruel as I was, as I had so briefly become. While Antares lashed himself to Triss, Morainn flew to me, her eyes blazing.

"Are you Eiren?" she shouted, but before I could consider what she meant, she clapped a hand around my wrist and pulled me to the vessel's highest point. The waters churned at my thighs, and the panic that rose within me was like a sickness. Would I die for what I had done? This was my fault. Whether it was with another mind or an alien purpose, it didn't matter. I was like a woman possessed, but I could not excuse my animal heart, the dread goddess that dwelled within. *Are you Eiren?* I wasn't sure.

The captain appeared before us, shouting something we couldn't hear, but before Morainn and I could reach him a wave struck against the vessel like a fist and she was parted in two. I plunged into the water before I could get a breath, thrashing. Morainn was torn away from me, or me from her.

Of course I couldn't swim; I had never been submerged in

water before. The roar of my fear filled my ears where the storm had, and my eyes began to burn in the black of the waves. I could see nothing, and though I had the sense at least to shut my lips tight against my last breath, my flailing limbs were useless. I was sinking and too selfish to want anything but to survive, even if it meant living with what parts of me had so recently proved themselves unworthy.

It grew so quiet that I was sure, so sure, that I would become light enough to rise to the surface again. I saw a glow like a lantern perceived through a colored screen, and a sense of disbelief flared in me, perhaps the last of my senses. The glow dispersed into many focused points of blue-green light, shimmering as they drew near. Only when one of them blinked did my last breath escape me in a bubble of surprise, and when the siren put her scaled hands upon my face, covering my mouth, when her children put forward their hands as though to pluck out my eyes, my hair, but lifted me instead on all sides, what I felt more than anything was fear. By my own power I could drown and die. In their hands I felt the power to drown the whole world, but the will to deny it.

I knew they would allow me to live. I didn't know if I deserved to.

CHAPTER TEN

Water and sand clotted my lungs, thicker than the blood that pumped sluggish from my heart to my hands and feet. I coughed and sputtered and rolled from the wave that retreated from the shore, dragging the hem of my dress and scrap from the hull of the ship with it. Tangled hair and seawater made it difficult to see, and I scraped both from my eyes. I thought perhaps my sight had been damaged, for though it had been midmorning when we had sailed out, the light now was twilight, purple as a bruise. Tongues of tide licked at my legs and feet, greedy, and I crawled forward until my nails dragged in dry sand. The time that I'd spent in the womb of the sea, her rollicking, wet belly, had seemed no more than a few minutes. Perhaps there was no such thing as time in the deeps where the sirens dwelled.

I was alive. Their light hands, like the touch of waves, had preserved me and carried me here. The desolation of the beach was a meager comfort, though how far I was from Cascar I didn't know. A world or years away, no amount of time or distance could be enough for me to accept what I had done and seen. When I had touched the sea and raged at the resistance I met, I had known then that what Gannet claimed was true: I was Theba. The shadowy encounter in Re'Kether had not have convinced me, but the delicate brush of the siren's finned hands had painted me with the certainty of it. I had been my whole life a girl whose heart raced at treachery in stories and shied from it in all worldly encounters, but it seemed I was becoming a woman that yearned for it. Some creature that craved it, at least, if not a woman.

The waves crashed and withdrew, and I was reminded of my

eldest sister, Anise, taking a brush to my hair, the smooth, thick sound as she combed to the roots, the crackle of static when she reached the ends. There was nothing for me but that sound and the sound of my breathing for a few moments, the one sure as the world had made it, the other a ragged interruption. I heard shouting, and figures emerged over the crest of a scrubby hill nearby. I didn't move as they quickened their pace at the sight of me but stared dumbly, their faces less real even than the siren's had been.

It was Antares and Imke, with several soldiers hustling after. Gannet wasn't with them.

"*Han'dra* Eiren!" Antares' exclamation was followed by hands upon me, pulling me to my feet, and then he simply lifted me bodily from the ground.

"She will need tending to," he said calmly, his tone in direct contrast with the wild surprise, the fear, on the faces of his men. "She doesn't appear harmed, but—"

"But where has she been?"

This from Imke. I dropped my head back against Antares' shoulder so I could see her, fix her with a stare that was remembering still what I had done and could do. She was silenced and everyone else, too, and though I sensed in others the same question. No one dared demand that I answer.

"I can walk, Antares," I said, grounding myself in the moment. I could worry for all that had happened when we returned to the city, could make my apologies, or try to. Antares lowered me to my feet, though I sensed that he knew my words were much weaker than my legs. Even as I moved them I thought of the sirens, my wet sandals slogging through the sand with none of the grace of their webbed toes.

We were not so far from Cascar, the lights rising as we rounded out of the cove where they had found me. The sounds of the city were quick to crash as loud as waves, and as we drew nearer still I noted the bodies crowded together, the angry humming of talk. Dark though it was, I felt Cascari eyes on me, sensed their thoughts churning as dangerously as the maelstrom I had conjured on the sea.

"This is my fault," Antares said softly, loud enough only so that I could hear him. He had let me walk, but hadn't left my side. "After Re'Kether, I should have known that you would not be completely in control of yourself. I should have heeded Gannet."

His words shocked me, but not as much as Morainn, breaking from a clutch of soldiers ahead of us and rushing forward. Triss trailed behind her, bedraggled hair but one marker of the wounds she had suffered on my account. Her eyes smoldered, but it was her mistress to whom I attended, for she took my hand in hers, demanding that I meet her eyes. Our steps slowed and the ring of soldiers tightened, and not because of the mob that waited before us.

"*Han'dra Eiren*, my father will be pleased that even the sea cannot claim his prize." Her first was full of command, of the bravado these people would expect. Under pretense of making sure that I was unharmed, she leaned forward, whispering. "I thought we had lost you."

It wasn't the tool, the weapon, that she had feared lost, but me. A grin wormed across my lips, surprising us both. Imke watched the exchange, her dark eyes calculating. But I didn't care. I could smile still, it seemed, for all the Cascari feared and hated me more for it. Even as I raised my head, as I warred with the part of me that wished to show them just how much they had to hate, the crowd surged, parting only to allow a single figure through.

"You cannot bring her back here." It was the captain. He had survived and for this I was grateful, for all it was clear he'd hoped for me a different fate. Did he know me? Did he suspect? He addressed Antares, purposefully avoiding Morainn's gaze. Without looking at her, I could hear in Morainn's words why the captain might fear to meet her eyes.

"The Cascari are renowned for their generosity, and their sense," she hissed. "*Han'dra* Eiren is my guest."

The captain didn't speak. In his mind I saw the ship splintered on the waves, knew that he believed me possessed by some terrible power, even if he could not name it. I didn't need to be a god for him to fear me. Any man or woman who could do the things that I had done was worthy of nothing less.

"*Dresha* Morainn, you are always welcome here, but it is too dangerous for her," he said at last, and I saw only his hands, shaking in pockets. What he meant was that I would not be safe, and neither would anyone be safe from me. His next made me want to crawl back into the waves. "Whatever she is, it is not of this world."

"She is a monster!" This from one among the crowd, and they began hollering all. What hurt more was the answering echo of feeling I felt in some of those who had returned with me from the beach. Morainn's thoughts, which would have been kindest, were eclipsed by the fervor of feeling from the Cascari. Torches were raised, but not to see better, and several stones were thrown. Morainn and I were immediately fenced on all sides by the spears of the guard.

"The horses, *Dresha* Morainn," Antares boomed over his shoulder, spear raised in both hands defensively. "They have torched the barge. We must ride now, through the Rogue's Ear."

Morainn's expression was all I needed to know that whatever the Rogue's Ear was, it wasn't a path Antares chose lightly. But even as he spoke I saw the bright flare at the city's eastern gate that could only be the barge, and with it any hope of another road. Like a drop of fat on the hearth it leapt and died, a spectacle I would under different circumstances have admired. If all we lost were goods it would be a lucky thing. The gorge of panic rose in my throat at those who were noticeably absent, namely, Gannet.

All of the power that I'd felt on the sea I couldn't conjure now, and I wasn't sure that I would if I could. If it came to defending myself against an attack, I felt far more comfortable taking up a fallen spear than rending flesh as easily as I had the hull of the ship. I knew that Antares wouldn't let it come to that, nor any of the others for Morainn's sake, at least. Their shoulders formed a wall around us. The Cascari menaced but most did not come near, their threats those of proximity only and their numbers dwindling the nearer we drew to the flaming barge.

The horses had all of the grace of their masters, corralled by a number of the guard well beyond the reach of the fire. We crossed the few Cascari who remained to oppose us, their cries silenced on blunt spear blows, bodies crumpled before my eyes like the storm-drenched sails of ship. This, too, was my fault. Guilt dragged my eyes down, heavier than any sleep.

"Can you ride, *Han'dra* Eiren?" Antares shouted, and my eyes lifted once more, cutting from the great blaze that was the barge to the circle of horses. Morainn was already astride, and many of the guard, as well. Where was Gannet? With my eyes on the fire again I nodded dumbly, which seemed to satisfy Antares.

""I'm glad to hear it, though Circa is a steady beast," Antares returned, lifting me bodily on to one of the horses. I could feel her heart beating through my legs, or maybe it was my own, pounding panic. If he didn't come, would he be left? Assumed dead or able to care for himself if not? The Cascari had struck indiscriminately, and I didn't think our hasty departure would leave them feeling any friendlier towards the Ambarians. That I might have caused trouble for my people, or what used to be my people, by what I had done here occurred to me only in the wake of my worry for what might have happened to Gannet, and shame and confusion joined the ranks of everything else I was feeling.

"Can you hold them?" Morainn's voice raised above the crash of the barge's flame-weakened beams, the screams of the Cascari mob as they descended in earnest down the streets toward us. She thought of her brother, as well, and though she asked Antares, I knew she would order him, if necessary. Antares knew this, and his resolve washed over me, cool in contrast to the belching flame.

"Not for long, *Dresha* Morainn," he said, words as brutal as the spear he hefted. "But long enough."

Even as Antares leapt from the horse he had only just mounted and many of the guard with him, their faces rising in the smoke, their ranks like columns of ash, a dark figure stumbled from the burning barge. My heart chased a sound of surprise and fear from my throat as the figure steadied, gait steady as one giving a lesson on maintaining dignity under pressure. He should've been dead, for taking such a risk. But he wasn't.

And my relief was as profound as my confusion in feeling it.

Gannet's expression was not so proud when stained with sweat and soot. His cloak was in ruins though not, curiously, any of his other garments. Neither Morainn nor I could express our relief, she for reasons explicit and me because I didn't know how to, not to him.

"What can possibly have been worth going back for?" Morainn shouted, her worry for her brother disguised by her outrage.

"Something I meant for *Han'dra* Eiren to have," he said, his words a puzzle until he pressed a warm volume into my hands, the leather supple from heat. No book was worth a life. I held it like I might a severed hand or the carcass of some beast found dead in the street before shoving it into one of the bags that hung from Circa's saddle. With this, as with so many increasing things, I would simply have to trust Gannet. My discomfort at such a thought eclipsed my relief that he was alive, and for that I was even more grateful.

Canvas destroyed and beams sagging, the barge groaned in chorus with the Cascari mob, and Antares mounted again. Now that we were all accounted for, I could see his measure of the crowd, his military training weighing his own numbers against those of the crowd. There would be another battle, another day, to reclaim Cascar. Not today.

"We haven't any more horses," Antares said, voice steady for all his eyes cut with the surety of a blade to the assembling crowd. The captain had joined them, and him I watched. The rightness that he felt was as mad of a fever as the one that had claimed me aboard his vessel. One did not need to be a god to do wrong.

My attention was drawn away from the captain by Gannet's abrupt weight, one leg thrown over either side of Circa's sturdy frame at Antares' words. Though the saddle had been fashioned for the well-muscled legs and gear of one of the guard, Gannet and I were not so slight together that it was not a tight fit. Uncomfortable for the horse, certainly, and for me.

"What has happened here will not be forgotten!" Morainn shouted, even as Antares turned the rump of his horse upon the mob and others followed suit. The chill in her voice was like something freed from underground, deep and secret. "You will be sorry."

There was no one to speak for the Cascari, or they elected not to speak. I was not sure of the depths of Morainn's threat, but I felt her anger and the edge of humiliation at being driven from the city in this way. I was glad only not to bear any of the weight of her outrage: any more and I believed I would be crushed as though in a landslide, not of stones but the burdens of my own heart and everyone else's, besides.

With the shifting of Circa's strong muscles beneath us, Gannet was pressed flush against my back, and without the reins or the horn of the saddle to steady him he was left to loop his arms around my waist. I had seen men and women ride in this fashion but their positions had always been reversed. I found I liked better having control of Circa, but not being unable to see what little of Gannet's expression the mask might've exposed. We were moving swiftly but not recklessly away from Cascar, for it was full dark now and there was nothing but scant moonlight to guide us. Antares meant to lead us to some safe distance—if there was such a thing as safety, with Theba in their midst—and break for camp. There were packs on all of the horses that I could see, and I vainly hoped that they would supply the comforts of shelter, hot food, and fire.

"We thought you had drowned, *Han'dra* Eiren," Gannet said over my shoulder, his voice mild, quiet. His mind was closed up tight against any feeling, and I did the same, or tried to.

"And I thought you dead, stabbed or burned up or worse."

"A lucky thing, that we were both wrong."

Though we rode among many, smoke and memory a hazy scent on our clothes and the manes of the horses, our conversation felt intimate. His sturdy warmth at my back, the delicate links his fingers made above my waist, these were no comforts following our escape from Cascar. My heart was pounding still. "Why did you go back for the book?"

Silence and darkness in his moment's consideration, and I considered, too, how much I should tell him, how much I could. If he had questions for me I wasn't sure that he would voice them, but my wonder was as great a blaze as we had left behind. The wildness of our departure was nothing compared to what had happened to me beneath the waves, who had delivered me from a watery death. I wanted to tell him, but I hesitated. Without sense, really, for how could a man who claimed to be the incarnation of a nameless god profess that such a thing as sirens couldn't be real?

"The book belongs to you. Or will belong to you. It used to be mine," he said mysteriously, tone resisting further clarification. I hadn't wanted to read it before, but now I wished there were light enough to flood all of its pages at once.

"*Dresha* Morainn would never have forgiven me if you had perished," I said, quieter than I needed to, given how close we were and how distant the others.

"Morainn has bigger problems than me," Gannet returned darkly. Circa's pace was uneven, hitching Gannet's hands tighter against me. "The ship you destroyed, among them. Did you know it was called *The Stout Lady*? Let us hope that captain's next vessel is stouter than the last. Perhaps he should name it after you."

My breath caught at his words, surprise and amusement both coloring my face. I turned, looking at what I could see of his face behind me. Gannet wanted to make me smile; I knew it even if nothing in the turn of his lips betrayed it. In these rare moments I could imagine the man Gannet might have been if he had been granted the privilege I had been given: the opportunity to grow up in ignorance of who I was, in love and lightheartedness, despite the war.

"I'm not sure *The Dread Goddess* makes a very good name for a ship," I managed in response, but my breath was lighter. The serpent of foul feeling that had curled in my gut unraveled a little, and I smirked. I couldn't help it. "Should we turn around, and you can suggest it to him?"

Though it would have been far less awkward for Gannet to try and look at me than it was for me to look at him, he stared straight ahead, hands held a fingers-width above my stomach now.

"How do you know I haven't already?"

If it had seemed a time to laugh I might have. For all of the mad wonders of the world I had experienced of late, Gannet making jokes with me was among the maddest of them. A lock of bright hair, usually swept tidily back from his face, fell pale over the cold brow of his mask. I returned my eyes to the road ahead. I didn't thank him for the book, nor for his attempt to cheer me. Still, my gratitude was a well that he could dip into at his choosing. I relaxed the walls he had taught me to construct. It was easier to be seen by someone who could understand than to struggle alone. I chose to share this with Gannet not because it meant I didn't have to say it out loud, but because it meant more not to.

CHAPTER ELEVEN

We were hours riding in the dark, and only having Gannet at my back kept me from falling asleep and from there onto the narrow track. Stiff failed to describe the state of my limbs, but I wasn't the only one whose discomfort was plain. Torches were lit when we were far enough from Cascar to risk it, and I watched as Morainn stretched, Triss offering a steadying hand for all she seemed as like to pass out herself. Imke had ridden elsewhere in our formation with one of the guard, a young man with features muted in the low light, but appeared near Morainn when it seemed we broke, at last, to make camp. She saw me watching the group and her eyes narrowed conspicuously, purposefully, as though she wanted me to see her disapproval. I refused to look away, the flare of anger I felt having nothing at all to do with the fires Theba stirred, and everything to do with me. I was relieved she had survived, if only because I wasn't eager to add anyone else's life to the grim tally I was keeping.

"Triss, help me," Imke muttered, looking away and loading Triss' arms and her own with Morainn's gear, or gear that had been given over for her comfort. What we had wasn't much. Gannet and I dismounted without looking at each other, as I was sure I had fallen asleep at some point and he had held me, seeing into my dreams of gill-fronded faces and feeling the press of webbed hands on his face as surely as I had felt them on mine. A shore of boiling water and waves of fire had woken me, and I hadn't been the only one to start suddenly in shock upon Circa's steady back.

Though I had felt the ebb and flow of Morainn's anger on our shamed ride from Cascar, she wasn't angry now. She was excited at the prospect of traveling by way of the Rogue's Ear, for all she had seemed at first to fear it. Her temper was the true tempest. How she could forget what had happened, or act as though she had, was a gift I would have traded my own for.

The Rogue's Ear, what is it?

Gannet hadn't gone far, but still he answered me in kind. First there were images of a narrow riding path, and darker impressions of a tunnel with more branches than I had hairs on my head. He withheld a picture of the valley at the tunnel's end, the wealth of green and running waters that no doubt awaited within. I had the distinct impression he did not want to spoil the pleasure of viewing that first myself, with my own eyes. I drew nearer to him, almost without meaning to, and this time I did speak.

"Have we rogues to fear, then?" I asked, attempting to make light of what I knew was an extremely tense situation. Gannet didn't grimace, but he might as well have done.

"Rogues will be the least of our worries."

"Ignore him," Morainn said, surprising us both in her approach and more with her dark grin. "He's only saying that because he's never had his pocket picked." Gannet would never rebuke her in front of everyone, but I could tell he wanted to and might even have risked a hard look if Triss hadn't called Morainn's attention away again. She bid her rest and eat, and crooned something about combing scent into her hair. Normally I would've thought it a stupid gesture, but we all stank of the flames that had consumed the barge.

Though the night was a mild one, I knew that colder ones were coming, and wondered at the fires that were springing to life around us. They were meant to protect us against something other than the elements, but reminded me too much of the fires we had fled. I felt now more than I ever had that the Ambarians had as much to fear from me as the Cascari had, that they were fools not to do as the Cascari had done and drive me before them with fire and spear. But they sheltered me, their treasured prisoner, despite the fact that each time I had lost control, my concern for those around me had vanished. Morainn had been on that ship with me, and I wouldn't have cared if she drowned until it was too late.

The greater threat for me was that I cared if she drowned at all. Six weeks ago I would have been glad of her death if it meant my freedom. Now, I had the distinct impression she was as much a prisoner as I was, for all the shape of her chains were different.

Gannet's gentle touch on my mind interrupted my thoughts, expressing a desire to speak with me. The little intimacy I had with him was another strange and guilty comfort, though I didn't know whether his actions were courtesy or protocol. I supposed that I would know when we reached Ambar and there were others, though the idea of being so vulnerable to so many was not one I was willing too much to imagine.

"There's still time to teach you," he announced softly, answering my unspoken fears. Perhaps I was not growing as disciplined as he claimed. I didn't answer, but there wasn't any lesson of his that I would refuse. I knew that soon enough there wouldn't be time.

"Perhaps you could teach me something practical?"

My tone was light as I unpacked a bedroll from Circa's saddle, testing its thickness against the chill. Though several fires were burning strong already, I wasn't sure I would be welcomed to sleep next to any of them. It was my hope that the soldiers who would no doubt be set to guard me while I slept would build a fire of their own.

"Like breathing underwater?"

He knew, and my surprise brought an image of one of the sirens unbidden to the surface of my mind. Gannet's expression changed as surely as if he had experienced my near-drowning himself, and he closed the little distance between us so that when he spoke next, it was as though he were making conversation with the pack he began urgently to remove from Circa's saddle.

"Did you tell anyone?"

His soft words blended perfectly with the smooth sound of leather strap sliding over saddle, and I shook my head, quickly attempting to appear as occupied as he. We faced Circa together, arms and shoulders brushing as we methodically removed saddle, bridle, and the single, achingly light pack.

"When would I have had time to do that? We were just chased out of Cascar." I paused, hoping my eagerness wasn't as plain as it felt to me. "Did you know about them?"

"Some stories are only stories, *Han'dra* Eiren," he said abruptly, as dull as though he remarked upon the sheen of Circa's coat. I could feel the turbulence in his touch and his mind, and while I had expected an unfavorable reaction from him when he learned of my rescue, this wasn't what I'd expected.

"Then you'd rather I were dead?"

"We can't talk about this right now. Tonight. Stay quiet and stay with Morainn."

He deposited a satchel of necessities into my arms, a reserve of rations and water following. It seemed he'd recovered more than the book from the burning barge. I couldn't carry these and all the rest without concentrating, and my anger dissolved into embarrassment as I moved awkwardly toward the fire. I wasn't surprised to find Morainn enthroned already on not one but several bedrolls, piled on top of each other.

"Triss will never forgive you for all of the clothes that have burned up. But she's taken to the foolish Cascari and is afraid of you, so she may prattle less when you're around. I must keep you close to lessen my own suffering," Morainn said plainly, teasing Triss, but more than a little bit serious. I wasn't sure if I was meant to laugh or not, but true to Morainn's words, Triss remained quiet, shooting me furtive looks. If Morainn and Gannet hoped to keep Theba a secret, they would do better to sedate me until we reached Ambar.

As though we had reached some agreement hours before on the shore or cast our hands together in blood, Morainn patted a square of bedroll beside her. I knew I could not refuse her, and I found I didn't want to.

"Then we've lost everything?" I asked quietly, eyeing the guard settling down on only hard earth to sleep, the few packs that I hoped would contain rations enough to see us through to Ambar. Why did I care about the backs and bellies of murderers? But I did, if only to counter the terrible feelings Theba conjured in me when she took control. When I let her take control.

"Not everything," Morainn replied. As though to punctuate her statement, she produced an assortment of Cascari delicacies: fruits elegantly cut and set into other fruits, sweet rice wrapped in tender leaves, crumbling spice bread. I did not feel guilty accepting her offer, for these things would not have traveled well: already the flesh of the fruit browned, the leaves wilted.

"Triss, go and get us some fresh water." Morainn's command interrupted Triss' hungry gaze at the fruit that remained, and for all I did not care much for the girl, I knew I owed it to her to save her one. I'd nearly drowned her, as well as myself. But as soon as she had departed, Morainn looked at me as though the water had merely been a diversion. We had a limited amount of privacy, sitting so close and talking low, and Morainn intended to take advantage of it.

"I want you to know," she began, casting her eyes as earnestly to the fire as she had at first to my face. "Gannet and others like him believe you to be Theba. I believe it, too, but I don't think it makes you any less than who you have been. Icons live many lives. I've met two Dsimahs," Morainn continued, mentioning another, gentler goddess, "and they were completely different. The first died an old woman before she could fulfill whatever purpose it was she returned for."

She paused, as though there was something she wanted to say, but wasn't sure how to, or if it should be said. Morainn being Morainn, she forged ahead.

"For most people, there will be no distinction between you and Theba. But what happened out there…you can't be blamed for Theba's violence any more than you can be faulted for telling Eiren's stories. You're a force of nature, and a victim of it, too."

Tears filled my eyes, and I was grateful for the haze of heat that obscured our faces. Her confession deserved something more from me than gratitude, though, and I found I wanted to talk with her as I had not wanted to with Gannet. He insisted that to be Theba meant I couldn't be anything else. With Morainn there was still room to be me.

"I don't understand how she has lain quiet in me all of this time." My voice was as hushed as hers had been. In stories Theba was a brutal and jealous force, but she wasn't easy to understand. She could be hurt and was most famously betrayed, but unlike her human counterparts, unlike *me*, she could feel no empathy, and preferred to wound many times over more deeply than she had ever been.

"I don't know how, either. Icons are always taken from their families at young ages and raised to know who and what they are. In Ambar, everyone knows what is expected of them," she mused grimly, and her expression darkened. "It's not just the icons, either."

I wanted to ask her what she meant, but even as I opened my mouth Triss returned with water. Imke was behind her and Morainn engaged them both as though our exchange had exhausted her. I allowed their idle conversation to continue without my input, searching instead the shadows beyond the fire's light for Gannet. I felt readier to speak with him, now that I had spoken with Morainn. Now that I had unwittingly begun to tell my secret, the rest felt like a wall of sand, ready to crumble at any moment. I waited, sucking the sticky grains of rice from my fingers and, despite the urgency of my heart, felt my eyes grow heavy with exhaustion. Even the stony ground beneath my too-thin bedroll seemed welcoming, but I wouldn't relinquish the world, not yet.

"I think I should face my fears, as *Han'dra* Eiren does."

Morainn's voice demanded my notice, and I realized that not only was she talking about me, she was looking at me also, and her handmaids, too. I blanched in surprise at the attention.

"What fears can *Han'dra* Eiren have?" Imke did not need to allude to what had happened to make her meaning any clearer. I didn't like being the center of any conversation, let alone this one.

"Perhaps she can tell us," Morainn said softly, but with an

air of command, eyes traveling from the inscrutable faces of her servants to mine. I didn't have the impression that Morainn was testing me, but was instead sounding the depths of the others circled around the fire. This was a move deft enough to mark her as Gannet's sister, and I found myself smirking despite my anxiety.

He was listening, too. I could sense him now, like a shadow more treacherous than any cast by the fire, a potent darkness. He was waiting, and I knew I wouldn't have what I needed until they had theirs.

As a girl I might have said that I feared the tribes of dawn and dusk, savage ghosts who stalked those hours for children who were out of bed when they shouldn't have been. Only a few years ago my nightmares would have been populated by Ambarian soldiers. Now an ancient tale came to me, one whose meaning couldn't be lost on anyone truly listening.

"There are crimes that no mortal punishment can atone for, and of one such crime was Herat guilty. Half as many years as she had been alive had she been imprisoned for the murder of her mother and father. Though she suffered greatly, she felt no regret, no remorse. This grieved her jailors but grieved most Adah, the immortal lord of justice."

Even as I said his name, I wondered if the Ambarians knew him as an icon. Imke's attention seemed to weigh no more or less upon me for all she had asked for this, though I was pleased to see that Morainn had relaxed even as I began the dark tale.

"Adah knew that he couldn't make Herat repent, not when she valued so little what she had taken. He knew he must cause her to want and to treasure, and then take from her what she would never know she had been given. But no matter how Adah tried to challenge Herat, he couldn't succeed in making her repent until he sought the counsel of Theba."

"Theba knew well the hearts of mortals, how fickle and weak they could be, how subject to flattery and covetousness; those hearts especially that were corrupted in some way, as Herat's was. Because of this, Theba urged Adah to take the guise of a mortal and pose as one of Herat's jailors. He would be kind to her, he would make her love him, and then he would leave her. It would be easy with a mortal, Theba insisted. This Adah did and readily, for he liked so well the plan's fruition that he was blind to the possibility of failure. But because Theba would not be satisfied without some sport, she wagered that Adah should have only a year and a day to make Herat love him, and if he could not, she would kill Herat.

"When Adah came to Herat and allowed her small pleasures, when he protected her and improved the conditions of the cramped and pest-ridden cell she had inhabited, she grew to trust, and later to love. It was easy, as Theba had said it would be, and when Herat and Adah had shared days and sleepless nights enough, the god chose to bring the murderess to her true punishment at last."

"Were there no other souls for the god to judge in that time?" Imke's peevish interruption was not an uncommon one. I recalled my brother Jurnus' exclamation, similarly timed, when first my mother had told us this tale. Unlike Jurnus, however, I expected Imke already knew the answer to her question.

But Morainn didn't give me the opportunity to silence her handmaid.

"Adah was no more immune to the thrill of vengeance than the goddess whose counsel he sought, nor the mortal woman he judged. Go on, Eiren."

No one would dare to contradict Morainn, and I could have no higher command at present. I continued.

"When Adah begged Herat to escape with him and laid out for her how it should be done, she seized upon his mouth with her own as readily as she did this chance for a new life. It was done in the night, with Adah's intervention to clear the way and dull the senses of the other jailors. Theba took the shape of a jailer outside of the prison, and when she advanced upon the pair as she and Adah had plotted, Herat froze, her instincts dull from neglect. Adah, however, was ready, and he fell upon Theba's blade even as he sunk his own into a critical organ so that Theba seemed to lay dead and Adah dying. If Herat attempted to escape even as her lover lay dying Theba would have her life, and if she stayed, Adah his justice.

"The god could not have wished for a finer end to his scheme. Herat fell to her knees, her muffled cries mere husks of the pleasured sounds they had made together in the dark. He felt nothing as he slipped from his mortal form, but Herat felt horror enough for many pairs of thwarted lovers. In his cold and lifeless face she saw the death masks of her parents, knew that she had lost what once she had taken. Instead of fleeing the prison she descended within and closed the door upon her cell, locking it from within before tossing the key out of reach down the dim, earthen corridor.

"The body Adah had inhabited disappeared, but Herat saw it before her every time she closed her eyes and often when they were open, too. She lived for many years with no companion but her grief and her regret, while Theba and Adah both found new schemes to amuse them."

The last of my words dissipated like smoke or starlight, the telling hanging like a curtain over the camp. Without speaking, those who had remained seated for the length of it tucked into their blankets, if they had them, and turned their faces away from me. The quiet that descended was not resentful, but each man and woman that settled around the fire that night bedded their own demons as willingly as Herat had bedded hers.

I didn't go to sleep, however, but rose and stepped around the already slumbering body of Triss, passed the fire that a lone guard stood awake to stoke and tend to those helpless in dreams. The guard didn't look at me as I passed her and out of the fire's light, but I could feel her attention as keen as the blade of her sheathed sword. I'd earned a moment's privacy, or perhaps she, too, was afraid of me now.

Gannet waited for me at the perimeter of the camp, sharing with me briefly his sense of the scout that had just begun another circuit around. If we left now, we would both be assumed asleep around the fire. Gannet took my hand, and we did.

Though we carried no light, my surprise at Gannet's touch was trumped by the dim outlines of the path ahead of us, the trees that had been growing increasingly thick as we had wended away from Cascar. This must be another of his gifts. In this strange semi-sight they seemed like straight-backed women in line at the well, their baskets and pots balanced upon their heads in the shapes of the stiff foliage.

"Why that story, Eiren?"

I sniffed and dropped his hand, though I knew the darkness couldn't disguise me from him. He seemed to drop my address in these moments, when I was most likely to be taken by surprise.

"Perhaps you should ask Imke why she challenges me to reveal what I fear. I suspect she knows already."

Gannet didn't reply. Herat's story crowded my heart. Her story made me sorrier now than it ever had before, that she had lived out her days in such grief, whether I believed it earned or not. Her life was more than just a lesson, now. She had suffered and caused suffering, and so had I. But I couldn't hope to simply be put in chains and left to have out my days.

But Gannet wasn't thinking about Herat. Not now.

"What you saw was an illusion," he said at last, and it was as though no time had passed between our exchange over Circa's saddle.

"But you saw it, too." I reminded him of the dream we'd shared on our flight from Cascar, the feathery brush of webbed fingers across my cheeks and so his, too.

"What I saw was what you believed you saw. It wasn't real."

"I don't know why you're afraid, but I'm sure that you have more to fear from insisting that I am a liar," I insisted. I couldn't be sure that Gannet *was* afraid, it just seemed like a reasonable assumption. Why else would he allow gods to walk among us, but not other equally unbelievable things?

"You're not a liar, *Han'dra* Eiren, but you're not always in control of what you see... or do." Gannet's tone had not exactly softened, but had approached something more like patience as he revisited his usual lecturing ground. I was Theba and Theba me, and in the case of my survival, no doubt, what had really happened would be outside the scope of my understanding.

"I don't need you to believe me. I saw what I saw." The words struggled from my lips, and I was uncomfortably aware of my rising ire. I wondered if it belonged to Theba, or to me. Gannet touched a hand lightly to my shoulder, illuminating his face and the stand of trees we occupied in the same instant.

"Just keep it to yourself. The *kr'oumae* belong in stories, only in stories," he answered, using a word that I did not recognize. We had very few stories featuring such creatures, perhaps he knew more. "The others will never understand."

And he was among them. Wishing to keep what little comfort I had in remembering the siren's scaled, alien face, I pressed the memory into a fold of my mind, a pocket even Gannet's deft hand might not reach. It didn't matter that he didn't believe me, or why. Gannet didn't own every mystery in the world.

"What is this?" I asked, retreating to a safe subject as I gestured around us at what moments ago had been only deepest shadow, but had been illuminated for me at Gannet's touch. The moment stirred his fingers slightly, and as though in accommodation, he pressed his hand more firmly against my shoulder. In the desert his proximity had been unnaturally cool, but here, where the night was chill, he seemed heated from within. As a stranger I had wanted nothing to do with him, but now I wasn't sure if I was more interested in what Gannet could tell me about me, or what he might reveal about himself.

"Something practical." Gannet answered, the fuzzy outline of his mouth an indeterminate smile as he quoted my earlier request. "I can show you, but I'll have to let it get dark again, first. Are you ready?"

That he posed the question before plunging me into sightlessness was generous. I nodded my agreement. When he released hold of me this time, I was prepared.

"Light is generated by all living things even in the night; you must simply learn to recognize and magnify that light. Close your eyes," he instructed, though I couldn't see the logic in what he asked. I could see no more with them open as I could when closed. Despite my reservations, I complied.

"Don't think about what you can't see," Gannet continued, though it was not a criticism. "You don't need to know the shapes of things to know that they are there: the outlines of the trees, your hands, the slope of the path. Even the smallest stone has friction and energy at its core; it is lit from within."

As he spoke my eyes probed the membranous depths behind my eyelids, that strange focus that comes when one is forbidden to open their eyes but is not truly resigned to the restfulness that closing them requires. I could imagine the spiney leaves of the trees, their tapered points ending each in a flare of light that issued from somewhere within their papery trunks. It was harder to imagine the stones and forested litter beneath our feet as charged and alive, but I pictured such things stirred by wind or water, and it was not so great a stretch to grant them a little energy, still as they were now.

"Good, Eiren," Gannet murmured. I allowed him the full scope of my musings, more than the little gleaning he could take for himself. He and I were grains tumbling to pebbles grown to boulders as we hastened down a mountainside, our insides fired before inevitably shattering at the mountain's base. But we had not hit bottom, not yet. I was drawn to imagine again where we now stood, our eyes populous as the knots on the trees, as curious as the heads of mushrooms that poked between their roots. I prized from the stars the points of each of his fingers, the prints of which I could feel still on my shoulder.

My breath caught as my eyes opened in surprise, my face and skin burning with a light I hoped he couldn't see. But I could, and with a clarity Gannet's touch had not granted. The night was not in the full color of day, but I could easily have navigated back to the camp, and even ahead into territory we had not yet covered.

As it was, I had plenty to question in the man who blocked the path before me. My marvels and my terrors had their start in him. His lips were parted slightly as though he intended to speak, but a tense moment fell between us that seemed to defy speech. Our eyes locked and a chill passed through me that no amount of heavy clothing would have been able to remedy.

"We should return to the camp."

I had expected something else, but foolishly. I didn't know why it made me suddenly so angry to have him behave just as he always did. I shut him out completely before the last syllable even wetted his lips. Embarrassment didn't settle well with me, and not with the pitch and groan in my belly and heart I thought to be Theba, either.

If I slept tonight, it would be the hard sleep of swallowed secrets.

CHAPTER TWELVE

Over the next several days I didn't speak to Gannet as we rode, made easier by the fact that I was behind him this time and didn't have to contend with his heavy gaze over my shoulder. Besides, I had plenty to occupy me in the changes to the landscape, the mountain ridge rising pale as Gannet's knuckles on the reins. The trees and undergrowth grew first thick and then thicker, green and hardy, with soil that Circa's hooves kicked up wet and rich. The cold was like a sentient thing, tight in every breath, stinging my fingers and toes and creeping to settle in my core. The cold weather supplies we had intended to purchase in Cascar remained there still, and I thought I would never be warm again. Pressed as close as I dared to Gannet's back under the pretense of keeping my balance, I shivered under my borrowed cloak.

My fatigue after that first flight out of Cascar was nothing compared to the soreness of my muscles after two and then three days of near constant travel, and when we made camp I was eager for nothing but to lie prone on my back and hope to sleep. Antares had promised that we would only be a few days traveling this way, and on our third morning out when the path allowed a little while for us to ride several abreast, he brought his horse into step with the tireless Circa.

"How are you faring?" It was not Gannet he addressed, but me. Antares' sympathy belied his military dress, and the question was merely a courtesy. My answer was plain as the hood I pulled continuously around my face, that I kept only one hand around Gannet's waist when I could and warmed the other inside my cloak.

"Death by knifepoint is increasingly preferable compared to

this," I said, gesturing weakly around us, not wanting to throw my arm too wide and dissipate what little heat I'd collected under my cloak. Antares' brow furrowed at my weary joke, but a smile shaved ten years from his features. He seemed about to say more, but the path had begun to narrow and someone signaled for him from the head of the column.

"We'll be there soon. By nightfall," he promised over his shoulder. I sighed. Though my proximity to Gannet betrayed his keen interest in our exchange, he didn't seem eager to take up in talking where Antares had left off. There was nothing to do instead, sadly, but brood on lesser things, and though I would no doubt be colder for it, I decided to retrieve the book from the satchel that hung on Circa's left side. Every night I had hoped to study the book that Gannet had recovered from the barge, but there had been little light for it. I'd made hardly any progress. Balancing the tome on my thigh with one hand, I secured the other around Gannet's waist but was careful not to brush my brow against his back as I turned to read. The temptation to rest my head against his shoulder was surprisingly strong.

"You're going to read?" he observed, voice quiet but pointedly lacking in intimacy. Gannet's eyes remained locked upon the back of the rider in front of us.

"Do you object?" For all I posed a question, my tone welcomed no judgment on his part. I wasn't angry with him; I wasn't sure what I was.

"Not in the slightest."

Theba had nothing to do with my reasons for ignoring him when I began to read.

The book was unlike anything I'd read before, in such an archaic form of the language we shared that I could hardly decipher it. What was legible, anyway. Much of the book was layers of text accompanied by drawings, one inked on top of the next, on top of the next, on top of the next. It made no sense to me, but I bit my lip against asking Gannet for clarification. The layers grew more numerous and more complex the deeper within the book one read, though I couldn't call it reading. I turned to a page that had no less than six separate passages of writing scribbled over each other, and a series of symbols that I could not even be sure were paired with the text, or had singular meanings themselves. On sight alone it seemed to me that in some places I was reading a later version of the text, for the characters changed slightly the way a language will in time, though I could not read enough yet to know if the meanings changed, too. In places the variety was so wild it seemed almost accidental, as though someone had attempted to rewrite history, if this were a history.

On that same page I recognized much altered versions of Aleynian characters—so much altered, if not even archaic, that I did not notice them at first—that spelled out Theba's name. What little text flowered out from her mention made little sense in translation:

And her breath is greed, and from her hands
the sky pours, a god mouth bruised.

I could not even be sure that I read it correctly, but I lingered on this passage for the little window it gave me into the book as a whole. For it *was* my book, as Gannet had said it was now. I was in it, after all.

"It will make sense, in time."

I didn't need to ask for Gannet to offer an answer. My eyes rose to the cut of his shoulders underneath his heavy cloak, the blond hair raked by the wind over his collar, bright against the black. I turned the page. I didn't want to share what I'd read with Gannet. He would correct me, or worse, would tell me precisely what terrible ills the passage promised, and coincidentally, so did I. Besides, if he were to look over his shoulder, he would no doubt find the sketch I had done of his own name on impulse in one of the few blank spaces of *this* page. I'd already searched the book for mention of him. It made no sense that he would carry the same name as his icon, but hardly anything about my world made sense anymore, and thus I indulged where and when I could.

Though I walled myself against him, we were touching still, and I didn't want him to know what I was thinking. That I was thinking of him. I drew the book closer to me, so even if he should glance aside to me he couldn't see it. I read like this for some time, relenting and resting my cheek against his back, turning pages and steadying the tome with my chilled hands only when it was completely necessary. As a particularly virulent gust of wind tore across the cliff side, I thought I would lose the book entirely, but I felt an unnatural cold enter my heart when the pages settled askew against each other, one rolled into the spine by the wind. There, flowing from one page to the back of the next, one of the seemingly senseless symbols joined with the thick inked lines of a second symbol, making one I would recognize were I to trace its shape in the dark. It was a holy symbol of my people, a weather ward. My mother had sketched it in the sand for me when I was old enough to toddle over the marks, and shown me later where it stood in relief in stone throughout our home and our city. I later found it in the strangest of places, embroidered or even dyed into our servant's tunics, and learned better the irony of its prevalence: it never rained.

Heedless of the cold, I lifted the book with my free hand so that I might better see it, and what might have seemed coincidence was clearly intentional. I could see now the creases in the paper where it had been drawn over one page and onto the next, muddying the lines beneath it in bold strokes. Circa's step caused the bound corners to bump against Gannet's back, and he stirred, chin raised as he glanced back at me. Growing more fond of my secrets, I took note of the place in the book where the symbol lay, and tucked it back into my satchel.

"Your studies in Ambar will be far more extensive," he observed, though he couldn't keep his eyes off the path without risking an accident and turned again.

"And you've said I'll have teachers," I returned, nerves giddy at my discovery and in trying to hide it. "It will be easier to study when I can make some sense of what I'm reading."

"You assume that's the point of study." Tone oblique, Gannet didn't offer any more, and I swallowed the retort that rolled between teeth and tongue. I didn't need to argue with Gannet to hasten the hours, and I sat as straight in the saddle as the needled trees we passed, arms and legs wound around him enough only to keep from falling off. With wondering over the presence of the symbol and the memories of my family it stirred, the hours we spent on the track seemed slim indeed. Antares delivered on his promise when we slowed well before sundown, my eyes sweeping over the vaulting landscape before us. I had sense enough to appreciate that the time we would take traveling through the mountains would be much less than what would be required to cross over them, but I didn't think the caverns here would be kindred to those I had called home the last few years in Aleyn.

Circa seemed uneasy as we came to join the others in circling a wide, crude opening in the mountain's side, like a mouth agape and stained wine-dark. I was far from easy myself.

"We'll hold here for now," Antares said, loud enough for all assembled to hear. I could feel his anxiety, like an animal leashed tightly, begrudgingly controlled. Already two of the soldiers had dismounted, the reins of their horses given to others: the scouting party. Circa's discomfort was like a current passing from her haunches to mine, and I was grateful for the prospect of firm ground. We dismounted, Gannet going first and offering me his hands. This contact was strangely more unnerving than what the ride had demanded, and no more welcome. And unlike the ride, this brief contact flooded me with his feelings. He was a man cornered, resigned to the nearness of something that was making him extremely nervous. I could not, in so sudden and abrupt a touch, ascertain whether or not that something was me or whatever lay ahead of us in the caves. I looked at his face, but there was nothing there, not even when he met my eyes.

"We'll have a fire and bread and beer before we go in," Morainn announced, suddenly upon us both. Her enthusiasm for this turn of events was evident, though I wondered how severe our trials were to come if we were rationing so much already. The three of us joined Triss and Imke, the latter crouched, busy making a fire. I couldn't keep my gaze from returning to the entrance to the Rogue's Ear.

"How did you move so many into Aleyn using such a narrow path?" My question was for no one in particular, and I avoided using language that expressly invited too much conversation about the war.

"We didn't," Morainn offered casually, as though she spoke of a trade route and not the massive movements of troops. "There's another way, and many that have come this far with us will turn and take the road to the east. We will not see them for many weeks after we have reached the capital."

"But we don't have that much time," I murmured, eyes snagged on the dark opening again, like a rent in my vision. They wanted to return to Ambar, and there was something that waited there for me, too. I didn't want to go in, but wanted to know very much what waited within.

"We can't reach Jhosch quickly enough."

This from Imke, whose face peeked above a blaze that had only just begun to lick the kindling she had gathered for it. Her fervor was matched among many of the soldiers, and even Morainn quelled excitement at being so near her home. That she didn't answer Imke's enthusiasm was a gift to me: I could not hope for such a homecoming.

The beer was poured into sturdy, resin-soaked vessels that could be nestled in the ash and earth near the fire to warm the drink, but not burn our hands when we retrieved them. Though tough, the bread was pitted with nuts and dried fruit, and I found that the meal was not an altogether unpleasant one, crowded around the fire for warmth and exchanging bolstering looks with Morainn when I did not stare into my lap or the darkened entrance to the caves.

While I sat next to Gannet, he seemed careful not to brush against me, or perhaps I imagined that he did. He had said nothing, done nothing, that gave me cause to believe he knew I had perceived his anxiety so briefly before. I felt as guilty for it as I did any inadvertent reading of something so intimate. I remembered that when I was very young, I would run and wiggle between my eldest sister's bedclothes when I had a bad dream. She would coddle me and cradle me, and I would sleep again, but one night, when I was surely too old for it, I stole into her bed only to touch her slim arm and feel with a shock the certainty of her racing heart, her mind heat-clouded over the young man who was apprenticed to our court physician. I had withdrawn from her as though burned, and never said anything to her about it nor gone into her chamber at night again. My sisters had teased her ruthlessly over him, and I supposed she fancied him. But we hadn't any need for a court physician, or even a court, when we were exiled. I never knew what became of him.

Somehow, I didn't think Gannet would appreciate my discretion. He would rather I had never known at all.

The men and women under Antares' direction did not seem to rest much, but patrolled the perimeter or secured our packs and rations with the horses, who would be led through the caves as a group, tethered together. Only when the two who had scouted ahead in the caves returned, appearing like ghosts in the tunnel's entrance, were any decisions made regarding our next course of action. A flurry of whispers passed among the guard, and Morainn, not to be ignored, approached Antares directly. When she returned, she brought her anxiety with her, chill as breath from the cave's mouth.

"He says we can't go together. Is it true?" She looked at Gannet, and I sensed in him the faintest flicker of surprise.

"They'd have no cause to lie," he returned, his eyes cutting despite his words to the two men who stood conversing softly with Antares.

"Haven't you been here before?" I was beginning to feel some of Gannet's nervousness. He gave me a look that suggested I should've known better.

"Yes. But it's not always the same."

His explanation was a sorry one, but he offered nothing more, not with Antares now approaching our fire. With various degrees of scrambling, we were all on our feet. Morainn had remained standing, and nodded impatiently as Antares sketched a bow before speaking.

"We'll have to take the paths in threes," he said, clearly distressed by this news. I had expected perhaps three groups, but he meant for us to travel three at a time. I was surprised that we would be so divided.

"Why only three at a time?"

Gannet shot me a look.

"Consider yourself lucky we don't have to go one at a time." He must've considered that explanation enough, for Gannet didn't say anymore. Perhaps the Rogue's Ear was no more bound by the rules of the mortal world than it was fashioned for mortal travel.

When Antares continued, it was with a greater measure of confidence. "If you would permit it, I believe you should travel with me, *Dresha* Morainn."

Morainn inclined her head in agreement, and her response assumed a tone that suggested she had come upon the idea herself. "I insist upon it, and *Han'dra* Eiren, too."

Gannet stepped forward. His posture neither challenged nor demanded, but I knew what he was going to say before he said it. "*Han'dra* Eiren cannot enter the Rogue's Ear without me."

His response was met with resistance from Morainn, but he didn't indulge it. Neither did he return the probing look I turned on him when he finished speaking. Triss and Imke remained silent, no doubt coveting the place I would've taken at Morainn's side, and at the side of her skillful captain.

"Kurdan will go with you, then," Antares named one of the guard, a stone-faced man I'd never spoken with taking several steps forward. "And you'll be the last three to enter."

With nearly an hour between each parting and Morainn, Antares, and Triss among the first, it was a dull time, simply waiting there, watching. I didn't want to draw any unnecessary attention to myself, even with my imagination running wild as it was, so I didn't seek to entertain us with a story, nor did I open the book again. I wasn't sure I could give either my full attention, anyway, contemplating four days in the dark with Gannet and Kurdan, each strangers in their own way.

When Imke and two soldiers whose names I didn't know passed into the depths of the tunnel, Imke's bright hair like a loose flag swallowed in the dark, I stood. I wanted to be ready.

I didn't feel the same apprehension that I'd felt when we'd waited at the docks in Cascar, nor the confidence that followed. But I didn't want to, for it had preceded a frightening recklessness. A quick glance at my companions confirmed that their thoughts ran along a similar vein. Kurdan didn't keep his hands on his weapons, but his posture betrayed a man ready at any moment to spring.

Gannet studied me openly, his look not unlike the one he had given me that day, mere moments before I had caused the ship to sink. That he blamed himself in part for what had happened wasn't a comfort, but a curse. It was hard enough to live with my guilt alone, but to know that he felt the same, that he considered me to be helpless as an infant, was maddening.

I focused on the cave's opening, the uncertainty of the journey ahead of us. Because there were only three of us now, and because I would not have much longer to ask, I spoke without looking at either man.

"What can we expect in there?"

The list of what we couldn't was no doubt far shorter, but I asked all the same. After Re'Kether, after Cascar, there was little that would surprise me. But still plenty to fear.

"It's not a way meant for mortal passage," Gannet answered. "We take it now only because we must."

"So we're in danger?"

Even as I asked, I glanced at Kurdan. He wasn't frightened, but I could smell the certainty of death on him. He didn't think he would see the other side, and the shade in his heart haunted me.

"If you do everything I say and don't stray from the path, we won't be in any danger."

The way he said it made me sure that Gannet thought there was no way I would do as he asked, and I wasn't sure what appealed to me more: doing as I wished, or doing what he told me and proving him wrong.

The hour expired after what seemed twice the usual length of time, and Kurdan, Gannet, and I approached the Rogue's Ear, the guard at the head of our party and Gannet at the rear.

"We should stay close together," Gannet said to Kurdan and I both, and though the older man bristled at being guided by someone without military rank, he made no motion but to acquiesce to Gannet's orders. "When the path divides, we must not hesitate in making our choice. We are headed north, and no other way."

I wasn't sure what Gannet meant by choices, but I followed Kurdan all the same. He hefted the torch he had taken from our fire in one hand and a little device for determining our course in the other. As he stepped forward I did, too, eager to be done with the anxiety I felt about going in, if not necessary eager to begin. Gannet put a hand on my shoulder, lightly, so much so that I wondered if it were a touch of another kind. I shivered, remembering that brief moment in the forest when there had been nothing between us but terrible honesty.

"You must follow Kurdan, *Han'dra* Eiren. Even should you want to go another way. If you do, I'll have to stop you."

His words were soft, but Kurdan could hear as well as I, and I could sense if not see his stiffening muscles. Would they restrain me, sedate me, something worse? I stepped out of Gannet's reach, and his hand fell to his side as casually as if he had never lifted it to touch me.

"I will stop myself, if it comes to it."

With that understanding between us, we entered the Rogue's Ear.

CHAPTER THIRTEEN

Our first hours underground were marked only by the sloping path, winding down within the mountain. When our course had leveled, I lost all sense of time and distance completely. But Kurdan followed Gannet's directions expressly, and I followed Kurdan. When the torch threatened to gutter out, Gannet coaxed the flame back with his hands and a bit of breath, giving me a look that suggested that I should not ask him to show me this particular trick, not now. I was happy to marvel, for a little while.

We didn't talk, but we weren't moving so quickly that I didn't want for something to distract me from my own thoughts. The caverns were tight and close, not at all like the spacious, vaulted chambers where I had grown to womanhood. Gannet had claimed the Rogue's Ear was not for mortal passage, but the tunnels we passed through were deliberate and featureless, far more like the craft of human industry than they were some natural phenomenon. I was surprised that I didn't feel the ghosts of those who had passed before us, and with a shuddering certainty I knew that they had not come this way, not any of them, for all that there had seemed only one sloping course to take when Gannet, Kurdan, and I first entered.

We could've traveled hours or minutes before Gannet suggested we rest for the night, the darkness and silence made it impossible to tell. I watched carefully, this time, as Gannet coaxed the last remnants of flame from the torch into a fire, using the wood that Kurdan had carried. It seemed to me that Gannet would not be able to create a fire, but could increase the potency of one already ablaze. It would not be so much greater a step than seeing light in the dark; the light was there already.

But I wanted to enjoy the brief light and warmth, and put away my curiosity for a little while. While Gannet produced our rations from his pack and Kurdan unburdened himself opposite the two of us, I took measure of our surroundings. In the natural light they seemed no more remarkable than they had to me earlier. Only the smoothness of the tunnel walls was worthy of note, especially here where the path had widened to a size reminiscent of a bedchamber. Enough for three to sleep comfortably, and for the tending of a fire. It was as though we had been expected.

That we didn't talk while we ate was not entirely strange, but that we didn't look at each other, either, made me swallow my food as though it were lumps of hard earth. Burdened though I might have been by what I would no doubt see in their eyes, it could not have rivaled what I imagined. I feared for Morainn and the others somewhere ahead of us, though I felt sure our paths would not cross. I didn't know if Gannet would worry: for all the reservations he expressed it was not in his nature to. Would I have allowed one of my sisters to walk ahead of me in this place? I didn't think so. But he hadn't been given a choice.

At last we readied for sleep, but even the finest down could not have compelled my eyes to close. The fire burned down to a glow so faint it ceased throwing shadows. I didn't need to hear Kurdan's steady breath to know that he slept, and neither did I need the too-silent stillness to know that Gannet remained awake and alert as I was on his pallet to my right. When he spoke, it was an invitation.

"Do you think your brother and sisters think of you as often as you think of them?"

Gannet's voice was low and curious, an open tone from lips usually shut against such simple confidences. He surprised me.

"I don't believe that I think of them often enough," I admitted, sharing with him a little of the shame I felt in having given myself over to the life that lay uncertain before me instead of the comfort and familiarity of what lay behind. "I don't know myself anymore, so I'm not sure I know them, either. I feel like I'm still the child I was when we were exiled."

I didn't want to be told what I could do better, or what I had better do instead. I only wanted him to know.

"Still," I continued, daring a little with the harmless soldier asleep on the other side of our cold fire, my words insulated between stones and our bundled bodies. "They are a part of me, like you and Morainn. You were separated as children, weren't you? And still you care for each other."

I wouldn't have employed my sight in the dark to see him then. It was enough that the sound of his breath all but halted before beginning again, a calculated rhythm.

"We lost many things we can never have again," he answered after a moment, and I was surprised by the obvious hesitancy as he continued. "When we get home, you'll see how it must be between Morainn and I. Between all of us."

His words were a warning, but not for me. Gannet was steeling himself for something, against something, but what little connection I had made with him was gone, as empty and formless as the black before my eyes. The light shuffling as he settled down to sleep confirmed that we would have no more confidences tonight, and I curled reluctantly on my own bedroll.

"If only you gave in to my demands as easily," I said softly, unwilling to let him go, not just yet. Gannet didn't respond to my baiting, and my disappointment could have lit the Rogue's Ear entire, if such feelings were fuel. I knew that the time we had left together was limited, that things would change in Ambar, and not only because he promised they would. More than what he could know would change, and I would, too.

What I hoped to preserve about the weeks we had troubled each other I wasn't sure, but the thought of going forward without him into Ambar, as Theba or Eiren or the torture that was both, that I could not imagine.

Only when I was nearly asleep, drifting along the pleasant edge of dreams soon to be, did Gannet speak.

"I have made more than my share of sacrifices, and I shall sacrifice more still. So will you."

In the morning, if it was morning, there were no embers left in the fire for Gannet to stir to life, and Kurdan resorted to one of his firestarters. He had a fair number of them, but neither man seemed comfortable in relying upon these means entirely for fire and light, and waiting in a darkness so thick and alive it seemed to crawl inside me, I couldn't blame them.

I panicked when I first attempted to employ the sight Gannet had taught to me, for nothing stirred in the absolute dark of the Rogue's Ear, and it became a struggle to find a particle of light upon which I could focus and expand. I didn't know if my troubles were my own or the result of where we were, but when I had the means to see again, our faces were cast grim in the ghostly glow. I would've preferred the limited light from Kurdan's torch, but worried that I wouldn't be able to gain again the sight I had wrangled from the dark, I held fast.

"If the path is anything like yesterday's, it won't take three days to cross, will it?" Kurdan asked the question as though he knew he wouldn't like the answer, but hoped anyway.

"It won't be anything like yesterday," Gannet said bluntly. There was a rawness about him, still, leftover from last night. I knew better than to ask how a natural passage through a mountain should be so unpredictable. I could feel in the first steps we took away from last night's fire that we were not walking within the mountain, at least not the one we had seen barring our way into Ambar. It was like being in another world, underground.

Gannet was right, of course, for we were no more than an hour from our camp when the path dipped sharply, growing rocky where it had been smooth, and so narrow in places that I thought perhaps I would become wedged between two sharp stone faces and have to be chiseled out. Kurdan had the hardest time of it, his build one for the swinging of weapons and not the carrying of books, as Gannet and I were. Still, he would pass through with struggle and then I would struggle, too, which made about as much sense to me as anything else. At one point we had to pass through one at a time, pushing and tugging from either end, and I couldn't breathe for the panic of it.

I had loosed my cloak and pack and handed them to Kurdan, out of reach where the path grew mercifully, marginally wide again. My limbs strained against the stone, but it was too late to consider removing my overdress as well, cold and modesty be damned. I was wedged so tightly I wasn't sure the fabric even had room enough to tear.

"I can't move." My voice quavered helplessly, muffled by the stone.

"If I could pass through, you can, as well. You are at the narrowest point, only a few steps more," Kurdan answered, his voice coming like something over a great distance, though it was my fear, and not the space between us, that his words had more trouble in crossing.

"I can't," I repeated, this time more shrill, feeling as though my heart was being squeezed into my head. The path had surely narrowed since Kurdan had passed through, by what means I couldn't know. I was being punished for what I had done. If this was no mortal path, it was where immortals paid their penance. Theba would have hers now, through me.

There was a scraping of boot upon stone, the creeping shuffle of someone moving deliberately behind me. I couldn't turn my head to see, but I felt the touch of Gannet's hand on my arm. How he had room to touch me I didn't know, for I felt as though there was not space enough to clench and unclench my fist.

Eiren.

His name in my mind was like birdsong, light and swift, like something carried on the wind, carried on airs sweeter than any these caverns had ever seen. My heart pounded. *I can't, I can't, I can't.*

You can. I need you to pull yourself through. Pull us both.

I could taste blood in my mouth, from my displaced heart or bitten tongue or both. My stomach and chest tightened as though

I might shrink myself through the passage, but that would not have been enough for both of us to reach the other side. I couldn't be any thinner than I was, nor Gannet, and what made the most sense to me then was that there was no course but for our path to widen.

My hands and feet scrabbled against the stone, the fingers of my left hand snagging a hold on Gannet's sleeve and those of my right tearing at the jagged wall of the passage. Like sand it crumbled, like the castles I had fashioned with Jurnus when we were children and had destroyed when we had no more use for them. I did the same thing now.

I scrabbled like an animal trapped, tearing at the stone. Kurdan's gasp was louder to me than the sound of falling rock. I could feel the ragged path underneath of my boots as I inched forward, and more littered down still as Gannet followed after me. The fabric of my dress tore and my hair tangled and pulled away from my scalp as my face and shoulders scraped against the stone. When I had planted my feet on the landing where Kurdan stood back, torch aloft, I used both hands to pull Gannet the rest of the way, coloring his skin and clothes with my blood.

"It was wide enough, I said," Kurdan began, though his bewildered tone and wandering eyes betraying him. He was as shocked as I was. For a moment I held Gannet's arm, the gesture like a misbegotten greeting, but he knew that I was thanking him.

You said that you felt the child you were when you were exiled. But you were a child when we took you, too.

His eyes were colorless and shallow in the half-sight we shared in the dark, but I saw more in them than he ever allowed by the light of day.

And now I'm not, I finished for him, releasing his arm but not turning away, daring him to say more, to confront Theba, to confront me. His secrets were of greater interest to me now than anything he could tell me about myself. He could not tell me how I had moved a mountain, but that he believed I was capable of moving much more was clear.

Gannet said nothing, but I left myself vulnerable to him, open as the chamber where I had first met him, to wind and weather and the high cries in the streets below. Still he didn't speak, but when we began to walk again he offered me a salve for the cuts on my face, arms, and hands. Though my body mended, my heart and head felt flooded, and I returned the salve to him without a word. For many hours I heard nothing, the Rogue's Ear as silent as a tomb and my traveling companions speechless as the dead.

We wouldn't die here, no matter how perilous the way. I knew if I wanted to I could burrow through solid stone to the other side, dragging both men along behind me without lifting a finger. Terrified by the certainty of this power, I kept to the path the Rogue's Ear had seen fit to give me.

CHAPTER FOURTEEN

On our second night underground, Kurdan woke from some night terror, and his cries were too near for my tastes to those of the young man who had died in our camp outside Re'Kether. But I felt none of the impulses I had suffered that night. Neither did Gannet seem alarmed, for all he ever did. Kurdan denied the offering of a tonic to help him sleep and tossed fitfully until we had rested enough to mark the beginning of a new day.

I couldn't manage the reserve I had mastered the day prior, but it was a difficult thing, finding some entertainment in the mindless dark. Kurdan and Gannet moved forward relentlessly, as though they weren't just trying to reach the end of the cavernous dark, but that passing through to that end was a battle. The tunnels we took at first didn't seem like they could have belonged to the same course as the narrow tortures of yesterday, open as avenues, warm and damp. By mid-morning, my desires were as pressing as the stones had been. If I had any control over the tones of my mind, I willed them innocuous as I reached for Gannet.

Have you anything left you want to teach me? We don't have much time left.

The last was not necessary, for he knew as well as I how close we were to his home. I darted a glance at Kurdan's back, wondering if we gave something away about ourselves when we communicated this way, if people like Kurdan even knew such speech was possible. People like Kurdan, of course, included my own family and every friend I'd ever had. I didn't think that I could call Gannet my friend, even if he was my only comfort in this place.

*You've grown quite adept at closing your mind against intrusion,
but you should know, too, how to combat a closed mind.*

My brow furrowed even as I opened and closed my mouth to
question him, my steps faltering slightly despite the evenness of
our path. Kurdan cast a look over his shoulder, blank and unas-
suming, as though he satisfied reflex and not curiosity. I smiled
apologetically, but he had already looked away again.

Why?

I wasn't at all sure how I felt about acquiring information
from an unwilling individual, or demanding entrance where the
door was barred. I wouldn't appreciate such force myself, and this
seemed basis enough for my skepticism.

Surely there are things you wish to know that I haven't told you?

Now it was my turn to look over my shoulder at Gannet, whose
lips bore the ghost of a grin, so slight I could have imagined it.

Is this some sort of test?

I don't administer tests.

His response seemed vague, as though he answered more
questions than the one I had posed, that though he didn't test
me, others would. My next gesture was every bit in answer to his
challenge, whether he meant it as a challenge or not. I brought a
battering weight against him, all the force of my will that was not
required to walk, to breathe, to bid my heart to beat. I could feel
him buckle against me slightly, our minds meeting like carpenter's mallet and raw wood. The shock of it caused me to pull away
immediately, and I flinched as though physically struck.

Again.

My lips parted in surprise, the tang of the cavern air sharp
on my tongue. This time, without prompting, I used the scene he
had given me when first we'd explored my own talents, and I was
standing at a mountain's snowy peak, ankle deep in his resistance.
In the valley below were all of his little houses of secrets. It was
night, their windows glowing and winking with what could be
mine, if I wanted it badly enough. I would sit by the warmth of
those fires, I would carry forth a lantern to wherever I wished.

I came tumbling down the mountain, gathering stones to me as I went, faster and heavier until I seemed to be made of stone, all my limbs and body built of them. The details of one of the houses came to me more clearly, a squat little place with gilded windows and shady, fragrant herbs growing along the path. I focused upon this place, but I didn't intend to slow enough to knock upon the door, rocketing forward as though I would tear it off its hinges entirely.

My stone body was gone; I had no body, and no eyes to look upon the woman who sat with her back to me, facing a fire that blackened the edges of a stone hearth. I circled like smoke to face her and the boy she cradled in her arms. He had the look about him of a child who is small for their age despite every attention of his parent, his gold hair pressed neatly against the crown of his head as he played intently with some object in his lap. I realized that it was a toy, a scroll case fitted with ribbons of many colors that he wound into the case and then out again, his tongue firmed between his teeth in concentration.

The woman whispered something in his ear, tickling his ribs, and the stern little face evaporated as a smile broke over his lips, eyes crinkled in the kind of joy that can only be witnessed among the toddling young. Not in the stoic attention he'd paid to the toy had I recognized him, but in the smile I saw that it was Gannet.

"It's time."

The voice was hard and male, but I was as frozen as the pair by the fire and could not turn to see to whom it belonged.

"If it must be," the mother said, Gannet's mother, and she lifted the boy from her lap and set him on his feet. She was striking and quite young, hardly older than I was now, and in her face I could see her regret but her faith, too, that what she was prepared to do she must do.

"It will be easier if you give it to him," the man continued, and the mother disappeared for a moment on the edges of what I could perceive, leaving me only the boy to contend with. His face, innocent, clear, and adoring, followed the form of his mother.

He resembled little the man that I knew, and when his mother returned, I could see in her hand what had changed him.

"Here, love," she said, and she bent down to him, holding forth a little scrap of leather with tethers on the side that she hooked over the boy's ears. She was crying, and I heard a sniff of disapproval from the man that waited in the shadows.

Gannet, for he was Gannet now, yielded patiently to her work in fixing the soft leather mask over his features. It was the sibling of the mask he wore now but dangled from his tender features. When she had finished, his bright eyes were lost in the shadows it cast upon his face.

The figures blurred as the man in the shadows stepped forward, the voices of the three lost as mother and son were parted and she was alone. I was alone then, too, drifting in the ether of Gannet's memories.

Come back, Eiren.

My eyes opened, though I didn't remember closing them. I was walking still, for my limbs had continued their tedious work while my mind was elsewhere. Now, though, I stopped, turning to face Gannet behind me. His eyes were cast down like a man careful of his footing, but I put my hand upon his arm, above his hand, where I could feel the warmth of his skin. My apology was given in a flood of detail: my own memories, fragmented and jumbling uncertainly as I tried to share with him what he had inadvertently shared with me. It was more than an apology, what I tried to do; it was a clumsy articulation of the desire I had now to sympathize with a man I had considered reluctantly my friend for having taken me from my home.

He had been taken, too.

I managed at last the earliest image that I had of my brother and sisters at prayer, bent with their brows and palms touching and lifting, fingers tickling each other when our father wasn't looking. I was in my mother's arms. She was observing our family with all of the love and devotion I could sense in her even then, the feelings that became a part of me even as I grew in the shadow of them all.

This strange and tender moment was brief, for when I had stopped Kurdan had, too. He watched as I put my hand upon Gannet, the other trembling at my side. When I released him we stood there a moment, facing each other. I didn't care what Kurdan thought, for I was seeking in the shielded eyes the boy that had once looked with fullness and feeling on the world. I didn't need to ask if my lesson was concluded, if I had met Gannet's expectations. It was, and he had none.

The powers he had taught me in shielding my mind from entrance were turned then to contain it for another purpose, to keep from the touch and taste of every memory in the men who traveled perilously with me, the temptation to know them because I *could* in ways they could never know me. Not now when I became more like Theba every day, and every day less the toddling girl cradled in her mother's arms.

So we began to walk again, Kurdan without question, Gannet ready with unasked for answers, and my feet heavy as quarry stones. I could feel my heart in my throat, though this was no false feeling brought on by panic and the mysteries in the Rogue's Ear. This was a mystery of another sort, a curiosity that turned on the sound of every footfall behind me, no matter how slight. I wanted to know the weight of his step, the curve of the ankle and calf within the boot. If it were a character that could be traced, I wanted to write it. As ink on my skin I would wear it. My face and neck were as hot as if I sat in front of a fire, fanning flames into my mouth.

The day might have seemed interminable were it not for the sudden and unexpected temperament of our course. We wound up as often as we wound down, and the choices Gannet had promised we would need to make and quickly were thrown every hour before us when the path forked and branched. Neither man hesitated, not Gannet to call our path nor Kurdan to follow it. I was grateful I had no play in this, for all of our options seemed equal to me. The focus required was great enough to prove a distraction from my thoughts, for which I was also grateful.

"We'll emerge at the Maiden's Brow, won't we?" Kurdan spoke

after many silent hours. The pressure was getting to him, as well. "It should be snowing, in this season."

"We may, yes," Gannet answered, the response little more than a reflex. He, too, was somewhere else.

"What's the Maiden's Brow?" I asked, the conversation harmless for all it was fueled by restlessness and worry.

"It's a low ridge of mountains, foothills, really, that line the Jhoschi Valley," Kurdan replied quickly, his haste written off easily as a need to fill the deep earth quiet that surrounded us. I knew that I wanted to. From behind me I sensed a hint of indignance that flared and fell again as quickly as it had come. Gannet had wanted to answer. He liked to tell me things, to teach me, for all he insisted he wasn't my teacher. My cheeks burned anew as Kurdan continued, his voice rising in pitch, words rushed together in an eagerness to speak.

"We call the valley The Braid, for it has the beauty of a lady, too. We are sustained by the harvest from the valley, what we grow, and what the valley gives us without tilling," he babbled, an odd hum of panic in his voice. "Jhosch lies opposite the Maiden's Brow, in the Re'Shran mountains."

Whatever I noted in his tone was lost at his words.

"Re'Shran?" I thought of our fabled king, the one that our people shared before his sons had sundered the kingdom. As I spoke his namesake my voice seemed like water dripping from wet stone.

"Do you know the name? You should."

"Third left," Gannet interrupted, a hand upon the small of my back, a push not in the direction he had stated aloud for Kurdan, but a different path. I stumbled and Kurdan wheeled upon the pair of us, his blade brandished. How long had he been holding it? Fear darted like a bird from a branch in me, and my dark sight fell away just as Kurdan threw his torch into my face and lunged with his sword.

In one instant I heard Gannet call my name as he had the night in Re'Kether, clear and without pretense of any kind, not worry but anticipation of things most terrible in whatever answer I would be able to give. I saw in a flash of fire my outstretched arms, like a child trying to avoid a fall, Kurdan's curved steel slicing through empty air. My senses were poised all in a moment and when I moved, it was with aching patience, as slow as clay and certain as death.

The torch flared to uncommon brilliance before my face, brighter than any rag and tinder could make, as I did what Gannet hadn't yet taught me to do and wouldn't have to. Bolder and brighter the flame grew in what seemed to me ages, but there was only a moment between Kurdan's tossing of the torch and my hurling it back to him. This time it was more than a source of meager light, it was a living blaze, suspended in the air like a body before it broke against Kurdan. He burst into flames, and time returned for me to its usual flow, my screams joined with his as I fell back against the stone to escape his flailing, blazing arms. Gannet tore off his cloak and threw it about the dying man, for he was dying. I could see his death like a cloud descending over the smoke that poured from his burning hair and clothes. I screamed and screamed, eyes blearing, long after Kurdan had stopped, when his life and body both had been snuffed out and there was no light to see by. No light to see what I had done.

"Eiren."

Gannet's voice was as delicate as moth's wings fluttering in the dark, but I curled more tightly into myself against the wall, as though I could flatten myself into stone. If I could destroy why could I not create? For all Kurdan had meant to kill me, had worked himself up to it under innocent pretense, I couldn't excuse myself what I had done. This was different than the howling man, than the foundering of the ship in Cascar. I had meant to do just what I had done. No matter what horrors lay within me, I didn't want to die. As soon as Kurdan had turned on me, it was him or me. And I hadn't hesitated.

"Eiren."

My sob gave me away, croaked into shadow and rock. Kurdan's

smell of smoke and charred flesh flooded my nose and mouth, and I gagged, retching against the wall I had turned to for comfort. When I turned away, lips slicked with tears and the contents of my belly, Gannet put his arms around me. I didn't struggle, relaxing against him as though I had lost control of my body with such horrible control of my mind so recently realized.

Any of my sisters' lovers might have whispered senseless things or stroked their olive cheeks, but I was filthy and had killed a man, and Gannet was neither lover nor a man inclined to whisper. Still, theirs were the only experiences I had to compare the weight of his arms as he supported me a few steps back down the path the way we had come, the gentle pressure and the noted hesitance. If he treated me thus because I was a murderer, I wouldn't blame him. I wanted to say his name as he had said mine, as though it would steady him as it had failed to steady me. Theba was a tempest. What manner of icon could he be, still as he was?

I allowed him to lower me to the ground, and I knew that he stood a moment before me in the dark for all I couldn't see him. Behind my pinched eyes Kurdan's blade arced through the air over and over again, his limbs danced forever in fire.

Sleep, Eiren.

His voice grew in my mind like a drop of oil in water. I could slip inside and ignore the rest, which was just what I did.

CHAPTER FIFTEEN

In my dream, my mother knelt beside my bed, dipping a cloth in herb-scented water and pressing it to my brow and neck. I could smell the braziers burning, the familiar, acrid scent of the oil she used when someone took sick. My light bedding stuck to me like a second skin, and I was sweating as though I were trying to shed them both.

"What were you dreaming about, Ren?" she asked, hands clasped patiently above the bowl as though in blessing.

My brow furrowed. I had been dreaming, hadn't I? I couldn't remember.

"I'm awake now," I insisted, refusing her question in the same moment that I reached for her hand. I wanted to take it and be sure that it was real, to trace the calluses and lines of her fingers and her palm.

She moved just out of reach, and I whimpered. I felt so weak; I couldn't touch her without great strain.

"What were you dreaming about, Ren?"

Her tone was the same and she fell upon each word like striking an instrument.

"I can't remember," I choked, hardly managing the words as my teeth began to chatter. I was cold, the sweat on my skin turned to a glimmer of ice. "May I have a fire in my room?"

Mother rose from my side, the damp cloth dropped from her hands like a hot stone, landing with a slop against the floor. Her face was hard and unfamiliar, and the eyes were empty, like blue stones in a human skull.

"Why don't you dream one?"

As she spoke her mouth seemed to glow until I realized her lips were red as a coal, her tongue a licking fire that spread from her mouth to her cheekbones and eyes, shriveling them in their sockets and racing over her dark hair. I screamed as she raised her arms, a woman turned inferno, and where she stretched her fingers the ceiling caught fire and the flame rolled like a wave the whole room across. My bed burned but I didn't, and when there was no more air to breathe I found enough to keep screaming.

Eiren.

Eiren.

"Wake up, Eiren."

That Gannet managed to hold me down against the ground was no mean feat, for I writhed and clawed in protest, trapped in the dream before my eyes could open fully, could register him there in the glow of a low campfire. This flame was a tame one, and he wasn't my mother, nor the creature in the dream that had seemed to be her.

Before I said anything I looked around, my gaze charged, but I didn't see Kurdan's body anywhere. I noticed, then, that while my face and hands were clean, Gannet's bore traces of stone dust and earth, no doubt gathered during a hasty burial. I blanched, but I couldn't be sick again. There was nothing in my stomach but air and swallowed screams.

Without speaking, Gannet observed me, my motives and thoughts as clear to him now as they must have been when I had acted against Kurdan. He offered me a skin of water with a gesture that demanded I drink. I obliged, watching as he returned to the fire and rolled in the embers what looked to be potatoes, wrapped in damp cloth to keep from burning. The tool he used I recognized as Kurdan's, and I was surprised first that it had survived, disgusted second that this was my first thought in reflecting upon the dead man's possessions.

I shuffled over to the fire, muscles corded still from the stress of my dream and what had preceded it, saying nothing and hoping that Gannet could, for a little while, say nothing, too. I didn't want to talk about what I had done, how I had done it, or what had driven the man whose life I had taken. Despite these affirmations, when I accepted my meager dinner from Gannet my mind was racing already from memory to limited memory that I had of Kurdan, if I had noticed him even once before Antares had named him as our guard for the journey through the Rogue's Ear. The hot mush in my mouth stilled my tongue, but I had no explanation to voice. I didn't remember him before the Rogue's Ear, he had been as peripheral to me as the howling man outside of Re'Kether. I knew them best because I had known them least, and they were both dead because of it.

"I don't know why he wanted to kill you, either," Gannet said after we had finished our potatoes, my brooding having given over entirely to hazardous musings. His words surprised me, for we had encountered nothing so far that Gannet had not been able to explain; better still, that he had not had some part and purpose in.

"I'm very dangerous. I'm responsible for the death of one of his friends," I offered, unsure, as afraid of being without answers as I was of failing to hesitate again. "He must've known who I was, or guessed."

"The man in Re'Kether killed himself."

Gannet seemed certain of this if nothing else, cleaning his hands on his tunic, a futile effort after so many days underground. He clasped them under his chin, fingers hooked together like a series of keys to be played. I noted his shoulders rounded forward without the cloak to cover them, the cloak that likely served now as Kurdan's burial shroud.

"Do you think they were working together?"

My question seemed paranoid, but it shouldn't have. I trembled as I spoke, as though some presence in the Rogue's Ear would judge me for what I had done.

"I don't know," Gannet said softly, burdening me a second time with his ignorance. I needed him to know. My way from home was laid down by him, and I couldn't abide a faltering of course.

"The war's end was only the beginning, like he said." I remembered the man who had died outside of Re'Kether, what he'd said, the grim portent that made more sense to me every time I dared to act on my power. I waved my arms, needing little more to illustrate my meaning when Gannet could see every insinuation of my mind, bared in fear as it was.

Gannet shook his head, staring through the fire, but not to the cavern wall that lay beyond it.

"It was always going to be this way. Theba will be realized in you, and only through blood."

"Whose blood? All those who died while I was raised a weapon in ignorance, all of the deaths that were indirectly mine? Kurdan's?" I breathed heavily, meeting his eyes in the dark with a demand greater than any words could convey. "Who's next, Gannet?"

And why can't it be me?

I railed against the crushing desire to break down into tears again, the guilt hot as lead in my veins that I did not, would not, cry for a man that had wanted me dead. Until that moment I had done him no personal ill, and something in me was sure that what had happened with the man at Re'Kether had nothing whatever to do with Kurdan's motives here.

"I don't know that, either," Gannet said. I was as sure as I was of the heat from the fire that he knew my thoughts, my will cast inevitable as a shadow across the cavern floor. "All will become clear when we arrive in Jhosch—"

"Don't make me promises you can't keep," I hissed. I could see his thoughts, too, the certainty of our parting when we arrived in the Ambarian capital, the darkness that followed. Did he know to what destiny I went there? And why I had to pursue it without him?

Gannet's lips closed over whatever he had been about to say, and we returned a moment to silence, to the murmur of the fire. I was inconsolable, alone. Despite my anger, I wanted him to put his arms around me again, but this I didn't let him know.

"Before Kurdan attacked you, what you saw and did after," Gannet began, and though I was sure my desire was shielded, we had arrived at the same place. I should have forgotten in the glut of my foul feeling over Kurdan what Gannet and I had shared, but I returned to it now in desperation. I nodded dumbly, waiting for him to continue, wanting him to. "Your power didn't surprise me, but it's…not common for such clarity following so much force. That memory is an old one, and one I would not have readily shared."

"I didn't seek it," I said hastily, though Gannet knew as well as I did that I had not sought anything. Had I coaxed that particular memory to the surface, or was it near enough then, or all of the time, for someone like me to see?

Though there wasn't anyone quite like me.

"I won't tell anyone," I offered lamely, as though this were some consolation. I wondered if he brought this up because he expected that it would make me feel better. But I only felt worse.

Gannet hesitated. When I cut my eyes to him, I saw that he was gazing into the fire, his lips brooding so that I didn't need to see his eyes to know it. His hands reached to either side of his head after a moment more, and he tugged at the straps there, far sturdier, more permanent, than the ones his mother had first fastened when he was a boy. I thought he might remove it and I swallowed my breath, but he didn't. He never did.

"Do you know why you wear it?"

My question was spoken so soft it was almost as though I had not asked it, that it had come whispering instead from the dark of the Rogue's Ear, one more secret for this place to keep.

Gannet's fingers stilled upon the bindings, but did not drop, poised as though he might work them loose at any moment. My heart was pounding and I wanted to put my hands over his, create laces with our fingers that would rival any that had been created for him to wear. The thought overfilled me, and I promised myself that it was his secret I wanted. His secret only, if I could just touch his hand, his head.

"It's a punishment."

He spoke, too, in hushed tones, though we were more alone

than we had been since we had first met. As alone as we could be, each of us someone else on the inside.

"No single lifetime contains suffering and time enough to repent for the crime, though I'll be the last to wear it, now that you're here." He looked at me then, hands falling to his sides, draining the air from me at the bare depths in his eyes. Conflict and curiosity and want, pools of it I could have dropped bodily into below the curved, molten brow.

"Gannet…" I began, and no will could have contested mine as I reached for him, laying a hand on his arm, fingers touching lightly where I had made contact with him before, given him my memories in apology for taking his. He flinched, but did not withdraw his arm. I allowed my thumb to brush lightly against his skin, smooth, wiped free of the grit of his work while I had been asleep. When he spoke his voice was as raw as his eyes.

"I begin to understand how my punishment will be gravest of all."

He did pull free of me then, and my hand hung in the air like a bird shot through with an arrow, a second frozen in flight before it plummeted down, dead. I clasped my hands together in my lap, heart grown sluggish. I couldn't put a name to what it was I wanted, but it wasn't this. I felt lamed, like Tara, the maid who was blinded and must find her way without this most fundamental sense. She didn't even know where she was going, but because it was in her nature, and the nature of all women, she went.

I felt Gannet gather himself together again beside me, the familiar severity, the certainty, what was steady and sure about his guise instead of whatever burdens he felt in it.

"It's late," Gannet said, though I was thinking of everything but the hour and he was, too. "You should sleep more."

I obliged, but only because I couldn't bear to sit beside him any longer before the fire as though it were natural, as though we could share anything without secrets and shames between us. If I'd found anything in him during our days within the Rogue's Ear, it was overshadowed all by what I'd had to do to see the other side.

When we began walking the next morning, our way soon felt easy and light. But my heart was the heaviest it had been. Though Gannet had buried Kurdan well out of the way of any course we might take, the Rogue's Ear wouldn't let us go without passing the mounded earth, covered over with crumbled stones. No matter what he had intended for me, I was sure Kurdan had never meant to come to such an end, buried in obscurity, far from any lover or mother who might've visited his grave. I didn't know the funereal practices of his people, didn't know what would be appropriate to say, if anything, being the one who had put him there. In death, it didn't matter that he'd meant to kill me, only that I'd killed him.

Hours passed before it was not my imagination but true light coloring our course, filtered in from somewhere above. I knew without asking that this meant we were near the end of our time here, and allowed my sight to fade in favor of navigating by the weak, natural light. I couldn't see as well the tight slant of Gannet's shoulders in this light, and this was a relief.

Something had stirred in me that could not now be stilled, and though I might not have the words for it, I had a story for everything. Last night I had killed a man, and today my mind was consumed with what it meant to love one.

I chose to tell it aloud because I couldn't stand the silence, what wasn't filling it. But I wouldn't have welcomed Gannet's protest or enthusiasm, either. I wasn't ready for it. If he felt anything at the start of my telling he kept it to himself, though it was a mercy for us both that I filled the uncomfortable quiet between us.

"Massoud was the son of the king and a prince, but he could not have been less the sort of son his family wanted. While he was as happy fighting and riding as other boys his age, he didn't go anywhere without the little snail that had been his companion since he toddled on two legs. When he took meals, the creature squatted beside his plate. During his lessons, the snail perched on his shoulder. When sparring, Massoud put the snail inside a sturdy case he had made to protect her and keep her close, hanging around his neck.

"What neither Massoud nor his parents knew was that the snail was not a snail at all but the goddess Alyona, who is known to prefer an animal shape to any other and is found more often in the company of mortals than others of her kind. Alyona delighted in mortals, and so thoroughly in Massoud that in his eighteenth year she decided that she would marry him.

"Alyona knew the hearts of mortals well, however, and didn't think that Massoud would take well to the ruse that had been her shape his whole life, and so one night, while he was asleep, she slithered near his ear and whispered that he must take her as a snail for his bride. When he had done so, she would be transformed to a beautiful woman."

Subtly, I shared with Gannet the face of Massoud I had always imagined, youthful and open as a book. Alyona as a snail had a shell of many colors, iridescent. As with the story, he gave me no sign that he appreciated my efforts, but neither did he close himself off to me. With Gannet, I could only consider this encouragement.

"Massoud met with great resistance from his family, who claimed they would forsake him if he insisted upon such a marriage. His brothers wouldn't speak to him and everyone in the court began to whisper that their prince had gone mad. Still, Massoud would marry her and had two rings fashioned from fine metals, one for himself and one for his snail bride.

"No one in the kingdom would perform the ceremony, so Massoud placed Alyona in the little case around his neck and traveled to the next kingdom, and when denied there, the next and the next until he came to a land so far away that no one had before heard his name or would even have known to worship the creature he carried. Married at last, Massoud slipped the ring around Alyona's shell, though once he had done so she was unable to transform to a shape that would please him, bound by the ceremony and his love.

"Alyona had not known her man as well as she imagined, for he didn't want her to change. He settled quietly in the village where they were married, making a small and honest living and whispering his secrets to her as he had always done. For thirty years they lived this way, the whole of Massoud's life they shared. As he lay upon his deathbed Alyona slithered to his ear and whispered the truth of what she was. Massoud replied that he had always known, but he could love her as an equal only when she occupied such a form. So he had done and didn't regret it.

"When he died, Alyona was freed from her snail form and brought his body to her sister, Dsimah, whose province is sowing and harvesting and who is known to bring life to any soil, no matter how infertile. Alyona begged Dsimah to bring life to Massoud again, for if any god could do so, it would be she.

"Dsimah couldn't do what Alyona asked, but from Massoud's body she grew a great, flowering tree. When Alyona swallowed a fruit from the tree, she bore a child that was cradled in its roots and raised dancing beneath its heavy boughs. So Alyona and her daughter, Massoud's daughter, can be found still, sheltered beneath her husband's arms."

My sisters had always sniffed and wiped at their eyes at the end, and Jurnus returned from wherever his attentions had wandered, nodding appreciatively and entirely for my mother's benefit. My interests had always lain in the art of the telling so that I could tell it myself in the future, perhaps to my own children. I'd wanted to be more like my mother, but all of the steps of womanhood between she and I were quite beyond me then. Now I could see how those years might be the most complicated in a lifetime's worth of years, how they might give and take away, or seem only to take without the scope of age to temper them. And those years were mine now, the weeks I had shared with the mysterious man walking before me the very heart of them.

Gannet passed beneath a wide patch of sunlight, cold and white as a flare upon his light hair. It did not seem natural to have so much to say and so much want to say it only to open and close one's lips without managing a word, but that was exactly what I did. When we rounded a rock face and saw before us the tunnel's opening, flooded with a light so blinding I had to shield my eyes, I knew that I had missed my opportunity to speak.

Before I could see properly hands were upon me, but they were not Gannet's. I was being guided out of the Rogue's Ear, the buzzing of voices settling finally into something like sense.

"Kurdan? Where is Kurdan?"

I closed my eyes, but it wasn't the light that hurt them.

"He was taken."

Gannet's stern assertion was met with greatest shock from me, for my eyes snapped open again to behold the others gathered around; Antares and Morainn nodding in grim acceptance.

"We lost several," Antares began, casting a quick look at Morainn before continuing. "Including Triss."

I gasped. Triss, gone? What terrors lurked in the Rogue's Ear that we had escaped, if not my own? No one asked any more about Kurdan, nor did they press Gannet and I immediately for any news of our passage. He didn't need to lay a hand upon me, didn't need to share more than a look that encouraged silence now, questions later. Exhausted from ordeals within and without, I obliged, turning instead to see where we had come. Their camp was not so lived in as to suggest that they had emerged much before we had, but any interest I had in the ground was given over immediately to the horizon.

The Rogue's Ear had deposited us above a valley that ran like an emerald ribbon laced in dark curls, mountains more treacherous than any in the low lands from which we had come. It was wild to see so much verdant below and sheer, white capped peaks above, dark trees like teeth cutting down the mountain's sides before giving over to rock, and then to rolling green. The fields did not spread uninterrupted, however, for I could see the little settlements clustered between forests and along a wide swath of blue, a river. Behind us, too, rose mountains as wicked as we faced, a fitting crown for the uncertain pass that ran beneath them. My lips parted, jaw askew, as though I hoped to swallow some part of the view or all.

"Eiren," Morainn said softly at my side, and I felt her hand upon my arm. The touch was a reminder that I was part woman, still, and incapable of devouring lands. The cold returned to me in that moment, as well, more virulent than what we had left on the other side of the Rogue's Ear. Already my fingertips and nose began to burn, and I stuffed the former under crossed arms.

"Where do you live?" I asked, trying to ground myself again for all my eyes drifted down, admiring the scene like I would the stage of a play. I hadn't known it would be like this, beauty cradled between the sheer, perilous arms of such mountains. How could this not be enough for them?

Morainn gestured, sure and heavy with the weight of what lay beneath her outstretched arm.

"There. At the base of the witch, *Zhaeha*."

I didn't need my sense of her to know to what she referred. The tallest peak was also the sharpest, seeming chiseled as though by great hands into a shape no natural stone could take, black and hooked against the cool blue of the sky. A peculiar feeling stirred in me at the feature's name, though I felt, if anything, that *Zhaeha* meant something else entirely, if not necessarily what.

"It's midmorning," Antares interrupted, casting his eyes from Morainn and I to Gannet, who stood apart, watchful of the valley below for reasons of his own. "If you're not overtired, we are well rested and ready to make the waypoint."

Gannet nodded without asking me, though I wouldn't have delayed near the Rogue's Ear for anything. After a draw of fresh water from a filled skin that Antares passed me, I greeted Circa like an old friend. The horse seemed no worse for her time in the Rogue's Ear, and I wondered if whatever forces designed the trials of that place considered beasts below their notice. Or, I wondered idly, above the trials required of their wicked masters.

We had more horses than riders now, I noted grimly. It was no longer necessary to ride in pairs, and what was a blessing for the horses and should have been for me did not seem so as I watched

Gannet mount a solitary mare. What I couldn't say I could perhaps have committed with a touch, but I could not, would not, now.

Our path allowed me to ride beside Morainn, and I grasped at this opportunity, heart hardened against the comfort of the formation I had fallen into with Gannet in the Rogue's Ear. If Imke had not planted herself on Morainn's other side, I would have been content. The air was fresh in my lungs, if cold. This was the proper north, it seemed, and the cloak I had neglected during my time underground was hugged close once more.

"We've been waiting a full day and night," Morainn began, relief in a voice I was sure had not an hour ago expressed only worry. Though she spoke with me, I knew her attention, too, was with her brother.

"We had some trouble," I admitted, pale with the guilt of lying to her even if I only did so to protect myself. Or perhaps because of it.

"The Rogue's Ear makes trouble for the wicked," Imke said, eyes dark on the trail ahead. A squirming heat filled my stomach at her words, and was not soothed by her next. "Kurdan wasn't the man he thought he was, nor was Triss a virtuous woman."

"Be quiet, Imke," Morainn spat, lip and brow shaking in anger. Foolish though she might sometimes have been, Triss was a great loss to her mistress, perhaps because she had not expressed as much when she was with her. I put a hand upon Morainn's shoulder, careful to shield her from my own foul feelings. Imke observed the touch with more discomfort than she had her mistress' scolding, and rode ahead, leaving us with only a guard riding with enough distance behind that we had something like privacy. It was clear they expected no danger here. If I hadn't escaped in the dark of the Rogue's Ear, it was unlikely I'd bolt now.

"I don't think it's possible to be prepared for the challenges of that place. I wasn't," I said, my sympathy touched with my own trials below ground. Morainn placed her hand upon mine, briefly, and I glimpsed Antares, ash-faced and up to his eyes in water, felt the blade-chill of it in my bones. She hadn't meant to share this memory with me, but it was so near to the surface of her mind that I could not help but live it with her. Gannet and I had not passed through water. The Rogue's Ear was truly no mortal place, to change as it did.

"You were lucky to have Gannet with you," Morainn murmured, looking ahead to her brother, stiff-backed on the mare. I shivered, and it had nothing to do with the cold. She couldn't know just how lucky.

"Why is it a secret, who he is?" The question leapt unbidden to my lips. Morainn's expression clouded completely now, and I worried I had pressed her too much. I wasn't the only one to have suffered in the Rogue's Ear. "I'm sorry, Morainn, I'm not supposed to know. He's said as much before."

"There's nothing to be sorry for. I can't tell you what I don't know. But if you think your hand poorly dealt for having been cast as Theba, count yourself lucky you're not whoever it is Gannet suffers himself to be."

"Hasn't anyone ever guessed?" I whispered, but still could see Gannet's chin sharp in outline as he turned and looked at the pair of us and away. His eyes were colder than any wind that threatened the hem of my cloak.

"Someone knows who he is, and that's exactly why we *aren't* allowed to know," Morainn said darkly. She sat straighter in her saddle, a princess again who would answer no more of my questions. For her own protection, and for mine.

But mostly, for his.

Was some greater evil anticipated of Gannet? I sifted through my memories for stories of a manifestation more foul than Theba, and while there were wrongful deeds aplenty, no god or goddess was as thoroughly ugly as she. I couldn't even see the sense in keeping something like that from him, for surely they would have done the same with me. I had been told so I might have some measure of control, though I hadn't showed any yet. Didn't Gannet deserve the same chance?

For all of the mystery Morainn had dispelled, I wasn't surprised that she had introduced yet more. It was easier to be quiet then, to suffer the pretense of a cheerful spirit. I was resigned as a sister even to Imke in our collective melancholy, though where her mind and Morainn's flew I did not pursue. I had sorrow enough for myself.

Ambar did not disappoint, for we were but halfway down the ridge, only a few hours from the Rogue's Ear, before a party approached us, military men all. Their hands were raised in greeting, and I could feel in them many efforts to restrain their relief to see Antares, who dismounted and moved towards them with no such self-control. I couldn't hear him, but I could see his smile, the hands clapped upon shoulders. His lips parted in speech that I imagined promised our well being, the victory he had returned to share with them.

And then their faces changed, all of them, and I wondered if perhaps Antares had given news of Kurdan, or the howling man, or others, men and women lost before even I had joined them. But it wasn't any of these things, for their eyes followed Antares' gesture to settle on me, a fervor there, and fear, and awe. They muttered to each other but didn't look away from me. Morainn's horse distanced itself a little, at her command, no doubt, and I saw on Antares' face resignation and sadness, but Gannet I saw best, sensed best. He reigned in his horse to turn his back on the men and inclined his head lightly to me, as though proving a point. But he had just had his point proven for him.

Things would change now, and I would change them.

CHAPTER SIXTEEN

The waypoint was a village with children at play, roaming dogs, folk returning from fields or woods or mines. I felt more apprehensive even than I had when we first arrived in Cascar. The sun was setting behind us, and I imagined we entered the village as shadows, figures thrown black and menacingly thin before us. Two weedy boys hovered uncertainly on a path, which had grown wide and beaten enough to be called a road. They held their hands above their eyes as though in a salute, but they were only attempting to make out our faces.

Recognizing no one, they scampered into a modest but well-built wooden building on the side of the road. We slowed, and a moment later a man appeared in the doorway, whiskered and bewildered. Antares dismounted once more and approached him, the colors he wore announcing him as a military man and eliciting a slight incline of the man's head. Behind him strode the scouts, and I was glad their attentions were for the moment diverted from me. Though I had traveled as usual ensconced between guards and servants and Gannet, they had been irritatingly preoccupied with me, where I was, the pace I drove Circa, which direction I looked. Ambar did not take many prisoners of war, it seemed.

"Is your lord in residence?"

I watched their exchange carefully, how the scouts seemed to assert themselves at either side, an unnecessary show of strength.

"He is," the bearded man answered, the children visible now on either side of him in the doorway, their eyes in shadow. He coughed nervously. "But if I may, does your return mean the war is over? It's ended?"

My attention was fixed. Though I didn't move lest I draw more attention to myself, I gave over my sense of things utterly to the speaking pair, silencing the vibrations and subtle sounds of the minds around me. Antares didn't seem to want to draw any attention to me, either, for though what he said next no doubt referred to me, he was careful not to gesture.

"Our victory was complete."

The man grinned widely and I was overwhelmed by the relief in him, washing out like a water tub overturned, or the whole of the sea itself. I couldn't see but could feel the happy hum of the children's backs underneath his two hands. I reached out to him tentatively and could see a woman of middle age but strong, hair coiled thick on her head in the style of the women who served in the Ambarian military. Antares didn't need my gifts to deduce the same.

"Your wife will be returned to you in time, by the southern pass," he offered, eyes falling carefully on the children who were beginning to smile, too, slowly aware of what was transpiring. "By midwinter she will come home to find you as tall as her shoulders."

There was such warmth in the words that I forgot for a moment that I was the enemy, the viper darting among the sheep, that it was my people who had been numberless slain and we who had lost. How could Antares be sure that their mother, the bearded man's wife, lived? That she hadn't been among the soldiers to remain in my home, enforcing the fragile peace of martial law? And I was here now, fangs sharpened with every shred of knowledge Gannet shared with me.

I caught Gannet, then, looking at me, and I stared him down, my anger and my longing as potent as any serpent's poison. There was a flash of surprise behind the mask. No amount of sun or shadow could keep his feelings from me now when I wanted them, when I didn't restrain myself. Roused by the violence of the scouts' attentions, I turned upon him, sharing with him a brief memory of my brother as a boy, a spotted viper easily as long as he was tall trapped between two hands. He had but grazed his palm against

143

the creature's fang and nearly died in a sweat that bedded him for two weeks. It was not difficult to imagine instead the face of one of the boys before us, clinging still to his father's trouser leg.

Gannet didn't turn away, surprising me by reshaping what I had given him: the snake turned slippery, a plait of hair unraveled from a weary head, the mother and son reunited on the doorstep we now faced. I shuddered and broke away from him, for if Antares spoke in ignorance, Gannet did not. He knew the mother lived by means I couldn't know. This was something new. It was a power I felt strangely certain we didn't share, and never would.

We didn't linger with the bearded man and his children. When they turned indoors, relief went with them and dread with me as we proceeded down the road. Now all of the village's inhabitants seemed to have gathered to watch and whisper, their movements subdued but hopeful. Morainn they either did not know or did not recognize, and they were too busy, besides, in gawking at me. She had pulled her hood over her dark hair, obscuring much of her face, so perhaps they might have known her if she'd wanted them to. Imke rode in confidence beside her with a cold little smirk for me before I looked away, embittered. I didn't want to be Imke's enemy. I had not wanted to be anyone's.

The lord of the village lived in a stone structure that was modest, or as modest as something three stories high and as many wide can be. A guard of two men—boys, really—lazed in the cold afternoon light, the colors on their jerkins faded but the same that Antares wore. They leapt to their feet at the sight of us, though how they had remained oblivious to the commotion within the village at our coming I didn't know. And then I remembered how my sisters had seemed to me at their ages: more distant and dull at thirteen than I had thought possible. While I'd wanted to storytell and run out of doors, they'd made time for little more than brooding and mirror gazing.

"If you will announce us to Lord Rhale," Antares began, but there was more cause for the boys' alarm yet, as a richly dressed man appeared in the doorway, waving dismissively at each young guard as they scampered to assist him from the step. I could see that he was quite frail, with no more hair than a newborn babe could boast, his clothes filling out a skeletal frame.

"How lucky for me that I am the first to welcome you," he announced, his voice light but shrewd. His eyes were milky and vague, and he couldn't have known Morainn or Antares by sight. He would've been lucky to see more than a few steps in front of him.

I had tact enough to keep from trying to read him, cutting my eye to Gannet. He nodded curtly at my restraint. One right thing could for a little while sustain me.

"Lord Rhale." Antares greeted the elderly man with a modest bow, which seemed to please him. Morainn stepped forward as well, her pretense abandoned when she pushed the hood from her head. She might have been placing a crown there for all the weight of the gesture, and she waited patiently for him to acknowledge her. Lord Rhale required the assistance of his youthful guards, one on each side of him, to bow and recover his footing again. Morainn's face was for the moment as stern as her brother's. I felt more certain now that we would be expected to behave quite differently than we had. Like children without the watchful eyes of their parents I could see that Morainn and Gannet had done as they pleased, but they were nearly home now, and already their roles seemed to me infinitely more complicated.

As for me, any certainty I had about myself vanished as I became increasingly unsure of my companions.

We were welcomed inside with a few words exchanged between Lord Rhale and Antares, his guard moving toward the smells of food and animals. Morainn, Imke, Gannet, and I were led upstairs. Lord Rhale didn't accompany us but servants appeared to be sure we didn't lose our way. I wasn't sure I could have watched the agonizing display that would have been the old man's slow ascent. I felt choked inside by the nearness of death, for I knew it now, and his decline was lingering like a bad smell over everything.

Morainn was given the best of rooms, one adjoining for Imke

and what protection was offered by her little knife. I was grateful to be further away from her than a few doors as both Gannet and I were led up again, to the third floor, and finally, to the fourth.

"Lord Rhale assumed you would want the chapel available to you," the servant explained, a coppery fringe escaping his tight cap. I had never seen hair his color and tried not to stare.

Gannet nodded his agreement, though shared nothing of what this meant with me, gesturing only that I take the room next to the one that would be his. I obliged, if only because the servant was beginning to fidget, avoiding looking at me but from the corners of his eyes. I didn't think his reticence had anything to do with my hair color.

The room was opulent, but sorely neglected. There was a thick layer of dust on two fine chests pushed up against the wall, and I didn't need to lay an experimental hand upon the heavy bedspread to know that it, too, would puff forth a cloud of disuse.

I waited patiently while the servant laid a modest fire, and more patiently still for him to leave so I might coax it hotter and higher, better for soothing my spirits and my chilled limbs. I was interrupted as soon as he'd gone, however, by Gannet opening and closing my door behind him, the flames settling low again as my concentration failed.

For a moment I studied him there, a frown creeping from my lips to my brow at the sight of a new cloak lain about his shoulders to replace the one he had left in the Rogue's Ear. He had seemed less severe without the cloak, the breadth of his shoulders more that of a young man than what this bulky wool belied: a burdened spirit, an icon with little need for youth or humanness.

"What is the chapel like?" I asked, quick to dismiss my thoughts of human need. I didn't want to dwell on his, not when mine were so mixed up. Gannet answered only because I suspected he had come on related purpose.

"It's not so different than what you're used to," he explained, but I was sure no sanctuary here could imitate the cool, secret stone places I had knelt in with my mother. I missed her so much

I felt almost blown over by it, like a weak tree in a storm. I didn't have any roots here.

I nodded, finally, neither denying nor confirming what Gannet had said. I rose from where I'd been seated before the hearth because I knew he wanted me to, but wouldn't ask. I felt like a child's toy manipulated with strings; would I feel them all, all of the other icons, as keenly? Would I do as they wanted simply because I knew it, and it was easier to comply?

Or was it only Gannet I sought to please?

"The chapel is usually a private place, but I'll go with you, this time," Gannet explained as we left my chamber, passing down the hall to a flight of narrow, worn stairs. Wooden frames had once reinforced the stone, and both had been well-polished by the traffic of human feet.

"Then it's not like what I am used to," I said, though I wasn't attempting to provoke him. "Are you afraid to leave me alone here, too?"

The cloak effectively masked whatever the set of Gannet's shoulders might have told me about his response, and without seeing his face, or daring the energies to peer beyond his guard, I could only assume he spoke in earnest.

"It has nothing to do with fear."

Curiosity piqued, I followed him up the stairs. I was surprised when I felt the sharp chill of outside air again, a simple wrought gate rising between us and a roof landing. I felt rewarded for my obedience when the scene before me unfolded to a familiar one, the nearest the Ambarians had yet to come in showing that we were anything alike.

Potted, scrubby winter trees were tangled with a canopy of vines, thick with waxy leaves and dark berries. Wood beams and altar stone provided some shelter from the wind, but only a little. Braziers burned in the four corners, and I could smell their incense on the air, a sweet, slightly bitter scent that could not have come from any herb but the same that we gathered underground: mudcap, light as air where it grew, but brittle as sculpted sand when harvested and dried. We burned it for the smell, which my mother claimed, usually within earshot of my more reckless siblings, could lull even the wickedest hearts to penitence.

The worship benches were organized just as they would've been at home, too, growing more narrow and squat the nearer the altar they were. In this fashion, those who came to offer their devotions would be forced to consider them fully on their knees with their head bent low, and to consider the needs and wants of their fellows in prayer. Only in desperation would someone approach the bench nearest their idol, where they would be almost completely prostrate on their bellies. None of the benches were now occupied, and I wondered if the Ambarians had learned humility as we had?

Or perhaps their temples were merely for show.

The irony of so many gods represented here, and each of them embodied somewhere in Ambar by a living being, made me wonder what exactly I was expected to do here. Was I meant to worship Theba? I certainly couldn't believe that she would deign to worship anyone else.

"We keep faith as Aleyn keeps it," Gannet said, though I didn't know if his words were in response to my thoughts, or simply in continuing the conversation we had begun earlier. When he continued, he wasn't speaking of Ambarians. "It isn't the same for us, of course."

"You mean I can't just ask myself for guidance?"

I knew I was being ridiculous, and in front of the gods, no less. But I didn't care.

Gannet ignored me, striding to the center of the prayer garden and to the left, out of sight. I followed, passing the stone faces of several benevolent idols whose eyes had been all but rubbed away by the wind. If they could see, I didn't think they would recognize one of their own, caged in wiry flesh and sullied cloth. Part of me was relieved, and the rest sure that it was inevitable that everyone would, in time, know me for what I was.

He had stopped before an altar that had only one bench for worship, so low that one's nose would meet the stone before their brow. There was no guide on the altar and no offerings, either, only a copper mirror, green with age and reflecting nothing. This altar I'd never seen before, and I knew why. Aleynians didn't worship monsters.

This was where the penitent came to seek Theba's favor, if she had such a thing.

Gannet hadn't knelt in approach, and neither did I. Instead we both stood at a respectful distance, side by side, as though something was represented there, nameless but powerful. But she had a name, and it was mine.

"I wanted you to see it, before you're tested."

"Tested?" There was an edge to my voice that hadn't been there, not before I'd seen the mirror.

"I know who you are, but like any icon, you must be tested." I was sure his voice had taken the tone he favored when his words were someone else's, repeated for my benefit but far from convincing.

"If you're so sure, what's the point?"

Gannet looked down at me, uncertainty and disappointment plain in his features.

"You more than anyone should understand that many things are done without a reason, even when it seems otherwise," he answered, looking away, gaze settling again on the copper mirror. He saw something there, more than anything it could reflect even if it had been highly polished. But it wasn't the same, the things I had done, the things I might still do. I put a hand upon his arm, fingers clutched against his sleeve.

"Haven't I been tried enough? I've done everything that you've asked. I can't do anymore."

It was a threat I hadn't intended until it was there upon my lips and then sprung from them, unfolding in the air between us like a hot breath. Gannet looked from the mirror to my face and then away, as though he could see my words between us and studied them. Without looking at me again, he took my hand deliberately from its desperate perch, holding the tight fist in one careful hand.

"What if I told you that people were brought into the world

with fists clenched, grew from sucking babes pounding at their mother's breast to children whose only games were violent ones. When men and women they come to be, no tool can they wield, no tender stroke can they make, for still their hands are balled.

"There are a few wise folk among them who want to open their fists, but they're afraid, sure that fingers wound so tightly from the womb can mean only one of two things: that within their fists they hold a great secret in need of protecting, or an evil that must remain forever caged."

He paused, drawing his thumb over my fingers, running it along the well created between my nails and my palm. The cold, or his touch, made me shiver from head to foot.

"I would like to know, do you think it a greater loss to go to their graves with hands clenched, never knowing, or open them and suffer, if that is what they're meant to do?"

When Gannet looked at me, it was as though I had commanded it, our eyes charged by my power, or his, or both. I didn't speak, and didn't need to, answering him when my hand unfurled like a flower, cupped within his larger one. With his other hand he lifted mine, clasping them both together with his hands a house to warm them. Because we were touching, I knew that he had suspected my answer already. It had once been his. More keenly than any sense of him I had in that moment, however, was the feeling of his skin against mine, the warmth, the cautious pressure of palm and fingertip.

A cough interrupted us, and Gannet dropped my hands with far less ceremony than he had gathered them. One of Rhale's servants stood a few paces away in the prayer garden.

"A meal has been prepared and will be served within the hour. Fresh clothes and hot water are ready in your rooms."

He seemed anxious to be away as soon as his message was delivered, and Gannet advanced upon him, signal enough that he could depart. I remained rooted to the spot, for sense and senses both had fallen to the stone when Gannet released my hands.

When he didn't look back, my voice rose like a bird's call from my lips, not a threat this time, but an entreaty.

"What did you find, when you opened your fist?" I asked, borrowing from his metaphor, whether it had been intended as one or not. He had taken the test, same as I would have to. Gannet stopped, but he didn't turn, didn't look.

"Another closed within it."

And down the stairs he went, leaving me to wonder if this second fist had been his own, closed still because there were things about himself he couldn't know, or if it had been mine, all along.

CHAPTER SEVENTEEN

Rhale was a gracious host, though his temper turned with every course brought out at dinner. It was ludicrous enough to be bathed and dressed and seated at a formal dinner, anyway, after having grown accustomed to taking my meals in my lap, that his company was doubly curious. I couldn't decide if his moods were the product of disposition or age, but when no one commented upon the eccentricities in his manner, I didn't, either.

I learned much as I sat quietly, eating everything that was put in front of me with a voracity that betrayed our last, lean days. Keeping my mouth full made it rude for anyone to ask me questions, and as there was nothing they could ask me about myself that I'd want to share, my strategy seemed sound. Antares supped with us, but none of his guard, as well as Morainn, Imke, Gannet, Rhale, and two young men I assumed at first were his sons. They had seated themselves on either side of him, and though they didn't feed him, they came near to it, filling his plate, wiping his chin free of dribbled gravy. Their tenderness had nothing in it of the love of sons, and more of love of another kind.

"I was never a campaigning man," Rhale announced over a dish of greens tossed with nuts, wilted slightly and heavily spiced. The comment seemed directed at no one, nothing preceding it but a polite compliment from Antares regarding the tenderness of the beef. "Though I could have led one of the Southern expeditions, if I'd wanted to."

I made a point not to stop my steady consumption, though my attention was far more attuned to the old man than it was to the meal. I needed a distraction after this afternoon, after Gannet.

I didn't look at him now, and had not, but wanted keenly to feel his eyes on me.

"It is a fine thing you did not, Lord Rhale, for we might not have the pleasure of your company now," Imke offered. I sensed from her a strange desire to please him, as though she were currying favor instead of speaking truth. Rhale huffed, and one of the young men steadied his glass as he nearly toppled it with a blind gesture down the table.

"I may speak ill of the dead as I lost a son to the damned sands, and I'll tell you that was a headless army if ever there was one. Men like your father," he said, gesturing to Morainn, who nodded dumb assent, and to Antares after, "and you, well, you're a breed apart from the rock skulls of my generation. Nobody else has lived as long as me, and why do you think that is?"

No one answered as Rhale dug into a pudding studded with fruit, and I gathered that such questions were not in want of answers. I was, however, and saw in Rhale an eagerness to speak that I hadn't encountered in anyone else. That he could speak so callously over the death of his own child chilled me, but did nothing to still my tongue.

"Surely your wisdom made you a great councilor in the late war," I speculated aloud, sorry to have followed Imke into blind flattery but not for what it might win me.

Rhale's head shot up as he made short work of the pudding. His eyes narrowed on me, little to be read in their milky age.

"What does the conquered have to say about the manner in which they're beaten? If I'd been consulted we would have had our victory years ago, you wrenched sucking from your mother's breast and not here a grown woman, with skills and troubles born of that condition and others, besides."

My heart quickened at how candid he could be where others could not, or would not. Did he know who I was? There was nothing explicit in his words to suggest that he did, but the nearer we drew to Jhosch the less faith I had in Gannet's insistence that my identity would remain a secret. I sensed that this man, at least, had little concern for keeping secrets.

Charged by his lack of discretion, I lifted my spoon as a bowl of soup was set to cool before me.

"You underestimate us. Had we known you wished to strike at the heart of my family, I think that I would be among them still."

Rhale laughed heartily at this, and I felt more than one pair of eyes upon me at the table. I had Gannet's attention, at last, but I didn't indulge in a glance, focusing instead upon the soup. My feigned disinterest drew the old man out further.

"In the hereafter, maybe. But with *their* kind," he gestured at Gannet with a chortle and a hiss, "everything must be done as it is written. Blood must be spilled, war must be raged. Death is her trade."

His words weren't the senseless ramblings of an old man, but I was sure now that he didn't know who I was. What role did the dread goddess play in the lives of these people, if he should mention her in such a way? Gannet had insisted I return with them, but he'd never been clear as to why. I took a deep breath before next I spoke, knowing that it would turn the tide of what came next, if not halt it completely.

"But where is it written that she must revel in it?"

No one had any answer for this, not even Gannet. I had looked to him when I spoke and not to Rhale, witnessed his lips parted slightly in anticipation. I wanted him to answer me that it was nowhere, nowhere, when both of us knew and everyone around the table, too, that the answer was everywhere. Even now, how could I reconcile myself to such a monstrous existence? I couldn't accept even that I had killed a man in my own defense. Would there be more graves for Gannet to dig?

I had a vision, then, of his face ashen, pale with grave sickness or near death, the same parting of lips with the intention to speak but no words issued forth. Hands swam before his face, many pairs and one of them mine. Were those my slim fingers weaving around his neck to strangle him, or clapped over his mouth to stifle his breath? Did I punch out his eyes with pointed fingers? The last pair of hands worked hurriedly among the others, and I saw the mask loose and dip from his brow, startling their terrible work, sparing his life.

When I returned to myself Morainn was speaking, had steered the conversation away from waters that I could disturb, and Gannet was looking at me still, the tight set of his lips like a seam in iron.

What did you see?

How did he know, always, how it was with me? I looked away, and as I summoned the will to deny him entry to my mind, I buried, too, the torturous images, hoping that they were nothing but my imagination.

It was not so late after we concluded our meal that I could retire to sleep, but neither did I want to suffer further the assembled company. One or two at a time I could manage, but I grew tired of the games played, and my part in them. I thought perhaps I could return to the prayer garden, but it was dark now and surely bitter cold. Resigned to my quarters but not to the warmth of the fire within, I was surprised on the stair by Morainn, following after me without servant, or guard, or brother.

"I've asked one of Rhale's men to bring us a cup of punch," she said, gesturing up the stair. "Shall we?"

I could do little but oblige her, and led the way up the remaining stair to the landing where Gannet and I had been quartered, his door closed and mine slightly ajar, spilling the fire's glow onto the stone. Inside, heavy robes that had not been there before were draped across the chairs by the fire, and a little table stood waiting between them for Morainn's promised punch.

"Lord Rhale is nothing if not hospitable," Morainn sighed, though her tone teased a little that he was known widely for many other things. Still, we bundled each into the robes provided, and were not seated but a minute before a servant arrived with a steaming flagon and two simple but finely made cups. He poured a healthy sum of the brew for us both, and didn't wait to be dismissed before going out again. As I raised the cup to my lips, I could smell the spice in it, the strong, sweet scent that promised a sore head in the morning if I drank too fast, or too much.

"You needn't pay him any mind, you know," Morainn began, and I sensed that she worried over how bold the old man had been, though needlessly. He didn't know. I took a drink before I spoke, wetting my lips and spirit both.

"I'm grateful for a little candor, now and then," I said, tucking my feet underneath me, shoes and all.

Morainn smiled, sampling her own punch. "I just hate being spoken of as though I am little more than my office, and thought perhaps it might be the same for you. Even if he didn't realize what an egregious ass he was being." She smirked and a laugh escaped me, as unwitting as Rhale's words.

"I am still getting used to attention of any kind, I suppose," I said, grateful for the opportunity to voice what I felt, instead of wondering if it had been read already. "At home I was the youngest of five, and hardly the best subject for admirers or gossips. Among my sisters, especially, one would think there were three of us, and not four."

Though I didn't speak in contempt, I was not so guarded as to disguise completely what petty jealousies I felt where my sisters were concerned, even now, when it seemed we were to lead such different lives. Even under Ambarian martial law, they would have options, while I would have even less than what I'd imagined as a child. Their leisure and their pursuits in the arts, in diplomacy; they would be mothers, wives, scholars. What would I be, or should I rend the world so that they might be robbed of their futures, too?

My face must have darkened, for Morainn reached across, laid a hand upon the arm that didn't steady my hot cup. My answering smile was weak. We had not much time now before she was properly home, and I didn't think there would be casual drinks by the fireside then.

"Imagine how it must've been for my brother," I exclaimed, stirring to the sentiment even as I feigned it. "Coddled and teased, with no one to coddle and tease himself but me, who was as mild as a nesting bird. No wonder he is the way he is."

Morainn's expression was thoughtful, even if a grin tugged at the corners of her mouth. I was reminded of her treatment of my brother when he had come for me near the start of our journey, which seemed so long ago I was sure it was another life, another person's life.

"What was his favorite of your stories, your brother?"

"He had many," I said softly. "Though he always asked me for the story of Goshi, who deals in secrets. Do you know it?" Even as Morainn made to answer, our attentions were both diverted, for in that moment a sound traveled through the thick tapestry hung in folds over the room's window. I rose and Morainn behind me, and I could feel her grin upon my back. Shivering slightly, I pulled the heavy weave aside and I could hear it better then, the rain.

"One of the last of the season. It will all turn to ice and snow after this," Morainn observed quietly at my shoulder, our faces framed in the window for anyone on the ground below, any spirit watching from above. I could give little thought to ice and snow with the gentle shower to distract me, steady as a dream, with drops that splashed fat against the stone of the window's frame. I could see several grooms below dashing from the stable toward what I assumed was the servant's entrance to the manor proper, their whoops and laughter born on a chill wind to our ears.

I could have gone on the rest of the night at the window, my fingers giving over to the pale cold, my eyes frozen open upon a scene that was more satisfying than strange. Morainn put her hand near mine, guiding the tapestry over the window once more to shut out the cold and the wet.

"No matter what happens, Eiren, you'll have me. I will be sister and brother to you, for having my hand forced in separating you from them."

Morainn left no room for a response and I didn't think I could manage one, my surprise and sadness, my pleasure, blended to mute gratitude on my face. She smiled.

"You can tell me of Goshi another night." Leaving her drained cup on the little table between the chairs, she departed.

Though compelled to pull the tapestry back again, or more daring still to go up to the prayer garden and feel the soft touch of the weather on my face, I didn't. The first because it was not so tempting as the latter, and that because I didn't want to see Gannet so soon. If there were ever a night fit for prayers, for seeking the guidance of whatever deity it was paid their penance upon his face, it was tonight.

I was sorely inclined to utter a few of my own, but retired instead, slipping fitfully into dreams bone dry.

We were expected next day to remain abed until his lordship did, which was too late even for travel weariness. I could only imagine the cost the delay would have for Antares, who was eager enough to be away that his want could stand in for each one of us. Despite the curtain heavy across the window, I woke with the sun, which, though later here than I was used to, was the only thing familiar to me. I dressed in my traveling clothes, which Rhale's servants had struggled to clean and repair the evening before, leaving them folded and showing little evidence of their efforts next to a basin for washing. Water in a pitcher was threatening to turn to ice, but I forced myself to wash before hurrying into my many layers. I only just refused myself the cloak as I descended the stairs, eager more for occupation than I was company as I scouted the corridors of the estate.

Only one door was thrown open on the second floor, and this to a room I thrilled to see: a library, shelves stuffed full of bright tomes and crumbling ones, tables and desks tumbled over by someone who had clearly studied at a length too great to clean up after themselves. Though there was no one in the library that I could see, I stepped hesitantly into the room, wondering if perhaps some of my secrets might be revealed here. I wouldn't need to wheedle or play to such teachers as these books could be. After a moment I hastened to a shelf, tilting my head to better examine the spines of the bound tomes, the scroll cases and trailing ties.

Many were in a script I didn't recognize, but not the same as the one Gannet had given to me.

Crouched on the floor, I pried from the lowest shelf a particularly ancient looking text, folded between two graying covers of some animal hide. I was tricked by my eyes or the gray light—for in this room Rhale had windows set with glass, a luxury he had not invested in the whole of his home—into thinking that the characters etched upon it were kin to those in my book. I rose, thinking perhaps to retrieve it, when I noticed a painting above the door that my original vantage had not shown.

A young man waited in the shadows of a circle of standing stones, his feature muted all but for his grin, which was at once charming as a babe's and as sly as a sand dog's might be if such a creature could smile. A few lines of glinting paint near his hand confirmed for me that he held a key.

"My great, great, great-grandfather," a voice announced, and I started, eyes sweeping down to the doorway beneath the painting, where Rhale stood, still in his dressing gown and heavy sleeping robe. His eyes were much sharper in the morning light than they had been last night. "Can't you see the likeness?"

I looked back up at the painting, my color betraying my worry at having been caught here, wondering if I was not allowed. Rhale, however, didn't seem to mind, hobbling over to one of the cluttered tables and taking a seat.

"He was a man who knew how to get what he wanted," he sighed, making a half-hearted motion towards one of the texts, but joining me in looking at the painting. A rendering of Charrum on the wall was not the same as seeing sirens beneath the waves outside of Cascar, but I found it curious that Rhale claimed him as an ancestor. He was toying with me, perhaps, or delusional.

But I could read him well enough to know that he, at least, believed what he was saying.

"What did he want?"

At this, Rhale chuckled, as though that had not been the response he'd anticipated.

"What every man wants, girl. Glory, riches, the love of a good woman, or, well," he finished abruptly, dropping a gnarled hand into his lap. "Charrum did as he pleased, followed his own course. I thought to do the same, but things haven't happened for me quite as they did for him."

My skin peppered with chill at his words, at the name he uttered. How had Charrum come to be in the home of an Ambarian lord claiming ancestry? I looked at the painting again, as though I might find some resemblance between the old man and the myth, as he'd asked. Rhale watched me, eyes narrowed, and I was glad he didn't have my skills. But when next he spoke, I wasn't so sure.

"I've seen the way he looks at you. Your life hasn't followed the course you thought it would, either, has it, icon?"

Either Rhale had come into the knowledge in the night or was more adept even than Gannet at hiding his true thoughts. He didn't name her, but he knew. What Gannet's attentions had to do with the dread goddess I didn't know, and didn't want to know. But there were other things I did.

"I don't suppose you have anything in here about me," I said evenly, not wanting to give Rhale the satisfaction of having surprised me.

"Icons have never interested me as much as other things," Rhale admitted, his creaky tenor betraying just how unpopular was the opinion he voiced. "But," and here he rose, sturdier than his slight frame first seemed, and moved slowly towards a shelf in the corner, gesturing to the highest shelf. "I have an account of Shran's histories you might be interested in."

As I crossed to where he stood, nerves balled in my feet at every step, Rhale turned his sharp eyes on me once more. I smiled a little, thinking to set him at his ease, or me, but his expression didn't change. While he clearly didn't perceive me as a threat, I was no harmless child, either. He tapped a finger against a tome, but as I reached for it, his fingers moved as effortlessly to grasp my wrist. He was stronger than he seemed, though I had the feeling he would let me go if I struggled. I didn't, at first, but leveled my gaze on him.

"Do you think you will find more in there than you can in here?" He spoke, moving the hand he clutched over my heart. I thought carefully about my words before I spoke, keenly aware of the pressure of his fingers against my skin. They felt like twisted paper, cool and frail.

"I am a stranger to myself," I said softly. "So yes, I do."

Rhale released my arm, and I dropped it to my side. I didn't reach for the book, for he retrieved it for me, setting it on the table with all of the others.

"Most fear the icons, but some, like me, do not." He paused, laying his stronger-than-it-seemed hand against the cover of the book, as though he were suppressing whatever lay within. "But everyone is afraid of you."

He trembled, but it was not from the stresses of his age, or even fear, exactly. The dread goddess was terrible but awesome, too, in her power. For the Ambarians, anyway.

"Then why am I here?" I asked. Gannet had never said, but I had never doubted that there must be some proof for such trouble, such cost. I had been an unexpected boon of their war, but after what Rhale had said last night, I knew that the dread goddess had played a role in its waging well before I'd entered that chamber with Gannet and Morainn.

Rhale looked surprised, but just as he opened his mouth to speak, our attentions were diverted by footfalls at the door. Gannet stood there, his hair untidy at his collar, his masked brow.

"It was written." His first words did not surprise me, predictable as bird song. Gannet's next, though, was new. "When we are in Jhosch, we will go to the opera. Then you'll know."

The way he said opera made it seem as though we would pay a visit to a sage or witness a great battle. My skepticism warred with irritation that he should interrupt now when I didn't want him, looking maddeningly well rested. I thought to take the book from the table just to spite him, but I knew I would only have to return it and seem more a pawn before Rhale than I did now. I liked the old man, and hoped this wouldn't be our last encounter. A nod, however, was all I could give him to indicate as much, for I was sure he did not exactly seek my favor, whatever he imagined me to be. I crossed the library to Gannet's side, my temper cooled as other fires were stirred by the heat I could feel radiating off of his body. He was dressed already for traveling.

"Strangers are more welcome some places than others," Rhale offered, an unusual goodbye but framed as one nevertheless. He was looking at me and not at Gannet, and I smiled.

"I'll remember that," I replied, hoping that we would someday have cause to return, and not just for the book the old man fingered lightly, as though he could read something upon its surface with just a touch.

Gannet didn't need to put a hand upon me to steer me out of the library and toward the landing where he would go down to see to our departure, and I up to ready myself for it. I would've shaken him off anyway. Without looking at him, I held his attention a moment, demanded it.

"You could've interrupted sooner," I said, for I hadn't guarded myself there. In fact, I was surprised he wasn't more critical of my lack of control. "Why didn't you?"

I could feel his eyes upon me, that he wanted me to meet them, but I looked away, focused upon a blank space over his shoulder. I had seen my mother often give this look to those who had displeased her, as though she listened but only out of obligation. It didn't matter that I had asked the question. I was owed something, and Gannet had kept it from me.

"You may think I know everything," Gannet answered without a hint of pride, only bald assumption. His attention was unrelenting, his eyes hot as palms on my cheeks, my eyelids, my brow. "But sometimes I have to wait for you to show me what it is you want."

At this I laughed, a cold cough of a thing.

"How could I want anything else, Gannet, but to know what it is I really am, and what I'm meant to do?" I couldn't maintain my charade of not wanting to look at him, meeting his eyes. The landing was not well lit, and I could see almost nothing in his face but smoldering shadow. "Don't you?"

"You are Theba. You know what she is. Isn't that enough?"

"Of course it isn't!" I exploded, a whisper that hissed like pressure from a pipe. I fancied I could feel steam heating my toes, my limbs bundled against the cold, my wet-hot heart. "I've done things and seen things that I don't understand. I don't have your faith."

There had been other moments like this one in the time we had spent together, moments where Gannet would share some part of his knowledge, open his mind to mine, and perhaps this was what I sought: an intimacy in what we were, if not with each other. But he had turned away from me not twelve hours ago, and he did so again now.

"You only have two days to acquire it."

Down he went, then, to the horses, to Antares, to the guard that remained. I wished then that I had a mask to disguise what I felt, but would settle for my hood and the fall of my hair.

CHAPTER EIGHTEEN

Morainn had been wrong about the rain. We were forced to stop early that evening when what rain had come and gone again throughout the day in a drizzle that delighted me turned to a downpour the likes of which I would never have been able to imagine. It was as though the sea we'd been meant to travel over had come to us, but in reverse: the valley was filling up, and we were at the bottom of a soon-to-be ocean instead of riding on its waves.

The Ambarians were prepared with supplies from Rhale's village. We took shelter under trees, meager enough cover until Antares and the guards that remained with us were able to construct a few hasty shelters from canvas and spikes driven into the ground. The shelters were hardly bigger than trunks but they were dry, and though arranged close together, conversation was hardly possible without shouting. I was irritated that when it became clear the shelters could hold no more than two comfortably, I had to wait out the storm with Gannet. I was still sore with him over interrupting me that morning with Rhale, but as we grew closer to Jhosch, remaining angry with him seemed like a waste of precious time. When we had our rations and the hour was all but impossible to determine through the thick sheets of rain, I thought it better to converse peaceably than to argue.

"You mentioned the opera. What is it? Why haven't you said anything about it before?"

There wasn't room enough in the shelter for much distance between us, so our meal was spread before our folded knees, our hands passing near to each other when we reached for water or bread.

"You have to see it to understand," he began, though gladly gave my temper no reason to rise again when he continued. "We learn about who we are as a people at the opera. Yours will be told soon after we arrive, I think."

I knew that the story he spoke of was not mine but Theba's, and I bit back the retort that wanted voiced. Still, he caught my eyes and knew what I felt despite the restraint I showed.

"You believe it but you do not accept it, *Han'dra* Eiren," he said softly. "How is that?"

"Rhale knew who I was. There are men here, I suspect, who know it, too. They know I am a killer, and still they follow me. How is that?" My voice was low, and my gesture to the camp of soldiers was a weak one, for my clothes were only now beginning to dry, and still I shivered. As I surveyed them, I was surprised to see Antares and Imke in a nearby shelter, he removing the blanket from his pack and laying it about the sturdy maid's shoulders. She had given her own to Morainn, no doubt. What I felt was not jealousy, or if it was, it came from that part of me I wouldn't claim, for I wasn't sure what I wanted. Even if I knew, Theba would only pervert it.

Gannet followed my gaze but when he turned back again I was looking off, my mind carefully walled against him. What he said next could only have been a guess, or the product of casual observation.

"If you're cold, *Han'dra* Eiren, you may have my cloak."

"I will be warm enough in a moment." My words were all heat and regret. I flushed despite the chill, the sensation a strange one, hot and cold.

Gannet seemed to accept this, and not looking at him meant I had to look out on the camp, imagining the conversations, the little intimacies that were none of them burdened as ours was. There were few safe avenues of conversation when I could not be sure of what I felt or why, what it meant for me to feel anything.

"You promised you would tell me of Karatan," I said, remembering the heated words we had exchanged after sharing Charrum's tale and thinking again of the painting in Rhale's library. The lines of what I knew to be real, and what I believed to be fiction, were blurred daily. It was no wonder I didn't know my own heart. "Will you tell me now?"

Gannet's surprise flashed but a moment in my sense of him, and he drained his cup of tea before responding, as though he needed the moment to compose himself.

"I don't think it's a story you will like. It's not really a story at all," he dodged, and I couldn't help but smile, casting a sidelong glance at him and inadvertently catching his eye.

"If you don't want to tell it, you don't have to."

There was some fiber of the usual man in Gannet, however slim, and he rose to my obvious challenge.

"Karatan was an icon, the icon of Adah," he said, and he remembered just as I did Herat's tale, and her fate at the hands of that god's particular brand of cruelty. "He lived many generations ago among my people, during a time when we turned upon each other for simple offenses, and murdered for greater ones."

Though he said this with as little emotion as he might convey a list of tasks or supplies, I could tell that the depths in their history, their real history, ran deep in him, too. Ambar had been forged in violence just as Aleyn had been in need and peace. Perhaps this is why of all the icons to have so integral in their culture, they had chosen Theba. Perhaps she had chosen them.

"The icons have power of a kind now, but their power then was even greater. There were no established houses, no lords, only the law of one man, one woman, against another. Icons were feared, revered, for their ability to bend and sometimes break the laws of nature. Karatan didn't abuse his influence. He knew that for the people of Ambar to survive they must learn to honor and preserve each other. His gifts, and the gifts of the other icons, some of whom were allies and others enemies, must be for some purpose. He wanted, he needed, to know what that was."

Gannet didn't allow anything like fervor to color his tone, but I felt the same want and need in him.

"He traveled far and dug deep into the living memory of his people. As the icon of Adah his was a balanced mind, and his meditations and questions led him to the tomb of Shran, abandoned but for a few generations in his time, and now lost. He heard the whispers of the First People there, of whom Shran was the last."

"Who were the First People?" I interrupted, this part of Shran's history a surprise to me. I had not thought there was anything of that family left to surprise me.

"You told the story of his sons," Gannet said carefully, avoiding speaking of the details of the brothers and their various betrayals, which surprised me, too. I had yet to see him waive an opportunity to mention Theba. "Salarahan was not the only one to be punished. Adah himself had judged the brothers, and through them all mortals. Shran and his sons, his wife Jemae and others were more akin to the gods than even you and I are, though they were not the equals of gods. Adah stripped from the First People their long lives, their physical prowess, the richness of their perceptions. His punishment we have been spared, as icons, for your family and mine pay it."

Gannet could teach me to see in the dark, to picture my mind a landscape and move in it as I would this terrain, but that he knew something like this, something from a story, that I didn't was the most surprising thing of all. And yet I believed him, my attention given over completely now. It was my turn to watch him while he found his words in the rain.

"In Shran's tomb Adah's icon heard the whispers of the god, and Karatan knew that he, too, must level some charge against his kind if they could not overcome their barbarism. Like the First People, they would be driven to death.

"He brought together those icons he felt could be trusted and together they sought the employ of one of the more powerful among the warring tribes, but also the easiest to manipulate. Through him they subdued the other icons, and the mortals who did not follow him were made to do so or die. It was through this lord that our line of kings was born, and myself, and Morainn."

"Surely this is not the story your people tell? It's far from glorious." I hadn't meant to interrupt again, but Gannet had been right. I didn't like this story.

"Real histories rarely are."

"But your first king a weak and power-hungry man? You cannot make peace from blood."

Gannet didn't respond for a moment, as though weighing what to say next. When he spoke I understood his hesitation.

"Isn't that what we've done in Aleyn?"

He implicated me in his statement, my role in the reconciliation that had come to our people. I remained unconvinced and angry besides.

"Is that it, then? You were right; it's not a very good story."

"It's not over," Gannet said coldly, though there was a blade's edge of sympathy in his voice that I chose to ignore. "When what needed to be done was done, Karatan offered his people something greater: a spiritual path. The icons, burdened with such profound gifts, were raised to serve and to advise, and the men and women of Ambar united to preserve what was in the past and plan for a shared future. It is very rare now that an Ambarian will turn against another Ambarian, and there is comfort in knowing the meanings of our lives."

I could only perceive such comforts meagerly, especially belonging to a people who had nearly the whole of my life suffered the Ambarians to pursue and subdue them. Sighing, I pulled my legs close to my chest, folds of fabric gathering around my body and still insufficient to combat the cold. During Gannet's telling the rain had abated, then stopped utterly, the clouds pulling apart like torn cloth to expose a bright moon. Though I would rather have resisted the urge to do so, I cast a look sidelong at Gannet, and met the eyes that had been fixed in study upon me. I didn't flinch or turn away from his gaze, the moon flooding his face with unusual clarity of expression, even with the mask. I knew that he wanted to speak, to open his mouth or his mind to me, but what he wanted to say he didn't share. Without the rain I felt exposed to the others in the camp, and though I hadn't believed then that I would ever want to return to such a place, I longed for the strange intimacy the Rogue's Ear had given us. I let him know this, let him live for a moment in the part of my mind that was not consumed with confusion and regret, but looked to a future no history of his could predict.

And then I wondered over a part of the tale Gannet had merely glossed over.

"Karatan visited the tomb of Shran. Why? He was our king."

His eyes were level with mine, his words soft.

"Have you never wondered how we share the same gods, the same stories? Shran was our king, too. Re'Kether was the seat of a kingdom we shared, many tens of generations ago."

Though my first thought was to resist him, as I did always, I wondered how it hadn't occurred to me before. The conspicuous absence of such detail from my stories also seemed deliberate, perhaps my mother's doing. With such tales as one of our few comforts during wartime, why shouldn't she omit a shared origin?

But how far we had come since Shran's time. How different we were now.

When I said nothing Gannet rose, and I thought he meant to leave. He did, but not before slipping his cloak from his shoulders. "You are still cold, *Han'dra* Eiren."

The heat of the heavy wool was for a moment increased by the pressure of his hands as he laid the cloak over my shoulders. It was his heat, the warmth his body had imparted, and I felt it sink into me as surely and naturally as the soil had drawn the rain. I didn't thank him, and I closed my mind before he could know the depth of my pleasure, my desire for him as strong as my distrust.

I hardly slept that night for fear of my dreams, and more that they might spill over from me to the camp and be seen or felt. It was not just Gannet that might have my secrets. They were strong and many, and when Morainn narrowed her gaze on me the following morning, I thought they must be obvious, too.

For several hours before we reached Jhosch, I had the pleasure of watching every detail of the city sharpen and grow. Eerily not unlike the ancient fortresses deep in the deserts of Aleyn, Jhosch was carved from the mountain itself, spires of natural stone cutting like teeth skyward, the hollows in the rock the windows and passages of human habitation. The sparse settlements we passed through lead me to believe that much of the Ambarian population must live in the capital. I could see the witch, *Zhaeha*, loom and curl beyond, more strange and surreal the nearer we came, instead of less. I hadn't spoken with Gannet since the rain, but because I had exhausted all possible conversations with Morainn since, I asked him about it.

"It's said that to pass beneath her crooked nose is to know the smell of your own death," Gannet said, managing to drain the horror and mystery from the statement entirely with his dull tone. "There's nothing beyond but more mountains, and more treacherous. No one lives there."

I quirked a brow playfully, not caring if he'd appreciate or even acknowledge my efforts.

"That sounds like the beginning of the story for those that do," I insisted, though I didn't have the will for stories, now, not even as Morainn perked at my mention, and one or two of our guard, as well. The only tale I could conjure was my own, half-finished and full of dark promise. Gannet, however, came as near to a slight chuckle as he had since before we entered the Rogue's Ear.

"It does indeed," he said softly, eyes fixed ahead of us on Jhosch or the witch, or both. "I've never been there, so how should I know? If you're willing to risk heralding your own demise, perhaps you should venture that way when we are near."

Even as Gannet made his own grim attempt at levity, I felt him retreat to a darker place, his own treacherous mindscape. If I put my hand upon him, would I see again the child Gannet, masked for the first time?

"You tease Eiren on purpose I think, Gannet," Morainn said lightly, her efforts to lift our spirits much appreciated, at least on my part. There was none of the glow in her cheeks that bespoke someone coming home after a lengthy absence, not the one I would imagine in my own if I had the pleasure, anyway. Neither sibling seemed to show particular excitement at having finally nearly reached our destination, though I wasn't surprised by Gannet's withholding of whatever it was he truly felt on the occasion.

"I would never tease her on accident," Gannet observed, and though his lips did not quirk in the slight fashion that usually signified a smile, I felt the tension dissipate even as we passed into the shadow cast by the great city. Imke perked in her saddle. I caught her eye, perceiving the scowl in it for all she turned quickly away. I wondered, not for the first time, if Imke and Kurdan had been close. She hadn't spoken expressly against me, not even in those veiled moments when she spoke with me alone. Still, I didn't trust her, not for the hungry way she looked when speaking of Ambarian conquests; not for her eyes, girded with the sort of careful, surreptitious observation normally seen among diplomats, not servants.

There was not much more talk after that, and I had my eyes and ears full, besides, of the sights and sounds of the approaching capital. It was like a living thing, moving as deliberately as we were, halving the distance between us with measured, subtle steps. We were expected here, for word had been sent ahead of us. There was no anonymity for Morainn, her people dropping to their knees, waving their hands or shielding their eyes from the setting sun so they could better see her. I imagined they were protecting themselves from her brilliance. My wonderings were cut short when I was seen a moment after, riding a few paces behind.

If Morainn inspired them, I drew them down again, lower than they had been before. Mothers and fathers looked on me with a mixture of awe and fear in their faces, holding their children against their chests and legs as though I might have reach enough to snatch them away. There was no confusion in their faces, nor in the faces of the armed among them, whose only doubts seemed to lie in whether they should raise or lower their weapons as my horse cantered near. If Gannet had thought himself keeping my secret, he was wrong. They knew. Here I would never be Eiren, storyteller, daughter, the youngest and mildest of many siblings. Here I was Theba, and I would not tell stories. I was one myself.

Almost as though it had been planned, I rode alone between grouped escorts. I wasn't a prisoner, but a terrible prize. More and more people tumbled out of doorways and stables, from gardens and groves heavy with fruit for harvest, all of their features awash at once with joy and moments later, trepidation. I couldn't look at them, but neither could I look down, as though ashamed of what I was. Would they think I was plotting some ill in the churning mud beneath the horse's hooves? I might tangle the legs of Morainn's mount and send her toppling. I might frenzy the soldiers that had served us so well to turn against their own. Theba wouldn't have settled for less.

My bold looks were not to be tolerated, for just as I thought perhaps we had passed through the bulk of the crowd, they pressed in upon us, and the anonymity of so many faces, limbs flailing, mouths open, allowed for insults to be shouted, curses and calls of a kind I had imagined, but never experienced. Wives called for their husbands, and mothers for their sons and daughters, blood was in their words and beneath the nails of the fingers that were clawing at the air. For those who had not the sense for words there were only wails, grief a language of its own.

I was more afraid of those that didn't speak, those that knew me and kept silent, brooding, as Gannet had the first time that I had met him. Did they know better than these common folk? Were they the powerful ones, the servants and protectors as Gannet had described them in the tale of Adah? I could feel my eyes burning as though smoke was building inside of me, a fire that the growing crowd fanned. It couldn't be tears for what I had become, because this had always been inside of me, waiting.

Gannet put a hand on my forearm. I could feel it despite the many layers the cold forced me to wear, and while it might've seemed to the watchers that he was restraining me, through the touch he flooded me with all the tenderness of friendship: my mother and father as clear as his brief memory of them could construct, the hands and abstract smiles of my siblings swarming around me. He hadn't known us, but he could understand, and as the crowd parted and we passed through, I didn't see them, but saw instead my memories and Gannet's imaginings pieced together. I could feel my sister Esbat's breath on my face as we waited beneath Lista's bed to grab her ankles and make her shriek, could trace the warmth of my brother's embrace after a rough practice with sword and stave.

Morainn he drew as well, and I realized he knew well what a comfort she was to me and I to her. I watched her riding tall before me with her guard on either side and I saw, too, those spare moments with her handmaids on the barge, our laughter over something insignificant breaking down the barriers between us. I could see that he played a role in this vision, too, for the shadows had space enough to accommodate a man who would only watch, could only.

"Gannet."

And without asking or allowing for hesitation, I slipped out of my glove and pressed my hand over his. Again the crowd might have imagined, and perhaps did by the few gasps I heard, that I sought to throw him off. What I did instead was thread my fingers in the hollows between his knuckles, imagined Morainn and Imke and Triss in those memories as formless, glowing light that made no room for shadows. We stood together in this memory turned dream, and as we came at last upon the entrance to Jhosch, the maw of stone and colored banners spilling like blood into the road, I took his hand there in the memory as I could not now. In the same moment I let him go in the physical world, unable to bear the disappointment of his letting go first.

The guard fell back, leaving Morainn, Imke, Gannet, Antares, and I mounted between the mob behind and an assembly ahead of citizens more orderly, formal, and no less reverent of Morainn and terrified of me. More guards appeared and when it seemed safe to dismount, we did.

"*Drech* Colaugh and *Dresha* Agathe celebrate your return."

No herald was needed to announce Gannet and Morainn's parents. Both were tall with the clear, bold eyes of their daughter, and the pretty mother I had encountered in Gannet's memory grown to her station. She was the rare sort of woman who acquires majesty with age. Her hair was fair as her son's, gathered on her crown in a thick, pale braid. No other artifact of her reign stood upon her brow.

Their father, Colaugh, had the darker curls and demanding carriage of his daughter, though his command seemed effortless as he strode forward, the grooms that had come for our horses scurrying away with reins in hand. Agathe followed behind, fingers pinning in the robes at her sides as her husband took both of Antares' gloved hands in his own.

"We are pleased to see you home and safely," Colaugh said, his voice rough and deep, furred like the great cloak he wore. Antares inclined his head in reverence, though stepped shortly out of the way for Morainn, who was gathered up by both parents, their words hushed enough that I couldn't hear, their gestures lingering and tight. I was uncomfortable with her homecoming, for I saw in it all of the things I couldn't have. I couldn't be happy for her. Was this selfishness Theba's, or mine?

Gannet stood apart from all of us, and I didn't know if this distance was because of a family he belonged to and couldn't share, or because their attentions turned immediately from their daughter to me. He wouldn't want to seem too close. Hadn't he said soon after our arrival here that I would be turned over to others, to teachers or worse? I could feel his eyes on me, could feel the slight weight in the air that was all of him contained against the world. And as my eyes passed between Colaugh and Agathe, I could see that he had inherited more from his mother than the brushed light of their hair. Even without a mask, her eyes were shadowed and full of secrets.

"*Han'dra* Eiren," Colaugh began, and unlike many of his people, he didn't struggle with the little inflections. But he met my eyes for only a moment before turning away, addressing the crowd. What I'd seen in that brief contact was mirrored in his words: brute intelligence, control, and a strength of will to rival that of both of his children.

"The war is over, and a new era begins. We welcome the icon of Theba."

His words were empty, exhausted of feeling. They weren't his, not originally. His thoughts were like a tense vibration, a note that I could hear but could not recognize. I noted the practiced way he avoided looking past me to his son.

"We welcome the icon of Theba," Agathe echoed, and as she did so the greeting seemed to swell like a tide in the gathered crowd, soft at first and firm soon enough.

"We welcome the icon of Theba."

I could feel Gannet like a pulse, like my own heart and blood threatening to spill from lips and eyelids and ears. I would drown us both.

"We welcome the icon of Theba."

Morainn had turned and uttered the same, Antares and Imke, too, without hesitation, each embellishing the greeting with hands that came together and parted again over their eyes. Imke's hands were shaking. Had I blinded them, or would they blind me?

"We welcome the icon of Theba."

"We welcome the icon of Theba."

"Theba, *matea tsisha a*," came the last, the loudest and surest. Gannet's feelings spiked behind me like a wave, like the waters I had conjured in Cascar and sent smashing through the ship. Several figures approached, repeating the greeting in a language I didn't understand. There were three, but I noticed most the one that strode a measured step in front of the other two, in the center.

Hello, Eiren.

I didn't quake but how I wanted to, as I could in an instant feel him rummaging about in my mind like a miser through his treasures, a beggar through trash. I could see both in him, this man with hair cut crudely but intentionally across his brow, blue eyes set like bits of glass in an ageless face.

I am Paivi. Did Gannet tell you about me?

I exhibited none of the control Gannet had warned me to maintain. I thought of the conversations when he had explained to me how things would change, the moods that had settled upon him darker even than usual. Paivi smiled softly. I blanched and struggled, aware of nothing but my own disappointment before he was standing in front of me, taking my hands in greeting as none of the others had. His smile widened.

He has never liked me, but you have no reason not to.

"Come, *Han'dra* Eiren, and let us make you welcome," he spoke aloud at last for the benefit of the others. He had caused me to forget them but they were still there, respectful and watching around me, their own greetings having fallen from their lips and leaving them with nothing but wearied silence. Colaugh was dwarfed by Paivi's presence, if not his stature, and I wasn't sure I believed Gannet now when he said that the icons had less power than in Ambar's turbulent past. From where I stood, they had all of it.

Paivi kept speaking but I wasn't listening. I looked at Gannet as one might contemplate shelter in a storm, the hands of Paivi's companions touching on either of my shoulders and leading me past where the royal family now waited. I didn't listen because I didn't need to. I already knew what he was saying.

Come, *Han'dra* Eiren, and let us make you.

CHAPTER NINETEEN

I was alone again before I could make room enough in my mind and heart for all that I had seen, for the people, my uncomfortably public entrance, and Paivi.

He had joined our escort, along with a host of servants and councilors, to the vaulted apartments where the royal family held court and conducted their lives behind closed doors. Jhosch was built within the mountain, not simply carved out of the side of it, with all manner of clever systems to carry the smoke and smells and waste out. The stone itself was delicate and webbed with designs that had been cut out by hands, human or otherwise, and here and there fountains splashed up water from beneath the ground. Spindly trees grew along lanes beaten by foot and cart wheels, and I wondered what ingenuity could compel them to grow within when so many generations of their kind had flourished only in the valley below. I wanted to sit down and simply look at the city, but I was hurried by the guard and everybody else besides. I felt Paivi's attention, harsh as the sun. Ambar didn't need the heat and the glare, for it seemed they had unnatural means for brilliance.

The royal family didn't keep a fortress or castle, though their home, which spiraled incomprehensibly forward out of the stone, balconies like wings unfolding, dominated the grand lane that wound through the center of Jhosch. A great deal of light was let in here, which though beautiful, served only to deepen the shadows that weren't touched by it. Once within, the walls were dark with secrets, like the deep places of the world. I touched them more than once, and they felt dry as bone.

I was tucked away into a room to rest, too exhausted and overwhelmed to admire it. I lay on top of the rich blanket, shivering, so I might stay awake and think better on my situation. There was a fire, but my chill had as much to do with the temperature as other things. I was sure that I should have been prepared for this, whatever it was. If Gannet hadn't seen fit to do so per his sense of duty, surely he might have done better by me as a friend?

He had shown me only one kindness since Paivi's appearance, the slight brushing of his hand against my sleeve, a gesture that was not lost on the former and illuminated him greatly for me. Paivi was the icon of Erutal, who was mild enough in the stories that I could recall, or, at least mild when compared to Theba. His province was for music, dance, and song, and there were many tales of his being seduced by the charms of mortal women. When they were pleased with him he, too, was pleased. When they were not he was as careless with human life as any of the pantheon. That Paivi was the icon of a fool god didn't make him any less a threat to me.

I didn't allow myself to grow too heated in thinking of him or of Gannet, fearful now of just how much I betrayed myself in the slightest rise or fall of my temper. Whatever his icon, Paivi was like the looking glass in one of my eldest sister's favorite stories, a mirror that saw right through you when you thought to see through to yourself. If you had a pure heart you would see yourself as you were, but if you were wicked, each sinful thought and hateful deed would plump like a wart upon your cheek. While the depth of Paivi's powers were unknown to me, I wasn't willing to take any sort of chance.

Despite my efforts to the contrary, I did sleep, and as I slept, I dreamed. I was Theba, or perhaps Theba was me, leaning out of the window of my childhood room. It had the width and breadth I remembered and my body was a girl's, hands gripping the stone sill and hair caught in a dance of wind. We laughed, Theba and me, and I could see her hanging in the air before me like a reflection just out of reach. We had the same eyes and crown of hair, but her mouth was cruel, teeth tearing a monstrous path in her lips. Our lips. I shrieked and the window closed around my growing form, woman again with the weight of me trusted too much on the sill. As I toppled forward Theba snaked her hands into my hair, and for a moment I felt the pain of being suspended by it.

She lowered me slowly onto the path below, a terrace walkway our guard had used and we, too, for pleasure. Theba passed into me again and we were the same. She propelled us forward.

The terrace was different, broad leaves like those of the plants I remembered in Cascar brushing against my calves, spilling and flowering out of contained spaces that bordered the path. It was a rooftop garden, but not one I recognized. I could see a figure ahead, cloaked. But it wasn't a cloak, only a shadow cast by a tree, curved unnatural to hang over a stone bench.

The figure stood and we sat, the bench warm from where he had recently reclined.

"Shran," we whispered, our breath hot as his body's heat, tumbled like a wave over us, over everything.

And then he tumbled over us, too, and I felt a touch I'd never known but had heard enough from sisters and servants gossiping to guess what it was. Theba rocked back on her thighs and I opened my arms to him, the little sound that escaped unraveling from us both.

His face in the moonlight was Gannet's.

I woke gasping, startling the servant that had slipped in while I was sleeping to build the fire back up when I toppled out of bed. I waved her away, knowing that even as she left she would return, and not alone. My hands covered my face as though what I'd dreamed was written upon it.

There was water in a shallow basin, resin-cracked, water so cold I wondered it had not yet turned to ice. I brushed a damp cloth over my eyes and hair. The color in my cheeks might be mistaken for illness, and why shouldn't it? What I felt, what I was, had no other explanation.

When Gannet appeared in my door way a few moments later, I wasn't sure which I felt in greater intensity: regret or relief. He closed the door right in the face of the servant at his heels, but I caught her brief, indignant look.

"You could've thanked her," I said, not looking at him, preoccupied with containing the dream as a thief might bury treasure, or a guilty man a body.

"So could you," he returned. Though he'd entered the room with purpose, the air about him now fairly vibrated with hesitation, and he hung back. Perhaps I hadn't given myself away then, and breathing a little, though not too much, I stepped back from the water basin, between Gannet and the bed. This stirred the dream again, and I stamped upon it, hard.

"She said you woke screaming," Gannet continued, stoking the fire himself with hardly a glance in the absence of the serving girl. "That you fell out of bed."

I couldn't lie to him, not completely. He could know that I dreamed without knowing the details of it.

"It was a nightmare. I was Theba," I began to explain, but the eyes that cut at me, sharpened by the lines of the mask, said what I didn't want to. *You are always Theba.*

"She had control, at first, but then what we wanted…was the same thing."

It was difficult to say as much and refuse the colors of the dream, my mind like a sketch, only, of what I remembered so clearly. That what I had dreamt was a story didn't calm me, but perverted what was dear to me. Shran and Jemae both had been used by Theba, and I wanted to believe that I was being used, too. How could that be true when she was me?

Flames licked softly at first at the logs in the hearth, and Gannet sat down in a chair before the fire. His posture welcomed me to join him and I did, caution like a brand on my face.

"Tonight they'll test you. There's no more time for uncertainty."

He didn't like what he had to say, but he knew that it needed to be said, and he wanted done with it. I closed up more tightly, not wanting this insight into his words, whether he meant for me to have it or not.

"Will Paivi conduct the test?" I asked, combing my fingers through the damp hair around my face. Paivi had said that Gannet did not like him, though Gannet's expression grew no more or less dour in speaking of the man.

"It's one of his duties," he answered. "Among others. Are you afraid of him?"

The question caught me off guard. "I trust him less than I did you, when we first met. That's not insignificant."

He smiled, and I felt something like threads pulled in my limbs and lungs at the turning up of the corners of his mouth.

"He doesn't trust you, either. But he's pleased to have you. More than pleased."

"How did they know it was me? Did you send word ahead?"

"No," he answered, tone wary. "But I'm not surprised. Someone must've sensed you, or dreamed you."

Or tried to kill me.

Before he could elaborate, a knock sounded on the door. Either the servant was far more polite than I would have given her credit for after being shut out, or someone else waited outside. As though he were responsible for who should be admitted to see me, and perhaps he was, Gannet rose and returned to the door, opening it wide enough for him to see but not me from where I remained seated. He whispered, and his words were lost. Not wanting to seem a petulant child at his elbow, I stayed where I was, impatient.

When he closed the door again, he looked at me, something shifting deep in his eyes.

"What is it?" I asked, though the answer I wanted had little to do with what had passed just now at the door.

"They're bringing you clothes and something to eat," he said simply. "I'll have to go."

"Why? What's wrong with this?" I lifted my arms, the traveling dress I wore wrinkled by my brief sleep but fine enough for anything, I felt. I realized at his expression—weariness and something else, too—that my first question was taken in regard to his leaving, and not my wardrobe. I blushed, crossing my arms over my stomach and taking an elbow in each hand.

"Eiren," he said, and surprised me by crossing the carpet, footsteps muted against the rich weave. He placed a hand over each of my hands. "I'll be called away soon, to other duties. You will have to become used to them."

He meant more than the attentions of the servants, of Paivi. He meant everyone, a life that would be different not only from the one I had known in Aleyn but the one that had, I realized, been a comfort to me on the road.

"What did you do before, that you return to now?" I whispered, thinking of the things he had yet to teach me, the stories I hadn't told him yet. I thought of other things, like the color of his hair in sunlight and firelight, the way his mask might feel if I pressed my thumbs around its base and under—not as an enemy might, to crush his eyes, but to see them better.

He stood there, holding my hands over my elbows in his awkwardly, but neither of us moved to break the contact.

"We're responsible for many things," he explained, though I could tell he struggled, with what he said or something else I wasn't sure. He had masterful control when he wanted to, when I was willing to show restraint. "We advise, we train others, we work to preserve our histories. The operas wouldn't exist without the work of icons, though we aren't suffered to participate."

Confused by this, I looked up, catching his eyes where I had avoided them the moment before.

"Suffered?"

Gannet's expression clouded. "Don't you think we have part enough already?"

I knew better than to translate his statement as some admittance that we were but players. Gannet believed wholeheartedly that he was whoever it was he had been confined to as a boy, that each of the icons was bound to do what they had been given mortal body to do. I didn't understand it, but I knew his life depended upon his belief. How else could one resign themselves to a life of service and sacrifice, disguise their face their whole lives and their own wants besides?

What Gannet meant was that any story worth telling would be about us, anyway.

I sighed and dropped my arms, feeling the warmth of his fingers against my elbows. He hadn't stepped back, and neither had I. The space between us seemed less, somehow, without arms crossed against it. I was looking at him still and thinking hard on what it really meant for him to go away, how it made me heavy and aching as a sun-baked stone to imagine this place without him. Hadn't we come this far together? Two days out of our capital and I would have made twice the journey alone to be spared his company, everyone's company. But his, especially.

Now he lifted his hands only slightly and I stepped into them, my arms circled like a ring about his back. I felt his hands, then, not linked as my hands were but pressed one each on my waist and mid-back. My face was turned away from his, but never had the space between his neck and shoulder seemed more intimate than it did then, my hot breath cupped in a hollow I thought I could occupy forever. With only cloth between our skin, Gannet couldn't guard himself, or perhaps he wasn't trying to. His heart was like a drum, each pump of blood as sure of the danger of what he did in holding me as it was in surrendering to wanting to.

It was as natural as breath, our bodies relaxed against each other. For the first time in months, I didn't feel as though I were holding mine.

An excruciating space seemed to build between us when he stepped away from me, eyes hooded, holding me at arms length a moment before releasing me altogether. He opened his mouth to speak, but the voice that emerged then didn't come from him, but from his sister in the doorway.

"*Han'dra* Eiren. I told Avery I would help you dress," she said carefully. The servant Gannet had disappointed earlier appeared from behind Morainn, arms laden with several wooly bundles. I didn't know how long Morainn had been there, and her manner betrayed little. She was looking at a space above us both, avoiding our faces, but there was an uncertain smile on her lips, tainted a little by the same fear her brother had shown when holding me. I could've fallen to the floor for want that he hold me again, and I made no mystery of my feelings. Gannet, however, had crossed the room to his sister, nodding at her before exiting without a word. My mouth opened and closed in protest or outrage or crippling desperation, but no words emerged.

The snap of heavy fabric shaken out behind me was an unwelcome distraction, but I turned despite myself. Avery was laying out a rich garment, plum colored and embroidered in great detail at the sleeves and hem. From the second bundle she produced what appeared to me at first to be a second gown, but when she unfolded it I realized the two were meant to be worn together, one over the other. The second was dark, too, blue-black and belted, sleeveless but with an ample cowl and hood. It was far finer, and would be far warmer, than the traveling dress I had insisted to Gannet would do for anything.

"I can manage, Avery." Morainn interrupted the servant's fussing, and I could tell by the expression on Avery's face that she didn't consider waiting on me to be among Morainn's duties. She did not, however, attempt to dissuade her mistress, merely excused herself with a curt nod and closed the door behind her.

Alone with Morainn, I felt immediately that some explanation, some apology, must be made, but she held up her hand, crossing to the last bundle and unrolling a pair of tall, soft boots.

"The less that I know the better," she insisted, and though I was confused by her words, I didn't continue. If there were some rule I had broken, I figured it was better not to know if I ever wanted to break it again.

Because I really wanted to.

"They've embroidered this dress in haste," Morainn observed, gathering a fold of cowl and allowing it to fall again. She smiled. "I hope it fits. I think they expected you to be taller."

I blushed at this, my heart reeling still but my head settling easier to this task than it might have another. Lista had dressed me for many occasions when I had let her, when we had lived in the capital still and had cause for fancy dressing.

"They made clothes for me?" I asked, approaching Morainn and the gown shyly, as though it represented someone I had yet to be acquainted with. Morainn nodded.

"The seamstresses did what they could, in the little time they were given. I wish I knew how they knew. Father was furious that I didn't notify him immediately, though it was safer that I didn't. But the icons…have means we don't. He resents it."

"Gannet doesn't know how my identity was known, either," I said quietly, fingering the fabric. I wanted to tell her that I wasn't as safe as she imagined me, hadn't been, but that would mean telling her the truth of what had happened in the Rogue's Ear.

And I wasn't sure I ever could.

"Gannet doesn't know everything, though I suspect he'd like us to think he did," she mused, again with the little smile. I let out a little breath of relief, grateful for some levity when my mind and body both seemed so tangled up. I lifted the heavy hem of the gown, and thought I'd get quite literally tangled in such a garment.

"I hope my test won't require running," I observed. "I'll trip."

Her eyes flickered at my comment.

"I don't know anything about it. We aren't permitted to know such things."

"Don't you govern the icons? You must know some of their business."

Morainn, however, shook her head. "It doesn't work like that. The icons are keepers of our history, and many secrets besides. The wars my father has begun…he's had encouragement."

This surprised me, but it shouldn't have.

"It's not over," I whispered, thinking of what the howling man had said. If the icons had a hand in Ambar's conquests, what would they plan now that they me?

Morainn misinterpreted my shuddering as a signal that I was cold, and helped me to shuffle into the unfamiliar gown. Though cumbersome and weighty as one tried to get into it, it moved comfortably on the body. The cowl, especially, I appreciated for the warmth it provided, and the embroidery on the inside, above my brow, attracted my attention. The characters reminded me of something from my book, if not lifted from it directly.

"What does it say?" I asked Morainn, pulling it back off of my head and holding the hood open for her to see. She turned her head, the angle an awkward one.

"It doesn't say anything," Morainn said, her voice a little like that used when one talks to a child who has limited means to communicate. "These aren't words, they're pictures. Symbols."

My brow furrowed, and Morainn held open her hands in a moment's frustration over how to illustrate what she meant before she crossed to the wash basin and dipped a finger in, tracing one of what I had assumed were characters on the stone.

"See, this is a house, and this, a carrion bird," she explained, then dipped her finger again, drawing the two together in one of the designs on my cowl. The images were not as clear when joined, though now that I knew what they were separately, it seemed obvious. She grimaced.

"It's not nice, what they're saying. Houses are traditionally seen as wombs, and well, it's like saying your belly is full of death."

Whatever Morainn expected it was not that I should laugh, but I did, wildly and full, scooping the hood back over my head.

"How fitting," I answered after a breath, thinking of the son Theba had torn from her own belly and planted in that of a mortal. I didn't know if she could bear life, but it didn't matter. What was important was that she chose not to. I laughed because they had branded the clothes I should wear with her spirit, as though I needed reminding. I had to laugh for fear of crying.

Morainn looked at me, eyes wavering in the fading light. The fire made us both seem haunted, and would more as night grew. With each moment I had the feeling that I knew just where to go, and I suspected it was because it was being shared with me, somewhere, by Paivi. He felt differently than Gannet did, enough that I had to dwell on the thought before I realized it wasn't my own.

Morainn touched a hand to her lips as though to stifle a question, but it followed the gesture anyway.

"Will you tell me one thing," she asked, each word weighted with her power, a life's privilege of simply getting to know and have what you wanted when you wanted it. "You're more like her every day, whether you want to be or not. Do you know, now, who he is?"

Pained by her pronouncement and the necessary distance it created between us, I shook my head. She pursed her lips.

"Then you should love him while you can."

CHAPTER TWENTY

Morainn had gone and the hour grew late. I'd been feeling more and more alone with every moment, beginning with the one that followed Gannet's hasty departure.

Avery had left a tray for me beside the fire. I was reminded of other evenings I had spent in company, but this drink I would take alone. I set myself beside the cooling hearth, sipping carefully the bittersweet brew.

As I drank I hoped for someone to come for me. I wasn't meant to follow Morainn or Gannet, but my path began there, in the door. I drained my cup. Hugging the folds of the hood against my cheeks and grateful for the warmth if not the message embroidered within, I exited the chamber and pulled the door closed behind me.

The palace was opulent, but the design was not a complicated one. Paivi didn't wait for me here, but I could sense him, was allowed to sense him, far above where I now stood. There were stairs winding at either end of the corridor in which I stood, and I chose to go up. I was surprised to find no one as I passed, crossing several floors and many stairs, higher each time. There were furnishings rich and clustered together, the many generations of wealth and rule in this place witness to my trial. I sensed that this was part of it, the need that I should lead myself to judgment. I had grown exceptionally skillful at acting on instinct since I'd met my first Ambarian, even better, begrudgingly, at doing what I was told. Why should I expect any differently here? Even when I wasn't told. Even when I was telling myself.

I knew I wouldn't have the comfort of Gannet waiting with

Paivi, or if I could look to Gannet for comfort of any kind again. Had he meant to reach out to me, or had I imagined the gesture as something other than what it had seemed, taken advantage? Perhaps he had only put his hands on me because to resist would have been to rouse my temper, Theba's temper. In the dream only moments before he had arrived, though, Shran had been eager. But he'd clutched Theba unwittingly. Gannet knew. Could our ancient king have known, too? Would it have changed him or his fate if he had? How much longer would I have to be Eiren, then, and worthy of such tenderness?

I faced a silvered mirror at the base of yet another stair landing, cleverly lit from an angled shaft that gathered and filtered the sunlight from well above. I didn't see a vengeful goddess in its depths but only a young woman, who looked more frightened even than she felt. There was nothing about this mirror to suggest the one I had seen in the prayer garden with Gannet, but it felt kindred to that object all the same.

I took a step forward, bolstered, but started when I didn't approach myself any nearer in the mirror. My reflection stood perfectly still and after a moment moved entirely out of the mirror's frame. A chill swept through me like the one that I had felt in Re'Kether. I looked quickly to the right and the left, sure that I couldn't be alone for all I appeared to be. I continued forward carefully, sure that at any moment I would see myself again, dark eyes and brow trembling within the mirror's confines. As I drew closer to the mirror, however, my surety faltered and escaped altogether, until I was flush with the mirror. I saw nothing there but the empty corridor, empty of me. A shadow darted across where my face would have been, and I looked about wildly. The shadow would have been on my face just like a mask, if my face had been where it was supposed to be.

The thought of Gannet, however fleeting or phantom his presence, was a little flame in my breast that threatened to devour my heart, lungs, and head entirely, and with hands as daring as those that had gone to him, my fingers grazed the mirror's edge. They dipped like water, like liquid and light, into the rippling surface of the mirror absent an occupant. For a moment I panicked at the uncanny nature of what I did. Though I had endured many strange things, there'd been nothing as physically and immediately impossible as the mirror's surface yielding to me as it did now. Where my fingers touched the reflection rippled, and when I withdrew them in alarm, the image of the corridor behind me didn't seem quite to settle. This was my path, however, and I had to take it. I didn't wait for someone to stop me. I braced my hands against the mirror's frame and plunged within.

It was not the soft pad of the carpet I felt against my palms when they hit against whatever ground lay beyond the mirror, but the cold damp of interior stone. I glanced up as soon as I regained my bearings, struggling first to my knees and then to my feet. I was in a cavern illuminated by a ghostly light filtered from above, a distant cousin of the kind I had known in the Rogue's Ear. There was no mirror behind me, nothing whatever to suggest that I had passed through anything but solid, unyielding stone. I pressed my hands against it as though to convince myself, but it was hard and real. Just like a story: the way in is never the way out.

A way out, however, wasn't of immediate importance. If Paivi hadn't compelled me here, something else had. I wasn't meant to leave, and didn't want to. Not yet, anyway.

I didn't know if it was the gown or some other force that affected me, but I wasn't cold, nor did my breath appear before my lips as I walked forward into the ample cavern. The shapes of the stone seemed common enough, but this was no natural place. Though lit, there were no visible openings for the light to pass through. The walls of the cavern were colored first like sand, then blood, before deepening to a bruise no stone could wear. As though wary that I would feel flesh instead, my touch was gentle, a guiding glance of fingertips across the rock.

There was a pool of water at the center of the cavern, where it was deepest, though the slope wasn't treacherous. I knelt at the water's edge. Unlike the mirror, which had seemed solid, the little pool was as liquid as it appeared to be. No other feature in the cavern stood out to me but this, and as far as I could see, there was neither exit nor entrance to be had in this place. So I settled down, if not to wait, then to think. Because my thoughts turned often to him now, it was Gannet that came first and most eagerly to mind.

Could Morainn have read what I wasn't sure was love, in him or in me? I'd never been in love, though I'd witnessed it many times in my sisters, and even in the boyish attentions my brother had once shown to a family scribe. There was little between Gannet and I that mirrored their enthusiasm, none of the careless tenderness, none of the little smiles and colorings that convinced me that my eldest sister had taken ill. As I dug my heels into the stone, my mouth filled with a taste as bitter as juice sucked from an unripe fruit. Wasn't I just like? Theba wouldn't abide flirtation, and Gannet was no ordinary, unburdened youth. It didn't matter what Morainn perceived or even what was there to be seen. Nothing like love could exist between us, and certainly not in me.

The pool opened up in waves, like a stone had disturbed the surface, though there were none for my feet to disturb. I looked quickly up and around. Though the light had faded a little, creating shadows where before there had been none, nothing in the cavern seemed to have changed. I could have been nervous, I supposed, to be trapped here with no means of coming and going, but I remembered the way I had shifted the stones in the tunnel in the Rogue's Ear, and I wasn't afraid. Though he'd been with me then, had made me act when inaction might have crippled us both, and he wasn't here now. I laced my arms together over my chest, feeling sore and sorry.

"It was your own heart you never knew."

The voice I recognized instantly, the sound as much a shock as looking up and seeing her there across the pool, slight and elegant as she had been in the last moment I had seen her.

"Mother," I started, but she raised her hand, and I could see in the fractured light that it was not as whole as mine. Should I rush to embrace her, I would gather nothing but air to me. I panicked, thinking perhaps the Ambarians had broken their word to me. "Are you a spirit?"

My mother, whatever she was, shook her head in the dismissive way she had used when one of her children came to her with some mild complaint. It was a gesture familiar enough to seize my throat, keep me from speaking again too soon.

"I am neither spirit nor fiction, only a little of each. But I am your mother. I am a great distance from here, well and whole. Don't worry."

It was a moment before I could respond, reconciling the vision before me with the memories I had of the woman who remained safely ensconced in Aleyn. If this shade was to be believed.

"How did you come to be here?"

Brows arched, my mother could have been chastising me for arriving late for a meal. "You summoned me, Eiren."

My eyes must have widened in disbelief or something more disturbed, for she continued in a more sympathetic tone, laying her hands flat against bare knees beneath the sheath that wrapped her sun-brown frame.

"Where are we? Is this Ambar?"

The request was so human that I answered without hesitation, grateful for this shred of normalcy. "I don't know. I was in the capital when I...when I came here, but I don't know if this is a real place."

I did not add that her presence led me to believe that it wasn't. I sensed this projection of my mother had the same easily wounded sensibilities as she.

"Do you like it there? Are you happy?" Her voice had softened completely, and I saw a visible change in her features as she became a picture of concern, of longing. I would touch her, if I could. I didn't think I would ever have the opportunity to touch my mother again.

"I have only just arrived," I replied honestly, not wanting to answer her questions directly. "It's cold and strange but I'm not alone, and they are not unkind to me."

Relief pebbled her austere face.

"We think of you so much, and want to give you news, but we haven't the means and," her face darkened with the pause, rendered for a moment almost invisible by the shifting light and her sorrow, "we were told that we could not."

This surprised me, almost as though I were speaking with her truly of the things that had passed since I had left. I didn't believe myself capable of conjuring any answer my conscious mind would believe.

"That is probably best," I answered, feeling instantly like someone else speaking the words, like Gannet. It was something he would say, favoring action that would spare him feeling, banish challenge. I felt like there was a great drain in my chest, and all of me sucked down into it. Lips pursed, only my next question could part them. "What did you mean when you first appeared, mother, when you said I didn't know my own heart?"

She was every bit my mother then, for all the real thing might have crossed to me and offered a comforting gesture for words spoken so frank.

"You have known us all, even the things we didn't want you to know, even when you didn't mean to. But you cannot turn that keenness upon yourself. Your surprise and sorrow, the things that bring you joy, I could name them better than you." She sighed, and I knew that this caused her great sadness. I knew, too, that she didn't expect me to understand.

"I know that I have loved and taken pleasure in the company of my family, and that I miss you still, always. I know the satisfaction of a story well told, of beauty observed," I answered her a little contentiously, though she had neither asked a question nor warranted my attitude. I didn't want to argue with her, only to show that she wasn't right about me.

Mother rose, but she didn't cross to me. Her gaze was every bit that of an imperious leader. She reminded me of Morainn, or, I realized with a start, Morainn reminded me of her. "Do you know why you really left home? It wasn't because you were told you must."

I balked at this, scrambling to my feet with haste enough to stir the pool with my boots and the hem of my dress. "I would be there still if the Ambarians hadn't come!"

Shaking her head, my mother turned, and I could see her becoming even more insubstantial. I panicked, waving my arms as though I could stop her, but the gesture seemed only to disperse more rapidly the shadows and light that made up her frame.

"Breech babes begin their lives with their feet. They are moving away from you before they have the words to tell you why," she said softly, her figure so ghostly now that the words could have come from the cavern walls. Tears burned hot streams down my cheeks, and now I felt the cold and keenly, my hood torn back by a wind that picked through an opening in the chamber that hadn't been there a moment before. Dragging my feet out of the pool, I was surprised to find two figures reflected there, my mother and me, looking watchful each and ahead, to the opening. Perhaps she'd never been there at all.

Because there was nothing to do but follow where I was clearly led or wait all my days out in this strange half world, I strode away from the pool, towards the opening. Though my boots dried with unnatural speed and my skirts, too, the cold was raking a chill into my bones unrivaled by any of our nights traveling. I didn't think of Gannet, or rather fought not to think of how he might warm me.

Outside, a path wound thin as lace between the mountain and a perilous fall. Trees clung to the cliff face like handfuls of hairs on an old man's head. Though there was only one way for me to go, I didn't see how I could, narrow and treacherous as it was. I couldn't even see where the path led, curving out of sight perhaps two hundred hands from me. While I was sure that I wasn't in Ambar but some other world, I was sure, too, that I wasn't safe from harm. If I should fall, consequences would be suffered, and as dire as those that would follow any great misstep in the real mountains that surrounded Jhosch. Still, there was nothing for it, and the tears I had not dashed from my cheeks had frozen there as I waited.

"This is a test Jurnus would recognize," I mused aloud, thinking of the training my brother had wanted for all he was never meant to go to war. Though we had all been encouraged, none of us had joined him but Esbat. I remembered the two of them perched upon a beam flanked on either side by our private guard. They were in a contest to land blows upon one another with knives too dull even for cutting bread, though their traded insults stuck plenty. Their cheers when the match was over, no matter the victor, would have had no place here. Still, their voices buoyed forth in my memory enough that it seemed when I laid my feet upon the path it was a little wider, the grit of the stone fit for feet.

As I walked, each foot placed one in front of the other with an increasing tremor in my legs, I wasn't sure if this was a test. I didn't anticipate another visit from my family for all they felt near to me now, nearer than they had in weeks. Guilt lingered at my mother's words, hanging like weights from my hips and knees. I had never given much thought to my future, if only because my present had always been so turbulent. The war certainly had not kept me from growing older, nor any of my siblings, though it had kept us from many of the things that might otherwise have filled our young lives. Our duties as leaders and diplomats, the possibility of marriage and families of our own, trades and crafts that extended beyond what could pass the time in the desert, none of these things had played as great a role in our lives as they would have if we hadn't been at war. I had been lucky to favor something that required nothing but my memory and my power of speech, and stories had filled nights that might have been made merrier with the crafts of peacetime.

I rounded the bend, and when the path continued around another, so did I.

With the arrival of the Ambarians and my departure, no doubt my siblings had grown where I could not, and I in ways they would not. It was easy for me to see the decisions that they would have made, perhaps had made already: Lista and Anise, positions of influence and power, or as much influence and power as they would be allowed. And husbands, certainly. Lista would have heaps of children and Anise only one to which she would be exceedingly devoted. Esbat would pursue some scholarship, turning her mind to invisible realities, to the abstracts of invention. Forbidden a weapon, Jurnus would punish his body in some physical discipline.

Or be killed, if he continued as foolishly as he had the night he'd visited the camp.

The path grew narrower still. I thought of all the ways that I was unfit to do what my siblings had and would do, how I wasn't so clever, so certain, so ambitious. Could I accept what my mother had said, that I would always have left? I couldn't. But neither did I see a future for myself in Aleyn, not as I might have had if Gannet and Morainn and all of the others had never entered my life, and certainly not now.

A figure stepped on to the path. It was Paivi.

"Theba, *matea tsisha a.*"

The words were the ones he had said to me when we had met at the gates of Jhosch. The language resonated with me, but even here I didn't understand it.

"I am the icon of Theba, not Theba herself. I would prefer you to address me as Eiren. You're not called Erutal, but Paivi."

If Paivi felt some surprise at my knowledge of who he was, he didn't show it. I wondered if this restraint had been taught to them all and was not, as I had suspected, Gannet's special province.

Paivi's broad smile, however, had no trace of Gannet's control. "If you wish, Eiren. I'm pleased you've dropped your title. You won't need it here."

There were maybe ten steps between us, and the path widened considerably when I had taken them by half. Whether I trusted the man on the other side or not, I wasn't going to linger on a mere thread of stone to avoid him.

"There are other things you'll find me less amenable to part with," I said, eyeing him with open distrust. Paivi nodded as though to suggest he was quite sure of that. He smiled and held his arm out not to take mine but in a gesture that guided the both of us away from the narrow path and up a steep, if thankfully wide, flight of stairs cut right into the mountain's side. I could see the top from where we stood and the fires that burned there. I didn't think it a great stretch to imagine them altar braziers, and the mountain's summit a prayer garden.

I laid my foot upon the first step and crumpled, my face smashed against the worn stone as though a weight pressed down upon me. I didn't feel hands holding me down, exactly, but I couldn't lift my head, couldn't even shift to keep blood from dripping into my eyes from a wound on my forehead. When Paivi spoke it was from a distance great enough that it couldn't have been he that held me there.

"Have you come so far to fail your last test, Eiren? You approach divine heights. There is no place for pride in your heart."

I could taste blood in my mouth, my tongue running over my salt-slicked teeth. I swallowed my curses, but I couldn't contain the groan that escaped my lips when I tried and failed again to lift my head. A load of rocks could have been laid upon it; it could have been a rock itself.

"Pride?" I whispered, freeing my arms from beneath my body with some struggle, palms pressed flat against the dusty path before the stairs. "I'm not proud of anything I've done lately. Just the opposite, actually."

"Are you sure? You have plumbed the depths of your companions' hearts and their enemies, too. You have defied the laws of the natural world, and conversed with creatures that have no claim in it." His pause was pregnant with a smile that rivaled the length of the horizon itself. "You *are* proud of these things."

Again I resisted the urge to shout at him, forced myself to consider his words. This, too, was a test. Blood began to dribble down my chin.

"Eiren." His face was close to mine now, his voice quiet, sympathetic. I opened my eyes and could see his through a film of blood, gold flecked with green, alien but honest. "I'm not here to try you, only to guide you. It is this place that tries us all."

Gannet had been my guide. I wanted him here now. He wouldn't have helped me to my feet, but he would've been there waiting for me when I'd done it for myself.

I closed my eyes again, remembering the strength and the caution I'd felt in his arms when he had held me. How long had I wanted him to do that without knowing that I wanted it? How could I ever hope to share such an embrace again if I didn't defeat what defeated me now? Paivi spoke of pride, but what I felt wasn't pride but wonder in the mysteries that my unique gifts gave me access to. My mind was strong, but it was mine. My powers might be Theba's, but she couldn't appreciate them as I did. She would not use them as I had to explore, but to conquer.

With a groan I lifted my head, cheeks caked with a mixture of blood and dirt. My arms and legs betrayed no lasting injury, and for this I was grateful. When my eyes met Paivi's again, they were dark with determination.

"I have a guide already," I said, gesturing to my heart. I didn't concern myself with how he might interpret the gesture, for I knew what I meant, and whatever waited for me in the prayer garden would, too.

I could do little more than crawl and this by will alone, struggling up the stairs at a measured pace, using the sleeve of my new gown to mop my face. I didn't know if the pressure had lessened or if I had found a way to overcome it. I knew Paivi was behind me still, but I didn't feel his attentions. Whether this was because he had withdrawn them completely or because what I approached so dominated my thoughts, I didn't know.

The scene at the apex of the stair was like what I had anticipated, but different from the garden at Rhale's estate. There was little foliage here, and none of the whimsy and wildness of the roof chapel. The mirror was the same, placed purposefully in a group of clustered stones. There was something reflective in their surfaces as well, chipped and mottled but glittering still. Only one altar stood, knee height, centered before the mirror. Because I wanted it done, and perhaps more because I wanted to know just what *it* was, exactly, I approached the altar. The mirror was angled so that one could not see themselves in it without kneeling at the altar. Though I'd considered wryly in Rhale's garden the ironies of worshipping oneself, I knelt as I knew I must.

Like the mirror in the corridor that had led me here, I saw nothing in the depths of this one save the reflected sky behind me. I wasn't immediately disappointed, for I had no desire to realize the full potential of Theba embodied there. I didn't want to see her face, or my own perverted. I threaded my fingers through each other in a penitent style, waiting. I remembered what Gannet had said about closed fists when he'd first explained that I would be tested. I considered that if his experience was anything like mine, his story was figurative, only. But representing what? Obviously the Ambarians kept secrets, as many secrets as we had stories. And from all that I had seen, Aleyn had the stories of the old world, and Ambar the living memory of it.

Until me.

Where there had been sky I saw myself, just as I was: my lip burst and bleeding, my chin stained, my nose purpling in a promise as dark as my eyes. How could this young woman be anything but what she seemed to be: human, vulnerable, sensitive of the hearts and minds of those she knew well and loved? If the goddess manifested herself in my anger, where was that anger now? Did she exist when it wasn't there? I didn't think so.

"Can you be sure?"

I was startled from the prayer bench by an unfamiliar voice, and when I turned I didn't recognize the face and form of the young woman who stood there. Her appearance was humble but her eyes were keen, her expression curious. She was also very, very pregnant.

She walked as she continued talking, to and fro a few steps away from me, nearer the stairs I had climbed than the altar. Her presence was commanding for all she could not have been but four- or five-and-twenty, and likely not even real.

"I see many things in the mirror, but I've never seen you," she said. "It seems you can't see yourself, either."

"Perhaps it's only that I didn't see what they expected me to see," I replied carefully, thinking of the purpose Gannet spoke of, the burden of all icons. I watched her. Who was she? Pacing still, her ghost-feet made no mark in the dirt. I stood from the prayer bench slowly, more out of habit than reverence.

"It doesn't work that way," she explained, moving still. Her hand moved now, too, in complementing patterns on her swollen belly. "You can't say that you are kind and have it believed of you, you must do kind things, speak kind words. You can't claim to be a house builder if you don't build houses, if you don't beat the dirt and dung from your clothing every night."

I stood next to the prayer bench with the mirror at my back, and when she fixed her eyes upon me, I felt the eyes of someone from the mirror on my back, too.

"If you act as Theba, then you are Theba. If you want to be Eiren, you must act as Eiren."

"But what if I'm both?" I struggled, feeling the weight of the judgment, the world, my words. My doubt was real and it terrified me. "What if in my head I'm one and in my heart another, not always the same, or at the same time?"

Her eyes were liquid, blue as aquamarines, blue as the sea that carried away little pieces of Cascar everyday. The hand on her stomach ceased to move, but I knew the child within was dancing still.

"Then you are not what they expected."

I didn't know if it was she or me that vanished, for I saw nothing in an instant, felt none of the solid certainty of a world beneath my feet. For the space of a breath I didn't exist, and then I was face down on the rug in front of the fire in my chamber, drained glass in hand.

Well done, Eiren.

Somewhere, far away from me but in the real world, Paivi laughed.

CHAPTER TWENTY-ONE

I was grateful for the summons to breakfast after a sleepless night, but I wasn't prepared for the clamor and opulence of the Ambarian court. Servants scuttled with trays and steaming pots of tea between tables that were heavy laden already with food and people, many of whom neglected their plates when I was led through. Though there were perhaps no more here than fifty, they ate and drank and reveled enough for twice that. These must be the affluent of Jhosch, the councilors, the wealthy, and other family, I supposed, titled if there was land enough in Ambar to allow for it. They looked on me, and I felt the press of embroidery on my hood like a brand.

At the head table I was disappointed not to see Gannet, but settled gratefully in the place that had been prepared for me beside Morainn. Imke hovered behind her mistress' chair, and I took particular note that no place was prepared for her here. I didn't think Imke would be happy that I had a seat but she didn't, for all she might be used to it. Morainn gave me a look that suggested quite strongly, and without my having to employ any of my gifts, that I reserve any serious conversation for elsewhere. In the same instant she gestured to Imke to pour me some tea.

"I will point everyone out to you and you won't remember anyone," Morainn insisted, eyes cutting around the room as though she dissected it, and would soon after its inhabitants. Her parents were deep in discussion with an advisor that sat beside her father. I noted Agathe's attentions drifted to Morainn, and to me. I saw Paivi, too, at a table situated below this one but above many of the others. I could only imagine the significance, though I wondered if the others at his table were icons as well, the men and women who looked much like the other men and women breakfasting but were set apart. There were young and old among them, and though their clothes were fine, the style was more simple, designed to draw less attention to the wearer, rather than more. I wanted to ask Morainn if it had been her doing that placed me here instead of there, and to ask, too, how it was that her brother had no place at any table. I didn't see him, and I was sure I would sense him if he were near. Perhaps because my gifts had grown to fledgling competency under his guidance, perhaps because of other reasons, I felt my senses altogether tied up in him.

My mind could not quiet my stomach, and I filled my plate eagerly with spiced root vegetables, bread, fruit, and little pies stuffed with sugared cream as Morainn talked and hardly touched her plate. I watched the ones I suspected to be icons, but Morainn drew my attentions away and I felt a strange relief for it. If I were scrutinizing them, they would surely be scrutinizing me.

"They've seven daughters, if you can imagine it, each prettier than the last," she claimed, gesturing to a couple seated further down the hall, and I grinned, knowing she meant instead that they were more homely, and couldn't say as much. She continued, inclining her head to a woman whose wrists and neck were heavy with precious stones. "And Beronda and her husband operate the mines on our Northern borders. Quite humble."

That Morainn wanted me to laugh made it that much harder to contain myself and keep from exposing her. If I let her go on, I *would* laugh, or choke trying not to.

"They don't live in Jhosch?" I asked, coming to the slow realization that perhaps this was not a typical morning for the royal family after all. Morainn's vigorous shaking of her head, the dark curls pinned under a modest circlet shifting against her brow, confirmed my suspicions.

"We have many visitors," she explained, but she didn't need to say that they were here for me, and were trouble for everyone. "They will stay for several weeks, until the opera. The ones here are finer than anything they have at home."

The opera. At the mention of it my gaze shifted unwittingly to Paivi, who looked like he had not taken his eyes from me since I had entered the hall. He didn't have about him the air that some men do, as a predator might, but there was something in his manner that desired knowledge of Theba and Eiren both. Gannet had given me the impression that all of the icons here were taken when they were young children, but it seemed unthinkable to me, to have no sense of oneself. I was alien and my notions, too.

"Do you enjoy the opera? Are you meant to?" I asked. In Aleyn we had our fires and our families and stories that grew a little with every telling. Ambar, I thought, would demand more formality.

A thoughtful crease appeared between Morainn's brows above the bridge of her nose, her eyes on either side like the pages of a book laid open at the fold.

"We are meant to, yes, and I do. For every icon there is an opera, and for many other of our histories, as well. The operas tell us what has been and what will be, and these are things we like to know." When she observed my expression, still somewhat dubious, Morainn only shrugged, as though I would simply have to experience it to understand. "Theba's opera is among the more popular, and is always performed when the moon is in darkness."

I wasn't sure if I was grateful for a few weeks to consider what she'd said, or if I would rather see the opera and have it over with. Imke poured more tea though neither of us required it, drawing Morainn's attention.

"Imke has never cared for Theba's opera. Dsimah's is your favorite, isn't it?"

Brows lifted, Imke withdrew with the tall, brass teapot, her hand in a quilted cloth to keep from being scalded as she held it. What did she see for herself in Dsimah, plowing and tending only to be herself harvested by livelier gods?

"There is more to gain for me in Dsimah's patience than there is in Theba's fury. I wouldn't say that I have a preference." Something flickered in her as she spoke, like a candle shielded by a hand. It was gone as soon as I had seen it, and Imke moved away, refilling the tea of all privileged enough to be seated at the highest table. I knew I could take from her what she kept from me, but I didn't want to prove myself the monster she so clearly believed me to be.

I wanted to ask Morainn to be more specific about Theba's opera, but as I turned to her a herald strode before the table to beg an audience for his lord. He began in a fashion that reminded me of home, speaking of Colaugh's benevolent spirit, Agathe's gracious heart, and the joy anticipated and expressed by all at Morainn's safe return. There was no mention of Gannet, which wasn't surprising, and nothing of me, either. I was grateful to have been spared. My relief, however, was short lived when Colaugh himself rose and welcomed his people. The first to stand and greet him, a man whose belly underneath a rich coat was no doubt as round and white as his bald pate, looked right at me before speaking and shifting his attentions to Colaugh.

"Your grace, we have given our lives in service to Ambar, and our victory in Aleyn is a boon indeed," he drawled, his voice plugged somewhere high in his nose. "As for Theba, has she been tested? Proven true?"

I saw Paivi and several of the others seated at his table look at each other, and I knew that they would rather this question had been addressed to one of them. Everyone else in the hall, however, was looking at me, and I felt for a moment like a lantern pricked through by so many pins, shedding light.

I didn't need to read Colaugh, for so great a personality he had that it seemed to fill the tureens full on the table.

"She's alive, isn't she? That should be all you need. Theba wouldn't suffer an imposter. If you continue to have doubts, perhaps a demonstration of her power is in order."

I wasn't sure if this was an invitation or a threat, but I didn't like it, either way. Colaugh's words were absolutely an endorsement, and an unwelcome one.

"It isn't that...I didn't mean..."

The bald man stammered, embarrassment losing the war to terror on his features.

"Sit down," Colaugh boomed. "Before you're forced to lie down."

Was he talking about me now, or himself? What I would do, or what he'd make me do? There was such a strange balance of power in the room, with Colaugh who seemed to have all of it but still leaned on mentioning me for more. Everyone looked at me, wanted for something, waited for something, and I quaked. I didn't have Gannet's hand upon my arm to steady me this time, and I felt a bitterness rising in my throat, as though I had swallowed smoke. The food that I'd eaten threatened to come up again, not as sickness, but as a fire spewed forth and cleansing the room of them all.

Careful, Eiren.

I could've cleaved my lip in struggle and surprise against the violent thoughts that threatened me and the fools, the innocents, that crowded the hall. Paivi's interruption encouraged more than it pushed back any swelling tide, and I refused to acknowledge him. It was this place driving me nearer my own destruction. It was Gannet's conspicuous absence, and the ambiguity I had found in my own heart during my test. Had my doubt confirmed it, allowed her to grow even more near my waking self until all would be obliterated? I would tell no more stories, and any told of me would speak of nothing but death.

I walled Paivi out and the anger within. Morainn laid her hand on the table, palm up and fingers curled slightly open. I focused on the gesture that was wordless but incredibly powerful. I remembered what Gannet had said in the chapel at Rhale's estate, and wondered if Morainn acted in knowledge of what he had told me. I believed she did. Did his mother know, too? Was this a table of confidence for a lost man, masked even unto himself? I could pity myself little when mother and sister couldn't acknowledge him, when the woman he had perhaps chosen recklessly to love was a monster.

But I couldn't be certain, not yet, neither of love nor of my own changing nature.

It was late enough that the servants could have laid out another meal upon the table by the time everyone had spoken. I was glad I had eaten heartily, though, because my nerves couldn't manage another meal like this. I'd rather never eat again.

Morainn rose and I was quick to follow, hoping my lot was not so soon to be cast with Paivi's. Even as the crowd exited he alone drew near the head table, and every person who had been seated with him waited, their eyes cast down but their spirits bent all in our direction. I hadn't felt their attention when the room was full of the heat and heart of so many bodies, but I felt it now, strangely benign. I wasn't even sure that they were aware of the depth of their curiosity and stranger still, their devotion. It felt like they'd been waiting their whole lives for me. They hadn't even known it would be within their lifetimes and still they had waited.

"*Dreshani,*" Paivi said, nodding in respect to father, mother, and daughter. "We will take her now."

This seemed explanation enough for the royal family, if it felt rather unsatisfactory to me. Morainn's look was sympathetic but brief, for she, too, had a part to play. To be my friend wasn't in her power just then. Parents watchful, she left my side to join them. I crossed around the table to Paivi. I was determined not to look as though I were being led, though his smile at my being so agreeable did little to rid me of the feeling that I was.

The others that had waited at the table, the ones that I felt I could now safely assume were icons, folded around us as we exited the hall. I noted the guards that lined the corridors, a presence that hadn't been in place the day before. An extra precaution on my account, no doubt.

"Where are we going?" I asked. Paivi managed to smile even when talking, and I began to think that perhaps this was not merely a response to me, but simply in keeping with his character. Erutal had hardly any stories about him and didn't make much trouble, so I supposed cheer could be his province where terror must be mine.

"Our quarters and our work spaces in Jhosch lay under the city. One of the entrances is here, in the royal palace."

I appreciated his candid answer, and couldn't help but thrill a little at seeing yet another side to this strange place. I decided to press him, to see if he would prove as taciturn as Gannet.

"Am I going to stay with the rest of the icons now that I have been tested?"

I wanted him to clarify many things about my test, but I wasn't yet sure if he had truly been present, or how much I wanted him to know if he had not been.

"We are in the same instant revered and reviled by the people of Ambar," Paivi explained without a hint of irritation or shame. His voice dipped slightly lower, but didn't take on the full character of subtlety. "*Drech* Colaugh wishes you to stay where you are for now. So for now, you will."

What he didn't say was that it was they, the icons, who would ultimately decide my fate.

And the fate of all in Ambar, I suspected.

The others nodded their assent at Paivi's declaration, murmuring here and there. As I had earlier, I noted again now that the icons were in many stages of life. The youngest was a boy who had yet to grow in the beard that was so fashionable among his people, and the eldest was an aged woman, paper-delicate and supported on the arm of another. My desire to make woefully uninformed guesses about which icon was which was curbed by my attention to the course we took.

Paivi led us out of the palace into what might have been dubbed out of doors a courtyard, though within the mountain it seemed a strange, unnaturally green place. Musky-scented mushrooms sprouted from the rocks, and lichens, herbs, and shade-loving foliage besides. Ferns trembled as we passed, their fronds closing up like hands retreating to pockets. A fountain like the ones I had admired on our arrival bubbled here, too, the stone splashed in a wild pattern and blank of the growth that asserted itself so thoroughly elsewhere. Near the fountain two columns rose, web-delicate, filtering the murky light. A great gulf of shadow opened up between them, and only when we moved closer did I realize we didn't approach a well, but a stair.

I watched as the icons that had walked with us from the hall began to file down the stairs. A glow trickled down the walls where some of them passed, and the faces and hands of others seemed to exude ghostly light. Our gifts were not all the same, but these little manipulations of the natural world were still amazing to me. I allowed them all to pass me, and even shared a light smile with two among them, a young man and woman who proceeded hand and hand down the stair, each fairer even than many of the Ambarians I had seen. As I had with the other icons, I didn't extend my mind to theirs, though I sensed that they were not as guarded, as resistant, as the others, and I couldn't help but compare the slim mouth and eyes of the woman with those of my sister, Esbat. Without Morainn, without Gannet, I wanted very much for a clever companion.

Paivi waited with me, and when the others had descended, his hand didn't need to make the gesture his eyes so strongly suggested. I should go down. I thought about suggesting that I could not conjure light as they had, but I had the power Gannet had taught me, to see the light of moving life even in deepest darkness.

And what else did Gannet teach you, Eiren?

I walled myself against him immediately, for hadn't Gannet warned me it would go this way with me in Ambar? Despite his lessons, I was as free with my thoughts here as I had been as an ignorant girl before he'd met me. I didn't respond, sorry for having been such a poor student, far more wretched even than my lessons as a child had given me reason to believe. The arts and sciences, diplomacy and history, these things I could master, but discipline I could not. As I descended the stair I thought to reach out for Gannet if he was here, but I could feel Paivi waiting like someone outside of a locked door and I didn't dare turn the key.

What I hadn't seen from above were the details along the spiraled stair that descended deep within the city. Characters like the ones in the book Gannet had given me, like those embroidered in my clothing, fled silvery down the stone walls, given a haunting glow when I employed my dark-sight. Paivi noted my attentions.

"He didn't teach you to read," he presumed, and for a fleeting moment I was grateful that the other icons were well ahead of us and couldn't hear. If I was to belong here, I wanted them to know me at least for who I was, if prejudice against Theba was something that could be surmounted.

"I know how to read," I snapped, not surprised at his ability to raise my ire, but ashamed of it. My next words were more level. "Morainn told me that these weren't words, anyway, but symbols."

Shrugging, Paivi touched a hand against one of the characters, and a little spark formed between his fingers and the symbol.

"*Dresha* Morainn isn't one of us," he explained, which was no explanation at all. My attentions narrowed with my eyes.

"And what does it mean, to be one of you?" It was a question I had asked Gannet in many ways, with and without words, though his conspicuous absence showed me that whatever Paivi and the rest were, Gannet was set purposefully apart. Again I wondered what terrors he stirred if even I were welcomed among them.

Paivi, however, seemed prepared to give a more direct answer. As his lips parted so did a little his mind, so that I could see him even as I guarded so closely my own thoughts.

"We preserve the future, we plan for it," he spoke, and as he did so I could see the icons as they were, as living memories of what had been and what would be again. I could see that Paivi was much older than he appeared, or carried with him the lives and experiences of other, older men. I saw births and deaths of icons, saw the flare in them that confirmed who they were, why they had come, and why they must again depart. Men and women and children whose lives were given freely in service of what must be. To live as I had done, in ignorance, was to squander a gift. As I loved stories, they lived them.

Though I hadn't intended it, my wonder and greed at what lay within him broadened the perception between us, and he spoke to me again in my mind.

You cannot know what it means to us, Eiren, to have you with us again.

Confused but hesitant, I didn't wall him out again, but stood my ground like a sentry at a gate. Paivi knew something lay beyond, but not what.

Again?

You will remember us soon. Theba will remember within you.

I kept my eyes fixed upon our footing, which had changed from stair to smooth stone, more tunnel than corridor, and unsettlingly like what I remembered from the Rogue's Ear.

I don't know what I'm meant to do.

My thought was more honest than any tone of voice could have conveyed. I saw Paivi, then, my image of a sentry become me, armored, and he stood with his hands open in a fashion that reminded me of Gannet's, just before we had held each other. Did Paivi know? My armor flashed and hardened.

You will change things, Eiren. Our time has come, the old time. Aleyn and Ambar will know again the pleasures of unity, of hands joined in common work.

I started, thinking of what Gannet had said, that we'd once shared a king, Shran. We'd known peace. Paivi must've known how this would appeal to me, which made me think he couldn't be telling me the whole truth. Ambar didn't seem to be a kingdom interested in peace, and if the icons had as much power as I suspected they did, they had even more to do with warring than their war-mongering king.

"If you've been as patient as I've been led to believe, then you can stand to be a little longer," I said aloud, my mind hurriedly closed, all images and metaphoric landscape drenched in black. I didn't want him to know any more, and so I couldn't ask for any more, either.

Paivi seemed not in the least disturbed at having been so violently ousted from my mind. No doubt he expected it, or appreciated my display of strength. The tunnel gave way to a floor of bright, mosaic tiles shining under torchlight that allowed for me to drop my dark-sight and revel in the warm, natural glow. The characters on the walls had been replaced by shelves carved at a comfortable height and filled with books, instruments, and curiosities. The corridor widened first into a foyer, and then into a room proper, with low tables and chairs and braziers positioned about that gave off a comfortable heat but no smoke. The icons that had arrived ahead of us had taken seats here, heads together talking or given over to study of some kind. Like a wheel, the room opened on to other corridors on many sides, no doubt leading to other common or private apartments. Paivi gestured that I take a seat at the table where three icons, including the pair who had smiled at me earlier, were seated.

Though I expected him to join me, he didn't, and we four were left looking at each other.

"Hello, Eiren," said the young man, my name a little strange on his tongue, as though the emphasis were misplaced. "I'm Jaken, icon of Alber. This is my twin sister, Shasa. She's also the icon of Alber."

My surprise prompted Shasa to continue seamlessly where her brother had left off.

"Alber has a dual nature. We're not the first twins, but the first in many generations," she said, smiling at her brother. "It is easier this way, to live as two minds, instead of one at war."

Her voice was light, but I sensed she was alluding to darker things. I didn't know this Alber, at least not by that name. He, or she, could perhaps be a variant on the mad carpenter, a figure who built his house up every day only to tear it down each night, driven by hope while the sun shone and plagued by demons when it set.

The third icon that sat with the pair filled the awkward silence. She had a few years on each of us, though not many.

"They think it the most natural thing in the world, though I remember when they were born, and how difficult it was to explain to everybody else what they were," she observed. Her tone, too, was as sisterly as Shasa's had been. I was surprised both by their openness and their honesty. Their minds, though lightly guarded, didn't seem to disguise fear or disgust. "I am Najat, the Dreamer."

That she announced no name beyond that of her icon made me shudder, her words planting a spreading chill in my bones. Najat I knew well, and I wondered that it wasn't she who led them, rather than Paivi. If they were preservers and protectors of history, as they claimed, of what had passed and what would come, she who could see all of hope and consequence in every moment would fall naturally into that place. Najat rewarded those who were generous and kind with fine dreams, and gave nightmares to those she deemed deserving of them. Unlike Adah, however, her judgment I trusted.

Najat smiled, oblivious of my considerations.

"Your birth I didn't witness, Eiren, though I would not have needed to say a word for all to know you."

"My mother always said I wasn't an attractive child, so perhaps it's for the best you neither witnessed my birth nor were forced to herald it," I replied, grateful for ready, if weak, wit. Their laughs were generous and Jaken rose to lift a pot that hung above one of the braziers, and as he brought it closer, I could smell the petal scent of flowery tea roll off with the heat. It smelled like home.

"We've heard that you are a great keeper of stories, Eiren," Shasa said softly, producing from clever compartments within the table itself palm-sized bowls for tea. I was happy to have a cup to look into when next I spoke.

"I am, though I've been led to believe they would not be to your liking."

It was neither true nor fair, really. Gannet had never said that he didn't like my stories and had sat through every one. It was only his response sometimes, or his lack of response, that never settled with me as well as the comfortable appreciation of my family, their praise and their little additions of sentiment or embellishment.

Najat didn't read me as he might have, but rather as a woman who has seen much and understands the nature of the heart.

"Perhaps you should reserve your judgment until you know us better."

Jaken poured me a little tea, flecks of dried leaf floating and settling. He smiled when he spoke.

"I would like to hear one of your stories, Eiren. I would like to hear your favorite story."

I was so used to being asked to tell listeners *their* favorite story that the request took me by surprise. But I already knew which story I wanted to tell.

"Before she was the wife of Shran and the mother of Salarahan, Jemae was a girl, and her temper was so fierce that her father and mother feared she would never be married, never mother a child. She stormed from her bed in the mornings and raged through her lessons by day. By evening time she was like a dying ember, smoldering and sulking. Many asked her, 'What makes you so angry, child?' Jemae responded the same every time: 'Everything.'

"In her eleventh year Jemae struck her riding master on the hand when he attempted to correct her posture, and in fear of what her parents might do to her if they discovered the abuse, she ran away and hid herself in a flowering bush."

Like it had been sometimes at the hearths of my youth, and more recently our resting places on the journey to Ambar, there were suddenly in the shadows listeners that hadn't been there at the start of my tale. I didn't falter in my telling to count them, though I took a sip of tea before continuing. It was sweet and hot enough to sharpen any lagging sense.

"Angry over having lost her temper, Jemae grew angrier still as she squatted in the bush, and began furiously to tear at the buds that had not yet flowered. As she reached for a particularly fat and ripe one, it unfurled before her, petals puckering like a mouth before speaking.

"'Why do you destroy us?'

"Jemae was taken by surprise, and did not tear at the plant again.

"'I was angry. I didn't think it would hurt you.'

"The bush shook, showering Jemae with pollen.

"'Any act of anger is like a stone dropped in the sea. The waves it makes touch many shores.'

"Jemae considered what the bush had said before she gathered the petals she had torn from the ground beneath the bush and buried them. Her tears watered where she had dug, and when she left her hiding place and sought her parents, no scolding could stop her crying."

I began to feel as though my listeners were doing more than just sitting idle. Like the times that I had shared my mind with Gannet, I felt images born between Najat and Jaken and Shasa and all of the rest. I had but sketched Jemae crouched beneath the bush, but my telling was buoyed by their imaginings as well, what they took from me and what they carried within themselves. What happened now was more than a simple telling, and I released an anxious breath before continuing.

"The rages that had been Jemae's domain before were replaced with tears that flowed in such volume that often she couldn't leave the side of the fountain in her family's courtyard. As quickly as she could drink she could cry out a cupful of water, and many superstitious villagers came to gather her tears to heal the sick or bottle them in charms. The girl Jemae would have been annoyed by such attentions, but the young woman she had become was only sorry she couldn't do more.

"In her fourteenth year Jemae's mother and father began to encourage suitors to visit Jemae, but their affections only caused her tears to flow faster and harder, so undeserving did she feel. They brought her gifts of flowers that reminded her of the bush that had sheltered her; they brought her sweets that tasted bitter on her tongue. One young man brought a great globe of brightly colored fish, but he was so startled by her crying that he dropped the bowl into the fountain and ran right out the way he had come.

"One fish swam to the top of the water near where Jemae was seated and began to speak in low, bubbling tones.

"'Why do you cry?'

"Though Jemae wiped at her eyes, there was room enough in her sorrow to be surprised at the talking fish.

"'Because I'm sorry for the things that I've done.'

"The fish gulped and splashed.

"'No apology is as potent as a deed. How you live your life will show that you are sorry.'"

In the minds of the gathered icons I could see the fish, for one his belly yellow and spotted, for another his whiskers as violet as the sky at twilight. It was as though there was a cauldron in the middle of the room and we were each pouring into it what we saw in the tale. I could hold in my mind the visions shared by everyone and my own besides. When Gannet's bold, silver fish darted across my notice, I found his dark eyes in the crowd and held them as I finished the story.

"When Jemae's last tear fell into the fish's open mouth, he shed his scales and climbed out of the fountain, a young man who looked quite like her riding instructor once had. He bowed to her before leaving the courtyard, and when he had gone Jemae rose and went to her parents. Her days after were spent reveling in what she could *do* instead of what she had done. It is said that despite her trials, Jemae died smiling, that there was nothing in the world that did not make her happy."

My blood pumped hot and certain as I finished, and I knew in that moment that I wouldn't need Theba to recommend these people to me. I didn't need to remember, for I knew now for myself that these were my people. Even if I didn't belong yet, I would soon. I looked at Gannet and didn't wonder where he had been or worry how soon he would go. If it was my lot that I should have him only for a little while, then have him I would.

But more than Gannet's eyes were upon me. Jaken and Shasa and Najat and Paivi watched me, and all of the others who had introduced themselves to me aloud with hesitant smiles and shining ones. Dsimah, Korse, Daggen, Lira. Tirce, Hamet, and Galen, still others who only nodded, who shined with no light other than one of service. Not all those gathered here were icons; some had made a choice to serve them. I wondered at their welcoming me so readily, but the feeling was fleeting as I felt myself pillowed upon their trust and anticipation. I released a breath I felt I had been holding since I'd left home.

Gannet's eyes behind the mask were shifting. His thoughts were loosed like a dart into my mind, hitting a mark I hadn't realized was there. I imagined my lips a cork, bottling my sense of things before it could be spoiled. In me, there was spiced perfume, scented oil, all promises made and kept. He turned to go.

Paivi's eyes were leveled on mine, and despite not having the cover of Gannet's mask, his were equally unreadable. What he saw I wasn't sure, but he lifted his hand from my arm.

"Eiren hasn't recovered fully from her test," he observed, and I felt sure it had been but a projection of him I had seen during my test, that he didn't know what I had suffered. What he offered me now, I realized, was an apology that was no more than a guess at what I had seen. His words alone were enough to put distance between the other icons and I. The hem of Gannet's cloak was just visible waving out of the chamber as he exited. Following him seemed like the most natural course, and so I did, hardly aware of the soft eyes of Najat on my back as I moved into shadow. They let me go.

It was dark, but I didn't try to see. I ran my hands along the wall, dipping into the little shelves, my fingers lost in the characters that were etched into the stone. I felt like Jemae in a later story, one that I liked nearly as well as the one I had told. After marrying Shran, she had parted the twelve curtains on their marriage bed to find him asleep. Her kiss had caused him to wake, and while I was sure despite what my mother had withheld in her telling that more than kisses followed that night, I could think of nothing but what pleasure there could be in being near enough the one you loved to share their breath.

"Would you like me to walk with you?"

Even without my sight I could sense Gannet in the dark, standing just out of reach. He had waited for me. Before I could respond he held out his hand. I took it. His palm was cool and smooth, the hand of a man who needed neither weapons nor tools, whose mind was both. He didn't hold my hand as he had in the chapel garden, but placed it upon his arm, against the crook of his elbow. I was very close to him, but it was a formal posture, and I struggled not to betray my hesitation.

When we reached the base of the stair I didn't want to ascend, didn't want to leave the strange magic that had been stirred below. If we could only stay, the horrors that had followed me here might not find me again. Though I was among those who had known me first as Theba, I had not, since Gannet had told me who I was, felt further from her than I did then.

"Eiren," he said softly, his free hand falling upon mine where it rested on his arm. It could've been a gesture of urgency, that we must climb the stairs and return to the world whether I wanted to or not, but his touch answered a want of another kind. My fingers bore into his sleeve and I lifted onto my toes, he was lifting me, his mouth and mine meeting with the sweet taste of intention. It was not at all like I had imagined, to be held and kissed, though our circumstances were as dire as any pair of lovers in my favorite tales. This was a closeness complemented by thoughts shared between the bridge that our bodies made, both of us thrilling, driving worry and regret as far as seeking lips and hands could banish them. I might at one time have considered him mad, another woman would perhaps have been flattered, but all I could think was that we had wasted so much time.

The kiss deepened but briefly; Gannet couldn't allow it to last. I felt his hands travel to my shoulders and he withdrew, holding me at arm's length as though to better study me.

"I have to leave tonight. I wanted you to know."

I laid my hands upon his and on an impulse raised them to my neck, the heels of his hands against my jaw. I wanted him to stroke my face there with his thumbs, and he did.

"Why do you have to go?" I asked, though I knew the answer before he spoke. The words were softened, though only slightly, by the gentle pressure of his fingers, cool against my flushed skin. My own hands moved against his arms, drawing us together again.

"There are things that I have to do."

"How can someone without a name have so much to do?"

Gannet didn't sigh, but he couldn't disguise himself from me when I stood with my cheek pressed against the throb of his chest. I could sense his worry, his hesitation, and already, his regret. I released a breath, gathering a great lungful of him before stepping back out of his reach.

"You hope that a few weeks here will rob me of the desire to ask such questions," I assumed, and Gannet shook his head, drawing his cloak against the cold that threatened where my body had been. When he spoke, he gestured his hand toward the stair, toward the palace and my chamber, where he couldn't follow.

"I hope that a few weeks here will grant you what you have always desired."

CHAPTER TWENTY-TWO

The next morning Gannet was gone as promised, and I knew better than to ask where. There was no breakfast with the court, and it was the twins, Jaken and Shasa, who came to collect me from the palace in Paivi's stead.

When I asked them where Gannet was, their grins were light, amused.

"You've passed your test, so he won't have as much to do with you now," Jaken began, his sister following his words almost without a pause for breath. "You may be Theba, but you're still coming to know her. It's better for you to be with the rest of us, for now."

"Will I be allowed to see Morainn?"

"Of course, but she has many duties, as do you. Perhaps later."

We descended through the gate in the garden into the strange underworld of the icons, and I was momentarily disturbed by how like a homecoming it felt to me. The feeling didn't last, and I accepted the comfort of Najat was waiting in the common room and others, too, the ease of a shared meal that had none of the discomfort, the current of gossip, as the morning meal in the court. Though of varying ages and surely having come from different classes, the icons seemed to have complete trust in one another. Jaken and Shasa confided to me that they had been born to a family of carpenters in the north, the youngest pair of children numbered fifteen altogether. I didn't bother to ask them if they missed their family, for it was clear that they had found another one. Again, I could be troubled only a moment by this, and then I was being passed warm bread and chutney, what chill had entered my body leaving through fingers that clasped an earthen cup of tea.

After breakfast, Najat shared with me what she had wanted to last night, and their work proved to be the greatest surprise of all. In addition to maintaining a library of ancient, crumbling texts, some of them kin to the strange book Gannet had shared with me and others in our shared tongue, they seemed to be a part of Jhosch in the way those who lived above could not be. I had wondered upon entering the city how it was that it could exist, seemingly carved out of the mountain, filled with ghostly architecture and trees besides. The tunnels below seemed to correspond in part with the avenues above, and when we came upon a narrow chamber where the icon of Dsimah sat at a crude table working in a great pot of soil, Najat paused in what had begun to seem like a tour.

"Dsimah, will you show Eiren what you can do?"

I wondered for the briefest of moments when they would begin to call me by the name of my icon, but the mild figure of Dsimah, rising and inclining her head to the both of us, captured my attention.

In many of the tunnels I had noted great bunches of roots hanging, some of them gathered together and bound up, others hung with lights, though the ones in this chamber were shaggy and rough, heavy and free of the mottled earth above. Dsimah placed her hands, stained with the soil she had moments ago been in up to her elbows, upon one great fat root and then another, and where she touched the roots began to glow a soft, buttery yellow. I watched the light, for that was what it was, spread from where Dsimah touched up and down the length of the root to the roof of the cavern. As though placed in my mind, I saw far above us a great tree, one of the many strange hybrids that grew throughout the capital, seem to shake and stretch, leaves flush with color. It was not a picture that came from Najat or Dsimah, but it was a true one. Perhaps it came from the tree itself.

Dsimah removed her hands and stepped away from the roots, and for a moment there was the blaze of her handprints visible and then nothing, the roots hanging just as they had the moment before. She returned to her pot, her smile one I was sure had more to do with the pleasure of what she did than in having been observed. When we had passed out of the chamber, Najat turned her eyes upon me, anticipating the questions I wasn't sure how to ask.

"Does she maintain all of the trees?"

"Some. Not all require her touch, at least not all of the time. As with all things, we use what we are given. We shape the elements of the natural world that are already there. The trees were planted with hands and fed first with water and soil. Dsimah gives them what others can't."

And there were others. Tirce we found working in stone, and I knew him responsible for the spidery archways and impossibly fragile constructions in the mountain's side. Hamet I would have liked to have had in the desert, for she worked in the deepest places, coaxing water from the unyielding rock. It was there already, Najat explained, buried and unreachable by human interference. But not Hamet's. Not ours.

What I noticed, too, was that everyone worked alone, and when again we came together in the library, the icons that worked there shared between them the love of brothers and sisters, nothing more and nothing less. There were no children, though the icon of Mehve was only just grown, perhaps twelve. In her uncanny way, Najat seemed to sense my interest, and we joined Mehve where she sat transcribing.

"Hello, Najat. Eiren."

Though her tone was more adult even than my sister Lista's had often been, her smile was that of a child eager to have their work interrupted. A cloud passed through me, if only for a moment. She should have been playing. Had Gannet, too, been robbed of play?

"Good afternoon, Mehve. What're you working on?"

Obliging, Mehve turned the bound text before her to face us both. I recognized some of the characters there, like the ones embroidered into my robe.

"It is an account of our exile," she continued, when her gesture failed to bring the light of understanding to my face. Like with the other icons, I had a sense of what she meant without prying into her mind. For Mehve, the exile she spoke of was for all Ambarians. "When Salarahan drove us out, and we were forced to make our own way in the cold and the dark."

I balked, but didn't know how to respond. I studied the characters in the book, willing them to make some sort of sense without my having to ask.

"Whay does this say about Salarahan?" I asked finally, curious how the Ambarians would paint a figure who was in Aleyn a paragon, his brothers demons.

Mehve, who perhaps knew less of me than every other person in the room, seemed puzzled by my question, but answered obediently.

"He betrayed those of his own blood, and denied his immortal mother, Theba." Mehve paused, casting her eyes at Najat. She didn't read in the older woman's face whatever it was she wished to, for she continued, but with some hesitation. "Surely you feel the pain of his betrayal, as the icon of Theba."

"I don't," I answered quickly, the color that flooded my cheeks surprise that this young woman, hardly a year out of her girlhood, could fail to mention Salarahan's betrayal at the hands of his own brothers. Either they told a different story, or the brothers' crimes were not deemed as grave as Salarahan's own. My obvious discomfort stirred Najat to speak.

"Mehve, Eiren isn't like any other icon you have met. She's still learning."

If Gannet had been there, nothing would have kept me from speaking. Asking the questions I might have put boldly to him was more difficult, however, with gentle, patient Najat. I found when it came to it I wished Mehve to answer.

"What do you know about Theba, Mehve?"

Perhaps it was a boon that Gannet had gone. I had the feeling he would've stopped her, or answered the question himself in a fashion that was not answering it at all. I couldn't even have laid a hand upon him to know better, for the touch would ignite, I knew, feelings of another kind.

Mehve sensed none of my struggle. Her attention was entirely diverted from the book now, and she glowed with the light of an eager student.

"Theba is the stonecutter who must break so we can build. She labors in the fields and forest, culling and harvesting, taking life so others may live. She brings balance. She'll take us home."

Najat didn't look at me as Mehve spoke, and I kept my eyes fixed upon the table, eyes swimming in the strange characters of the book the young woman had abandoned in favor of talking to me. I could see why she might, for her words glowed with a fanatic's devotion. Like Gannet, she spoke of the future in riddles, and I began to wonder if what they knew, or thought they knew, about what was coming was all like this: vague feelings and predictions, certainty grounded in metaphor.

"Thank you, Mehve," I replied lightly, tightening the grip I had around my own mind for all I was sure no one in the room would be able to see into me. If Shran's ancient throne was out there somewhere empty, and they wanted it, they could have it. When I had led them home, would I, too, be allowed to go?

But Gannet wouldn't come with me, and I would return with yet more gifts my family wouldn't understand. I would know there was a darkness in me that had not been there before. Even if I still refused to believe that I was the icon of Theba, something had been stirred by the suggestion that had given rise to terrible deeds.

"Perhaps you would like to eat," Najat offered. Mehve assumed this as some cue that she return to her work, and as I looked at her slight profile inclined above the ancient tome, I wondered what her real name was, if she even knew. Had she borne the name of her goddess all of her remembering life? Was a birth name a gift that only Gannet had been given, to know who he had been meant to be, if not who he was? I didn't ask, but rose in response to Najat's suggestion.

We returned to the common room, Najat and I, and she did

not moralize with me as Gannet might have after such an encounter. Still I wanted him there with me more fiercely than I had ever thought I could want anyone who wasn't my family in those first few hard weeks on the barge. I thought of the sacrifices made in the story of Massoud and his snail-bride, of Alyona who after his death lived her immortal life in the shadow of her love for him. Her daughter, too, half-mortal, had perished, and Alyona had gone on still. How was it that something that could knit two people together could rend them from each other, from themselves, just as easily?

Jaken and Shasa met us for tea just as they had that first evening, and after a time others joined us. I wasn't asked to tell a tale and was given instead the rare pleasure of listening. I couldn't deny the comfort I felt in the company of the other icons. These were different feelings than those I had known with my family. Then I had not been able to understand what a gift it was to be accepted and welcome, I had never been separate or alone. Because the icons shared burdens akin to mine, because their senses were uncanny in a way my sisters' and brother's never had been, I began to understand what Gannet had meant when he said he wanted what I desired to be mine. I had thought that I belonged, but now I *knew* that I did. Whatever the icons wanted with me, whatever they intended for me to do wittingly or unwittingly, I claimed them, and this place, in my heart.

"Najat, do you know the tale of the sandal maker's daughters?" I asked during a moment when the room quieted, as if in anticipation. My hands had moved almost of their own will to refill our tea, my eyes to light warmly upon first Shasa, and then Jaken.

Najat inclined her head in thanks before replying. "I do."

"Will you tell it, please?"

And she did, just as I remembered and, with the sighs and soft murmurings of the other icons as evidence, so did they all.

More than a week passed this way. Someone would come for me and underground we would go. Though the others always had work to attend to, I was left to observation and idleness. Paivi spent some time with me each day engaged in what I could only presume were measures of my skill, though for what purpose he didn't share. As I had with Gannet he would attempt to enter my mind, and while it seemed to me that I'd succeeded in keeping him out, I didn't trust my perception. On the one occasion I did allow him some access, simply to have some basis for comparison, there was none of the warmth and energy of Gannet's mind. Paivi was as cold and as calculated on the inside as Gannet appeared to be on the outside.

I learned, too, that Paivi's initial use of his given name with me was an affectation. The others called him Erutal. I struggled to do the same, for all it seemed strange to me that he could be the icon of such a temperamental fool. A god, surely, but a fool.

In addition to his failed explorations of my mind, Paivi wished, too, to see my performance in complete darkness. He would place several objects within a chamber, some as miniscule as a pin, and shut me inside. When I took too long to recover them all to his satisfaction, I argued that even natural light would have made for a challenge.

"I'm not interested in excuses, Eiren."

His response maddened me, and being shut up in a room made me madder still. As surprisingly content as I felt in the company of the icons, sharing their meals and stories, I felt my temper all of the time, too. I didn't know why I was so angry. There had been lessons I disliked in the past and powerfully, but they hadn't made me feel as I did now, and I wasn't even sure that it was Paivi who was the source of my increasing frustration.

His work seemed to be, in addition to tormenting me, arranging for special audiences with various icons. Though there were any number of chapel gardens in Jhosch, it seemed that many came to the city to lay their complaints and desires directly at the feet of the icons. I watched several of these meetings from behind a latticework screen, and it made me uncomfortable to see those who I knew merely as individuals, for all their names and their work, accepting tribute and making promises. The coin that was exchanged to arrange these encounters provided for the living of the icons, their food, clothing, fuel for their fires. I could see the necessity, but it felt like a charade.

There were, of course, many who had requested already to speak with me, and Paivi denied them all.

"I explained to them that you're like a child. One doesn't seek an audience with an icon until they are more than Mehve's age, at least."

He cut his eyes to me when he spoke, his words a subtle barb. I refused to look at him, though I could feel his eyes on me when he continued all the same. We were sitting alone in the chamber where only moments before Dsimah had met with a prosperous farmer, and left with her deep robe pockets jingling.

"They don't understand that you were raised in ignorance. They don't know what life is like in Aleyn."

He knew he was provoking me. I was glad there were no other icons about, for I didn't want to offend them, for all I, in some ways, still failed to understand them.

"And yet you've been at war for more than a dozen years."

"They're not the only ones who are ignorant of their enemies," Paivi had said, a note of irritation in his voice. We hadn't talked anymore after that.

I learned to expect less from Paivi than I'd enjoyed even in my earliest acquaintance with Gannet. In Gannet there had always been the desire to disclose, if not necessarily the will, but Paivi had neither. It was clear they answered to the same master, though whether that was some innate knowledge of their icon or some leader among them I had yet to meet, I didn't know.

The longing I felt for Gannet I couldn't have anticipated. It troubled me, too, for I had seen no lovers among the icons, nor did they appear to have any relationships of that kind with the folk of Jhosch. I didn't know if what I wanted was allowed, though I was sure with Theba's influence it wasn't wise. Morainn could neither confirm nor deny my suspicions about the other icons' lack of entanglements, and didn't seem to care either way.

"I may not have yours or my brother's presence of mind," she claimed delicately ten days after he had departed, "but you should pursue what brings you peace."

"No matter what it may bring to others?" I said, thinking of what Theba was capable of when she couldn't have what she wanted, or when the consequences were unexpected. She wasn't alone in never having an intimate among the gods, for they rarely, at least in the stories that I knew, desired each other, preferring the temperate hearts of mortals. Perhaps it was merely in observance of this habit that the icons treated each other only as siblings. But everyone else?

Morainn didn't answer, but poured instead tea for the both of us into clever little vessels of Ambarian make whose hollow walls kept the drink warm but didn't burn our hands. When we were together, she often dismissed her servants and preferred to do those things that they considered inappropriate for her to do. Preparing tea might have been an insignificant gesture, but I knew what a gift it was for the both of us.

"I saw more of Gannet within the past few months than I have in as many years," she admitted, lips pursed above a steaming cup. "You're lucky that he'll return before the opera. I know he's often elsewhere, though I suppose it's possible he's below ground, and it isn't safe to see me."

The stigma she mentioned so idly I was beginning in part to understand. The icons were, as Paivi had said, both revered and reviled. Though the icons kept mostly to themselves when their services, or blessings, weren't required, this meant only that their hands were invisible, but no less responsible for steering the course of this land.

"What was it like for you as a girl, knowing that he was out there, but you weren't allowed to see him?" My question was one that could only have blossomed between friends, and Morainn answered in kind.

"When I was young, it didn't seem fair that I must learn and do so much, and Gannet didn't have to. When I got older, of course, I realized there were demands made of him as well, though I don't even now know what they are." Morainn held her cup in two hands, her face thoughtful. "I wonder if he was ever like you, unguarded. If he could be that way with you now."

This surprised me, and the color that rose to my cheeks betrayed my surprise.

"I can sense sometimes, what he's feeling, what he's hiding," I admitted, guessing rightly that this would be a comfort to her. "But I think he wants to keep more from me than anyone."

"I'm sure it is because of who you are, Eiren." Morainn drained her cup, her knowing smile rather like one I might've seen on my eldest sister's face. "And I don't mean Theba."

Though I knew her words were meant to comfort me, I couldn't help but think of all of the ways that I was more Theba, and less everything I had been. I was shamed by how little thought I had given my misdeeds since arriving in Jhosch, that I was only reminded of Kurdan when Najat had taken me to a place where some of the icons had been buried. I had been unnerved by the markers on the tomb, by so many bodies identified by the same name and the knowledge that another who walked below ground now would someday join them in anonymity. No one would know Kurdan, either, if they found his grave in a hundred years.

"Sometimes she is more me than me," I muttered, but didn't say more.

The next morning it was Avery who came for me instead of one of the icons, though she offered little in the way of explanation. I could only suppose that Morainn awaited me, and so I followed her without question or complaint. Before we left my chamber she crossed to one of the chests where robes and blankets were stored, taking out a great, heavy robe to rival even the substantial one I wore within the palace and below ground.

"Are we going outside?" I asked, and Avery nodded. I slipped obediently into the extra layer, lifting the many hoods that settled now around my shoulders over my head. I hadn't been outside since we had arrived in Jhosch, not properly, the streets of the capital mostly sheltered from the elements and great braziers providing heat for the laborers and merchants that worked out of doors. When we exited the palace, however, even the custodians of the city, hard at work sweeping the streets, couldn't clear them entirely of the white powder that settled where it passed through the lattice-like openings carved out of the mountain. I didn't know what I was looking at, and Avery didn't stop me when I pulled my hand free of the great robe sleeves to collect a handful in my palm. It was cold and wet and slippery, and began to melt from my body's heat almost immediately.

Just as I was about to ask Avery what, exactly, I was holding, Morainn approached with Imke and several other servants, none of whom I recognized. I was pleased enough to see her, and my pleasure increased at the sight of Antares towering over the women with a number of the palace guard with him. If we must have an armed guard to travel outside of the city proper, I would have chosen him. Though we couldn't greet each other with as much familiarity as we might have if Morainn had visited my chamber in the palace, her smile was warm and she noted immediately the clutch of white powder in my hand, now rendered almost entirely to water. Even after all I'd seen, it was like magic to me.

"As soon as I knew it was snowing today I decided we should go out," she explained.

So this was snow. I knew of it in stories, of course, but it was a phenomenon singular to Ambar. Even the mountain ranges in Aleyn were absent of it, and though I had seen it at a distance as we approached Ambar, this was the first snow of their winter.

Morainn paid no attention whatsoever to Antares or the others who were armed as we made our way out of the city, but I could sense her irritation at their presence, and knew that they were more for my benefit than for hers. The question of whether or not they were protecting me or protecting everyone else *from* me wasn't one I had to ask: I knew the answer was both.

We did not ride but walked out of the city. We were in Jhosch still but this was the part of the capital that had more to do with providing for the body of the Ambarian citizen than the mind. There were farms and groves, dusted all with white, and labor animals lowing as they took shelter from the snow. Men, women, and children didn't retire from work because of the weather, but their hands and feet slowed as we approached, bowing their heads to Morainn but raising them again just as quickly to have a look at me. I thought again of the conversation with Paivi, of all they didn't know. Was it my responsibility to lead them in ignorance? When I was in Theba's thrall fully, would I care?

And yet I couldn't believe that it would be so. I saw the other icons and they were individuals whole, not simply incarnations. Though I had been seized in the past by the alien force I had taken to be the dread goddess, I hadn't felt it for some time. Even when Kurdan had fallen in the Rogue's Ear, I knew that it had been me who had slain him. In my own defense, but still by my own hand.

What leaves hadn't fallen from the trees were borne down by the weight of the snow, both crunching delightfully under foot. I felt the cold only after my wonder was exhausted, and my dark thoughts were banished entirely by the serenity of the scene, of our quiet but merry company. It could have been sweeter only for me to have Gannet at my side. I wanted for him more than I did my mother or father, my brother, my sisters. Had I become a woman, or a monster?

Monster.

Monster.

"Monster!"

It wasn't my thought that amplified but a scream, a screeching that was followed by a whistling arrow and the thunk of the point against one of Antares' armored guards. The one nearest to *me*. There was a flurry of swirling cloaks and drawn swords, and someone pressed me hard into the snow and earth. I heard shouts that could only have been orders given. Even if I'd wanted to lift my head and see, the pounding of my heart seemed to pin me to the earth. More screams, and a dark fall of hair near my face confirmed that Morainn was beside me, her eyes wide and white and flashing when they caught mine. She was alive, and for that I rejoiced. There was room in my fear to hope that no one had been hurt because of me, though not much.

"Eiren, get up."

It was Antares' voice, and a moment later there was a hand gripping my forearm. I rose with his assistance and met his eyes only briefly before my gaze traveled beyond him, behind him to the hooded figure that struggled against three of the guard. I saw the bow, the glove the assassin wore to provide a steady hand when firing, and a great surge of anger flooded through me. I could have struck him down with a blow, by my hand or my mind I didn't know. My violence was barely checked by Morainn's charging forward and raking the hood away. The face of a man of middle years was revealed, one I didn't recognize and it seemed neither did she. His face was stubbled out of neglect rather than fashion, his eyes severe.

"Who dares to attack me?"

She didn't need to say any more, for though I hadn't seen Morainn or her family mingle much with the common folk of Jhosch, it was clear to one and all who she was. His expression did not falter.

"It was not you whose heart my arrow sought, *dresha*, but *hers*." He looked past Morainn, right at me, eyes burning with a hatred I was sure even knowledge of my sorriest deeds could not have stirred. It was like hatred from another world, born of more than what man could feel. He stopped struggling against the guards who were trying to hold him, looking at me as though I were the only person who existed for him in that moment.

"You will never do what you have come to do, Theba. I will go to my grave if I cannot bring you to yours."

I felt again the surge of anger, but again before I could act Antares stepped away from me and toward the captive man.

"Easily done."

And Antares drew his sword, which I had never seen him do for all he had worn it since the moment I had met him, and plunged it deep into the belly of the man. I gasped as he withdrew it and drove it again into the man's chest. He didn't scream but remained still and silent. Though the man's eyes fell from me, I felt that they had burned through me in his last moments.

"Why did you do that?" I asked, shocked as the man crumpled to the ground, the serene beauty of the snow splattered with his blood. In Aleyn even such a blatant attempt to take another's life would have resulted in an inquiry, his motives examined, questions asked.

Antares cleaned his sword in the snow. I knew I'd never be able to see white again without also seeing red.

"Such men aren't given the right to defend themselves, or foul the world with their lies," he returned quietly, looking up from his work to Morainn. I could see in his face that this was not the first judgment he had delivered so swiftly. "We should return to the palace, *dresha*."

Morainn nodded dumbly. In her countenance I could see that she, too, while she wasn't surprised at Antares' work, she was surprised at the act that had required it. I didn't need either of them to explain to me that attacks of this kind against icons were always met with immediate and deadliest force. I didn't know what Antares would have done if Morainn had been the man's target, but it didn't matter. It had been me.

I thought of Kurdan, ranked now in my mind with his nameless attacker, each of them consumed with a blind desire to hurt, to kill, to put an end to my life and in so doing thwart Theba's work. Neither of them would have me, neither Theba nor those who would destroy her. My will and my life would be my own.

CHAPTER TWENTY-THREE

There wasn't time enough to reason away what had happened out in the snow before the day of the opera arrived. Najat banished me back to my chamber early, and soon I was accosted by Avery and several other servants, all arrived to dress and paint and plait me. Though I was no stranger to such attentions, I had often encouraged our servants to shift their passions to my sisters, who were far readier to be coaxed and teased than I was. These women, however, had no one to tend but me. My mood wasn't improved in thinking of my sisters, nor by the guilt I felt for not having thought of them but a few hours earlier, ensconced among the icons as I might be in a family.

Avery was the bearer of some new torture, however, for the great rug in my chamber was rolled up off of the floor and a tub three times my size was carried in and placed before the fire. One servant stood by without any other purpose but to heat bucket after bucket of water. With the fire roaring hot and high I almost imagined I was warmed through, and when Avery instructed that I strip all of my clothes and climb into the tub, I thought at first she might be crazy. Still, there was no arguing with her, nor with the servants that crowded once I was in to scrub and pick at my nails, my feet, their hands kneading scented soaps into my scalp and shoulders. With the steam in my face they plucked the stray hairs on my brow, giving not one moment's pity to my yelps of pain. There were some cosmetic habits my adolescence in the desert had never required, and when I was finally freed from the tub and wrapped shivering in a thick robe, I felt like a cooked bird.

Though I had worn the robe and gown I had been given on

my first day each day thereafter, Avery unfolded now a flame-gold bundle of a similar style, if richer in every other way. The fabric itself reminded me of the light, airy stuffs we used for clothing at home, but this was only the topmost layer, shimmering and settling over a soft, downy underdress the color of honey. Embroidered along the hood and sleeves were not the characters of the other, but detailed renderings, scenes and figures playing out the details of their lives.

But it was not any life, it was mine. My mother carried me as an infant from the birthing chair to my father's arms, Jurnus and I raced through the streets and the sand. I bent my head in prayer, I burned ritual herbs, I braided Esbat's hair and soothed Lista's vanity. I went into exile with my parents, brother, and sisters. The figures were tiny and but a handful of knots each, but I recognized them all, and could see when Morainn and Gannet entered my life, crawling dark and glinting with gilded thread in the capital tower. The sand barge rolled over the breast of the garment, plagued by troubles and shadow-spirits, the ruins of Re'Kether sketched in thread that seemed to shift as that place had.

The Rogue's Ear was at my throat, darkness giving way to light in the world and in my heart. What I had experienced there not even the most skilled seamstress could have rendered. But there was still something clairvoyant in the stitches. Did I imagine that Gannet stood in stitches taller and finer than he had at first, in contrast to my first impression of him? My arrival in Jhosch stood at the back of the stiff collar, and though there was greater space for a more detailed rendering of faces, the artist went instead with more color, an abstract sense of myself and all of my traveling companions. We looked like figures of myth, all splashes of color and fine, spidery features. It was breathtaking, and I could hardly imagine wearing such a life for all I had lived it.

Avery gave me as much time as I needed to examine the dress before she helped me into it. I submitted to the tucking and lacing, the many layers of skirts hitched in a way that allowed them all to be shown to greatest effect. The hood was left gathered at my shoulders while my hair was dressed, lightly oiled but softened around my face. I was patient as they painted my eyes, cheeks, and lips, trusting that their skills were greater than that of a ten-year-old Lista, using me as canvas and plaything. I fingered one of the thread figures that I imagined to be her, and wondered how the artist could have known so much, or perhaps only guessed. I didn't fathom that such business would have kept Gannet away, or that he would have relinquished my secrets even if this had been his errand. I touched a hand to my neck only to have it brushed lightly away, thinking that there were some secrets in the dress he couldn't know.

When Avery relented, I was sore for having been seated so still for so long. At least the dress wasn't uncomfortable.

I followed Avery to a part of the palace that I had not yet entered, though I hadn't strayed far from my room and the great hall, and couldn't call myself familiar with the place. The royal chambers, though somehow finer even than what I had already seen, seemed also the most lived in. It wasn't that anything appeared worn or weathered, but the touch of lives fully lived was on everything, appearing to me in a sight that was not unlike what I employed in the dark.

Colaugh and Agathe shamed even the elegance of my garment, and I pitied the artisan who had fashioned mine when I looked upon the king and queen in their finest. They could have been in rags and still outshone me, possessed of the same lofty carriage as my own mother and to a lesser extent, my father. Anise had grown into it, too, and I suspected Lista would if she could leave off flirtation with every glance and gesture.

Yet my family was far removed from me now, and their warmth, too. I was welcomed with only civility by Colaugh and Agathe, and Morainn when she lifted herself from a chair. Gannet wasn't there, of course. When would he return? He'd promised he'd be here for the opera, hadn't he?

I inclined my head to each of them in turn, but did not drop into the deeper bow of Avery behind me. I saw Imke at a far door with two other servants. When Avery had presented herself, she withdrew and joined the others in shadow.

"Eat, if you like."

Agathe gestured to the table where Morainn had been seated, cold meats and fruit laid out on platters and looking as though they hadn't been touched. Having had nothing in hours, my appetite was far from delicate. I did my best to disguise it as I sat and gathered a plate. Morainn returned to her chair, and Colaugh and Agathe joined us.

I was allowed to eat quietly for a moment, but their eyes upon me were full of questions, and I didn't want to test their patience or their generosity. Their minds had hunger of a different kind. Unsure of my place with them, I allowed my mind, already open, to settle like a mist delicately upon the room, sensing their superficial concerns only. They were thinking of Gannet, and I was immediately alarmed, wondering if perhaps they knew already of what had passed between he and me. I darted a glance at Morainn, but her face gave nothing away, and I resisted the urge to delve deeper into the mind of a woman I called friend.

"I wish that we could meet as families, without so much blood between us," I said carefully, thinking what a poor diplomat I made. I wanted to stress to them, though, how great in my heart their son and daughter had become.

Agathe's brows lifted and settled again in a moment. Whether she was aware of how easily I read her or not, this was the only sign she gave of anything less than studied regality.

"We meet as we must," she said.

"Our people have for many generations worked together with yours. Blood calls to blood," Colaugh said. He spoke of the Ambarians and the icons among them, not at all in ignorance of his exclusion of Aleyn. It was purposeful. For Morainn I might've been more than Theba, and perhaps even for her mother, but not for him. I looked at Morainn, my discomfort growing. I didn't know what to say, so I didn't say anything. Perhaps Morainn could join me in my quarters after the opera, and we could talk as we had, freely, breaking bread and passing a cup. I almost thought then to suggest as much, but a herald was admitted by one of the servants. I could see his intentions as if they waved on a flag before him, the whole of his speech to the royal family, to me, and later, to the opera's audience, embroidered in the air.

It spared me having to listen, at least.

I rose at the appropriate time to follow behind the royal family, thinking of such processions at home before we had been driven into the desert. As the youngest, I had always come last, and now I was more distant from them than I'd ever dreamed I could be. I imagined my mother and father, my siblings, turning their faces toward the north in wonder over me, and my heart ached with regret and with guilt, too. I'd felt something like family with the icons during the past few weeks, but nothing, nothing could compare to what was written in my blood and on my body, the press of a lifetime's worth of embraces, pinches, and other affections. What had been there first, I wondered? The body born of my mother and my mother's love, or Theba?

The opera house was deeper within the mountain than the palace, and I had the sense that it served as a center for the city in a way the palace could not. The palace was private, but this place was for public gathering. The face of the house was carved much as the palace was, seeming to spring from the stone itself, but where the palace had all of the impressions and comforts of a structure that is human made and one whose sole purpose is for human shelter, the opera house boasted no such familiarity. The latticed stone at the front and sides glowed with an unnatural light, and I saw within that mineral-doused fires burned green and blue. There was no gate but the lane deadened, grown broad with the stones laid in beautiful, intentional patterns. If there were characters or images I couldn't pick them out, but the delicate tracery of mortar between suggested more than simple labor.

I recognized none of the guard who stood at attention outside, and wondered if perhaps the soldiers that had accompanied Antares had been given well-deserved leave from their posts. They hadn't been friends, not remotely, but I was grateful that the eerie shadows drawn down the liveried, armored men were not across faces that I would have recognized by fireside. I didn't see Antares, either, and hadn't seen him since the morning he'd slain the man in the snow. I'd learned from Morainn that while attacks of that kind were far from common, Ambarian law did not leave much room for such offenders to explain themselves.

I felt my heart hammering as the guards that had accompanied us parted to join their company in lines outside the opera house, spear points muted in the strange light but made somehow more deadly. I wanted to walk beside Morainn, but she followed immediately behind her parents, and I several steps behind, as though I were both a guest they wished to distinguish and a leashed animal, padding in deference behind her masters.

My heart found no rest, of course, when the wonders immediately within the opera house were muted by the sight of Gannet standing to one side. He didn't look at me, he didn't even look up. I read nothing in the bowed, golden brow, and I noticed all the icons that waited with him. Unlike the guard that stood outside the opera house, they were in two lines to one side, their eyes fixed on the ground, their garb as rich and bright as mine. Braziers were burning with the strange glow all around. At first glance it seemed like the night sky, populated by scattered and senseless constellations. The ceilings glowed with runes, a masterwork of some precious metal inlaid in the stone, tier upon tier of private boxes pocketed in the mountain's walls and looking down upon a many-seated ground floor. An oval-shaped stage was lit by fires of green and gold and blue at the center of the opera chamber. I marveled only briefly for the opera and Gannet both, for Colaugh and Agathe were proceeding up a flight of spidery stairs to our left, Morainn flowing up an identical set on our right. Witless, I looked from mother and father to daughter and back again, but it was Morainn who gestured to me, and she I followed.

Two guards trailed behind me but remained at some distance. Despite this opportunity to speak with Morainn, my attention was

hushed conversation. Morainn passed back through the curtain. I looked down toward the ground floor seats and I couldn't distinguish between one person and another. I felt exposed all the same, not wanting to draw too near the edge of the box lest I be noticed by some keen, distant observer. I could see the shadows at the stage's back, and I wondered if even now they disguised the players. What sort of people could they be, playing at icons playing at gods? My gaze traveled from the stage to the curtain entrance to my box and back again, waiting for some appearance in either place, something to attract my attention away from dark thoughts. Though I'd hoped to speak with Gannet privately before the opera began, my curiosity got the better of me at the sight of movement on the stage.

Two figures, a man and a woman, moved towards each other from opposite ends of the oval. Their skin and clothing glowed in the firelight, making them far easier to see than the patrons who were level with them. I wondered what alchemical work was this, some powder or paste that gathered and reflected the light from the strange fires. As they neared the center, all conversation ceased abruptly, and seats were taken in startling silence. The pair on stage moved in study around each other, circling as prey and predator might, as uncertain lovers, establishing trust or dominance or both. Unwittingly, I moved nearer the box edge, taking a seat for fear I might now miss something.

"In the beginning of the world there were many gods capable of creation, but only one who could destroy." The voice emerged from the shadows, bodiless but clear. "It was Theba who claimed the broken blade in the forge, the fallow crop, the stillborn babe. If we didn't have her to reap, how could we ever know the value of our sowing?"

"She taught us. In our earliest history Theba lay with the mortal Shran and conceived with him a child."

There were other figures in the shadows but only just visible, their limbs thrashing out onto the stage in a wild, soundless dance. The man and woman collapsed onstage and I bit my lip, my chest tightening in the moment before the woman rose slowly again, climbing over the man and coming finally to stand with one foot on his chest. One of the figures at the edge of the stage crawled forward on her belly before rolling over onto her back, offering herself to the woman standing. I knew this story already, but not like this.

"Theba does not suffer life and so the child was cast from Theba's womb and into the body of Shran's mortal wife, Jemae. She didn't survive his birth, and Salarahan grew to manhood in ignorance of his true mother."

I felt a chill slip through my body, followed by the heat of anger. It came from another place and was simply thrust through me, like a spear point, like a man, like a babe. It didn't matter that I hadn't known a man or borne a child, I felt the alien presence of each. Was I the only one affected this way, or did the opera have some unnatural hold on the whole audience?

"When Salarahan came of age he betrayed his true mother in word and deed, and for one hundred years Theba punished him. His brothers ruled the kingdom their father had left behind, true in their service to Theba. Their rewards were great, and they would be living still if Salarahan hadn't thrown off the yoke of death and returned to the world of the living."

"He cast Theba from his heart and from the hearts of those who would follow him, parting the kingdom and slaying his brothers. He made war. Those who remained faithful to the dread goddess, she who had provided for them, fled north, and Salarahan and those like him abandoned Re'Kether for the south."

My breath stopped. I should've guessed that Re'Kether would play some part, but the perversion of the gentle Salarahan, the lies about our people and the quiet lives we had led before the Ambarian invasion, were too much. We had not been parted by force, but abandoned.

My shock and what happened next on the stage distracted me from arguing the validity of what the opera's narrator claimed. The figures around the periphery of the stage threw themselves in part into the light, and their bodies, too, were cleverly painted, so only this leg or arm or even only a head would shine in the light, the rest obscured. It looked to be a massacre of bodies behind the woman, who neither looked at them nor shook at the horror that fanned out on all sides. The man I had taken to be Shran was so still and so lifeless I wondered if perhaps he hadn't actually been killed. The woman that was Theba bent, however, and touched his cheek with such profound tenderness that I could feel it like it were my own cheek, my own hand, and his eyes fluttered open and I knew that he lived. He rose like a man on a string, and she led him off stage.

The curtain rustled softly, and I tore my eyes away from the stage, sensing Gannet before I could see him as he crossed quickly and quietly to the chair beside mine. I imagined lifting a hand as the woman on the stage had and trailing my fingers from brow to mask lip to cheek, but even as my fingers twitched Gannet looked at me, his expression unreadable.

Watch, Eiren.

It was difficult to do as I was bid, but in the moment I had given to Gannet the figures on the edges of the stage had come forward, and the woman was nowhere to be seen. There were two groups now, and while one powdered themselves with white, the other smeared their faces and limbs with gold. Snow and sand. Ambar and Aleyn. I wondered then that it hadn't occurred to me that the Ambarians would think Theba's story this story, the sundering of our world, but I was more curious still if there could be something I didn't know about so ancient and frequently told a tale?

The woman who was Theba appeared in the midst of the white-powdered bodies. They quaked at her presence and I quaked with them. It was difficult enough to imagine myself, let alone a third, as some representative of the vengeful goddess.

"In their trials to cross first the desert and then the mountains they forgot her, what she had done for them, what she had done to them. Theba wanted Salarahan no more, and she would forge her own kingdom in the north. But they were weak, and must be made strong. She lit in their breasts the fires of ambition, and they fought to win her favor."

At these words, the white-powdered figures began to turn on each other, wrestling and inarticulate as animals. From their hands sprayed red, and whether it was blood or some other concoction I couldn't tell. Half of the stage grew slick with it as figure after figure fell, gurgling, scrambling, spitting. Theba stood among them untouched, and when they had finished their numbers were much diminished.

The gold-powdered figures had played no role in this conflict, gathered together in tight groups, heads turned inwards and bodies inclined completely towards each other in protective circles. Theirs was the isolation of Aleyn, their survival dependent upon a commitment to harmony. The contrast between the groups, the white now bloodied red, brought tears to my eyes, and I watched Theba pass between them, embraced by Ambar and shunned by Aleyn. She hadn't been content to destroy the world, but would remake it in blood and darkness and pin the blame upon her mortal son. When next the narrator spoke, the voice was magnified to haunting clarity.

"Many hundreds of years passed, a thousand, and Theba brought forward her servants, the icons, to work her will in the world. She told them that she would return in body herself when their greatest moment was upon them, when they would return to Re'Kether and reclaim what had been taken. They worked and waited, icons and mortals alike, for her coming. They were told they would know her in the stars and in the air when she came again."

I had not forgotten that Gannet sat beside me, but I was suddenly keenly and painfully aware of my body, that they were speaking of me and yet somehow not. Gently, Gannet placed a hand upon mine, which had gone white with tension in my lap. We looked together. I didn't need the audience's rapt attention to know that what came after was new.

"Eighteen years it took to claim her."

The Ambarians followed obediently behind Theba, their footprints wet and red as they crossed the stage. The Aleynians didn't resist them, but lay down one by one in positions of subservience. I felt my face grow hot as Theba surveyed, her eyes dark hollows in the strange light on the stage. The fires guttered low and my heart grew wilder and heavier still as Gannet's hand tightened over mine. I couldn't keep from looking at him now, wondering if I might find as many answers in his eyes as the would-be Theba on the stage withheld.

"Please forgive me," he whispered, his hand transmitting nothing to me but his body's heat. I started when his fingers found my jaw amidst the folds of hood and robe, but his touch was achingly gentle, brushed from chin to cheek and settling against my pulse.

He spoke but I didn't hear his words, for even as I thought to return the tenderness of his gesture in countless ways my attention was tugged inexorably back to the stage. All were in shadow but Theba. She stood as still as though she were made of stone, and if there had been gasps and whispers in the audience in response to earlier scenes, all were grave-silent now.

"You've made yourselves worthy of me," she began, her voice wholly unlike the narrator's, low and cold like a sound that begins in the earth and grows to topple mountains. "Free me and what Salarahan divided I will reconcile, from blood and boiling sea a kingdom will rise again and that kingdom will be yours."

The figures that had retreated to the shadows begin to sing, crawling forth on their bellies and broken limbs to kneel at Theba's feet. I couldn't understand them, and wouldn't even if the language had been one I knew. I was clouded with anger and horror and triumph and desire from the pressure of Gannet's fingers still on my skin. I couldn't pick out what emotions were mine and which belonged to the fierce figure on the stage, but I refused to be afraid. I met his eyes, and his seemed to suggest some knowledge I should've gathered from the Theba figure's last words.

"Eiren," Gannet whispered, and I turned back to him as the chorus continued, swelling even as the fires' light diminished further. His thumb traced a pattern now, one that sent a strange fire dancing down my limbs. "Eiren, do you understand now? That Theba must be freed?"

I shook my head, searching his face for answers when his mind remained closed to me.

"Haven't you already? You took me from my home. You've wakened her within me. Your people no doubt consider that liberation."

It was Gannet's turn to shake his head, a slight, sorry gesture. His mouth was lined with grief, and the impulse to press those lines smooth with my lips almost overwhelmed me.

"It is more literal than that," he said softly, not looking at me, his fingers falling slack against my skin. "The gods walked amongst us before, not as icons, but as creatures of flesh and intention. Theba will be…will be the first. To herald in a new age of godhood. Of order."

Of submission.

I took his hand but wasn't sure if I meant to throw it off or hold it tighter.

"And what will happen to me? Will I die? Will she…will she take over my body completely?"

His wordlessness now was born of lack of knowledge, rather than an unwillingness to speak an ugly truth. There was a long moment before he answered, and I sensed, rather than saw, the chaotic dance of victory on the stage below, the voices of the players raised in wild riot.

"I don't know. It has never been attempted. But most believe— and will lay down their lives to see it done. I—I can't stop what's coming."

His voice cracked at the last, and the hand that I had seized I drew to my lips. An impulse, but a true one.

But would you try?

The words were not spoken but pounded out, a beat of my heart at a time, my eyes commanding his. I realized then that I was not afraid, not of him, not of what they had planned for me, not for the first time of the darkness I felt coiled in my heart. They would expect me to submit, but I would not. I could not.

Was I willing to die to keep her from living?

My mind was open to him, every desperation, each thought hardening to a determination as certain as bone.

I will.

And then what he could not stop was something it was clear he did not want to, more than what happened on the stage, what it represented, what he had said and what I had rejected, more than my sliding easily from my chair to his lap. I loosed his hand and he found finer purchase for it where my neck sloped down to my breast. I felt a parting like two pages in a book splayed open for an herb to press, like my lips against a hot cup, eager for the sweet tea below the humid rim.

I knew enough of thirst to recognize in him a deep desire to drink, and he was in the same moment hard and sweet and soft, practiced severity entirely absent as he kissed me. There was none of the restraint he had shown weeks before, and I wouldn't have known how to stop had I wanted to. Little more than a breath passed between us; only the most witless sound of pleasure was given room between lips parting and pressing again. I couldn't hear the chorus on stage for the rebellion in my ears, the fire burning up my chest that had nothing, nothing, nothing whatever to do with Theba. It was Eiren who claimed him with a hand fixed just so above where his heart pounded, the lines in my palm pulsing with a rhythm they could not forget. A human hand, a human heart.

Theba could not make me take anyone, or kill anyone, or betray my people. Not in my body, and not without. Theba, who knew so much of betrayal. If I were to build a kingdom it would be in peace, as Salarahan had done. They could not compel me. I wouldn't allow it.

And I wouldn't be alone in resisting.

"Eiren, Eiren," Gannet's lips hummed against mine, but my attention was drawn suddenly below. The players had moved to the top of the stage and were bowing not at Theba any longer but out, towards us. It seemed they were finished, for there were no fierce visages among them, but smiles, and hand holding, and even the fires had grown brighter. But then there was a scream, and chaos burst through the line of happy players. Dark figures moved among powdered ones, and as they did the players fell, shadowy stains spreading over their spare clothing. This was not the trick they had played earlier, but real blood. I couldn't see their faces in detail, but their thrashing was like none of the mimicry that had come before it. Gannet rose and I was lifted in part by my own will and his hands, which had dropped to my arms and gently, if urgently, tugged me up.

I saw her then, the Theba figure, held between two others covered from head to foot. I saw, too, the glint of knifepoint against her throat. I half expected that she would look at me, accusing, terrified that she should die in Theba's name, my name, but her eyes were fixed on a spot on the ground floor of the opera, where no doubt a lover, mother, or friend stood. She was only a girl, so young; I could see that now that the guise of Theba was gone.

There was a swelling in me as the knife slashed across her throat, as her blood splashed across her garment and on to the stage. So much, vibrant and thick, and as it ran so, too, did my sense of myself. While Gannet had held me I had been completely Eiren, but now I was Theba, all cold and outrage.

"We know she's here. Give us the icon of Theba or more will die!"

Each word was the strike of a hammer against an anvil, a mallet on the warped side of a long-neglected bell. There was a cold, deadly thrill in some dark heart of myself at the challenge. I felt Gannet stiffen beside me, sensed his attentions on me shift from desire to fear. I stood, feeling something ages simmering within rise to a boil.

Yes, I thought, or Theba did, stealing from heart to vein to head. *More will die.*

Even as I felt myself ready and wanting to unleash some judgment upon the killers below, Gannet locked my arms against my sides, forcing me to look at him.

"Eiren, no. You can't. You have to get out of here. Find Paivi."

He kissed me but it wasn't enough to bring me back to some part of myself before he was thrusting me away, his keen eyes on my face, his mouth bright with blood where I had bitten him. I saw the fires flare there, shock and pain and something more.

When I spoke again, it wasn't me, or was some part of me I didn't recognize.

"You said you would fight. *Prove it.*"

I felt the cold anger rising in me again, blotting out the heart of me that might have heeded him. There was a tremor in my bones that was less fear of what waited for me below, and more vengeance born of what had been woken within.

I did not wait to see if he would follow.

CHAPTER TWENTY-FOUR

Below was chaos. There was a tangle of mad limbs and shredding clothing as everyone who had been in the opera house tried desperately to get out. The cries for help, the howls of terror, the weeping and wailing, seemed to me a great and terrible music. At first I was tossed about in the panicked crush, but then the opera goers weren't just trying to flee, they were fleeing from me, too. My body pulsed with heat and light. This wasn't the sparking, ineffectual lightning I had unwittingly conjured in Re'Kether, not the heady whipping of the sea near Cascar, nor the wild, impulsive flame triggered by Kurdan's attack in the Rogue's Ear. This was far, far more dangerous. I felt in me volatility but a dread control, too, violence a tool that I could lift and use at the moment of my choosing.

I was the weapon and the wielder, both.

I walked toward the stage, unimpeded as a funeral procession despite the chaos that surrounded me. I didn't feel my feet, my hands, my head, but felt instead that I was a living flame, ready to scorch, to swallow, to purge. There was no room in me for horror, only ruthless will. The attackers had not halted their slaughter, perhaps had not believed I would come, and when I reached the stage I was confronted by the slick reflection of blood in the brazier light. There was more pooling on the stage than seemed like could have come from only one woman, or even ten. The fleeing citizens of Jhosch still swelled and shrieked at my back, and I searched for the ones that had called.

Though I knew it was all, *all*, who had been waiting for me.

"You wanted me?" I screamed, my monstrous roar shredding the wild sounds issued by the masses. Did it grow quiet, or was it only a prescient pulse of silence to come? I leapt to the stage, vision black, seeing all of the scrambling, shrieking bodies as they would be soon: still, blackened, condemned to ash.

"Eiren!"

Gannet's voice was a bright string picked in disharmony, and I raised my hand as though I could swat the sound away. Still my eyes were drawn to study individual faces, and I shut them quickly. I did not want to see his face in the crowd. I did not need him. Not now. I could still taste his blood in my mouth, and I wanted more.

I opened my eyes just in time to confront the hooded figure who swooped near to me, those behind standing their ground amidst the broken bodies of their victims, the backdrop of those who still sought to escape them. The foremost figure rushed me with a wicked blade, ready and wet, and I grabbed the wrist where it had been sheathed, grinning as the figure collapsed to their knees with a howl of pain and outrage. Smoke poured out where flesh met flesh, and it was not I who burned. The others stopped, hesitated, began to step backward.

But I did not need to be close to finish them all.

"Eiren, don't—there are things you don't know!"

Gannet's voice again, and this time I saw him, launching himself onto the stage and slipping as I had done in the standing blood. Already it thickened as it cooled. I didn't want to wait but his eyes, wide and steady behind the mask above a mouth fighting hard to keep from curling in terror or horror or both, gave me pause. Behind him I saw more familiar faces fighting toward us, faces set in desperation. Morainn. Her parents. Antares.

But it was Gannet I addressed.

"What more is there to know? You wanted this. A killer. Ambar worships death, why should I not give them what they want?"

I felt a strangled cry that this wasn't so, this wasn't what *I* wanted. I didn't want to be the murderous Theba I had seen upon the stage, a young woman who was dead now for having played such a part. Neither was it enough simply to be Eiren. Not for these people.

But not for me, either. Eiren was powerless, hesitant, guilty, and I crushed her even as I forced the hooded figure, still whimpering, aside.

"I need you to know the truth." He came no nearer but was heedless, too, of the hooded figures that advanced upon him. It was Antares who rushed them, and I raged, for these deaths were meant to be mine. Great gouts of flame were squeezed between my fists, illuminating the depths of Gannet's eyes. He did not shrink from me. He was a fool.

But I was still listening.

Gannet held my eyes, his own reflecting the brawling forms before him. "What we have kept from you, we have kept from everyone. I need you to know that you are not the first."

I cooled, only a fraction, searching his face. There was nothing there, only images like the ones on the stage, blood and murder.

"*What?*" My voice was as deep as stone, as sure as a rock fall. I shook and the world shook with me. I sensed an eagerness in Gannet to be rid of this weight, and though he came no closer, he leaned forward slightly, as though his head were heavy with it.

"I told you that we have been waiting for you, for Theba, for a very long time, but this isn't true. You are not the first icon of Theba, but the *nineteenth*."

I gasped. I might have gathered all the shadow in the room into my mouth, making it impossible to breathe or speak. Gannet took advantage of the opening in the fighting and my shock to tackle me, his arms gathering me to him and immobilizing me in the same moment. Tenderness and control. The instant he touched me I was flooded with knowledge, what he had learned in his own lifetime and the lifetimes of icons before him.

"Each and every one, murdered in her infancy, or soon after," he whispered, holding me tightly, and I saw with crippling detail the broken bodies of babes, swaddled still or on their first legs, hair dark as earth or light as candle flame. "Her will to live again no doubt drove her to Aleyn."

I could not listen, could not breathe, was for a moment neither Theba nor Eiren, living instead in the last memory he had shared with me: a girl grown enough to be called such, her features showing the distinct promise of beauty in adulthood. Her throat was cut as neatly as if a thread had simply bit into her neck, and a woman held her, wailing. There was no sound in the memory, only their faces, one forever frozen, the other desperate and torn.

"She was my aunt. Or she would have been," he said, and I wondered I could even hear him, over the screams of the dying, those that stayed to mourn them, those who could not or would not run. Behind Gannet his family and many guards rallied, more heretics circling. Their hearts were pounding, their heads swimming, and I was dashed about with every rogue thought, every bloody memory. They'd known. They'd all known. The last icon of Theba, the child, her wailing mother was the king's sister. An aunt and a cousin Morainn had been robbed of, just as she had been robbed of her brother. A king who had been twice cursed: a niece and a son. But he had surrendered to it, just as Gannet had, just as they all did.

It was too much.

"This changes nothing."

I pushed Gannet away from me, oblivious to the force I had shown until he stumbled back hard, tripped over the broken body of a heretic, or a player. It didn't matter. All were guilty. Icon or assassin, idiot or sage, they had stolen from so many all the sufferings and joys of a true and full life, and I wanted to do the same to them.

My face was flooded with color, blood pumping hot and high like a river pulsing at its banks after a wild rain. I couldn't deny now the edge of Theba in my anger, the excitement, but this served only to drive me to greater fury. Were it not for her, for them, I could have been simply Eiren, a sister and daughter, not a leader but a follower, living a quiet life instead of this wrecked one.

If this was it, if this was all I could be, I would wreck it completely.

If Gannet had any sense, he would run. There was no room in my heart for longing for him, only the horrors at hand.

"Don't get in my way."

I didn't address any of them, not directly, and I briefly considered opening Colaugh's mind as I might crack the rind of a melon, spill the insides and sort them for myself if there were more secrets to be had. There was a flicker of zealotry on his features, but my rage doused it as easily as a candle flame. When the nearest guard raised a spear against me, the point softened and dropped to the floor with a single hot breath.

"Please, Eiren, don't," Morainn shouted, racing forward with soldiers at her back too stunned to stop her. She had none of her brother's skill, but she knew me. She knew what I meant to do. "You're not like Theba. If there is a terrible thing *we* have done it, waking her in you."

Her breath came fast, her doubt and her fear as plain to me as they would've been in the minds of any of my sisters, my brother, my parents. She had a place in my heart, just as they had. I knew what she needed in the same way that I had known as a girl when Esbat had a nightmare and wanted waking, when Lista needed most to be told she was pretty, when Jurnus needed an ear for his boasting, and when my father wished he had been a better man, a better leader, a better father. I wanted to comfort her, and I wanted to tell her about Gannet's kiss, his hooded eyes, his hands, but I burned up instead over the flash of knives on the stage, the memories Gannet had shared; they were knitted together in my memory, a tangle of beauty and blood.

I couldn't give her what she wanted, couldn't have what I wanted, either. Not the sister, not the brother. Theba had claimed my heart, and everything else besides.

The figure I had cast aside earlier had been crawling away, and my strides were so long, stretching, unnatural to reach their prone body. I lifted them up and tore the hood away to look straight into Imke's eyes, shining with the desperation that comes before death. A chill passed through me as I saw her draw the little knife, her movements calculated, expert. Her lips were set in a thin line but in the corners there were shadows, and like a child wandering into a darkness that hosts more monsters than any story, I followed them into memory. She had been working against me, against the royal family, for a very long time. The intelligence she and Kurdan had supplied the heretics had painted me weak, malleable, unworthy. A perverse imitation of a smile splintered my lips. When I spoke, it was my voice, my will, my want to hurt that left my lips.

"Do not presume me as weak as the children that have died at your hands," I said softly, and my mouth tasted acrid, like smoke. I thought I might rub my hands together and build a fire between my palms. Imke's look was one of fearlessness and fervor. My bones were grinding to keep from extinguishing her, but Imke alone would not do. She hadn't operated alone, and wouldn't die alone, either.

The heat that threatened to cook me in my skin I expelled, and it started first smoldering at my feet, waves of heat passing off of my hands. This was more than the manipulation that Gannet had shown me, more than firing a spark that existed already. I grew the fire as though from my own gut, bellowing forth like a volcano all of the anger and ash of rage enough for all of the lives cut senselessly short.

"You were foolish to underestimate me," I muttered, shouted, stormed, my body racked as flames poured off my skin. I didn't see Morainn or her parents or the soldiers, merely the blur of bodies as they rushed away from me. In that moment I didn't care for their lives, nor did I spare a thought for the hordes that still crushed against each other below, neither their bodies nor minds fleet enough to escape the wave of flame that crashed against the floor of the opera house. Their screams did not reach me, for my ears and mind were crowded with fury, with the faces and cries of the players, the babes who had not grown as I had, to be able to do what I could. I would be a force enough for them all.

I was party to Imke's death, though, because she was nearest, because I pressed my burning hands against her face, feeling her features bubble and fail against the heat, losing all human shape. The thrill, terrible and dark, filled me, and I stepped over her body to face the fleeing crowd. They disgusted me; this land disgusted me—what it had been and what it had become. I would start here. I would cleanse what had been sullied.

Smoke belched from my ears and mouth, flame roiling from my hair and fingertips, whipping like lashes on the ground and in the air around me. Even as the fires raged under my control and all fled from me, one did not. I sensed Colaugh's mind, his triumph, his exultation, *his* plans startlingly and suddenly clear to me. Colaugh had known Imke's face, her motives and deeds, hers and a score of others. He had failed to quell the heretics' rebellion, and he had stayed his vengeance until now because he had lacked the tool required to deliver that vengeance: me.

With that knowledge, the fires failed as surely as if the air had been sucked from the room. I stood a lone and trembling woman amidst the smell of seared flesh and smoldering stone, the screams of the fleeing and the pained silence of the dead or dying. My vision blurred and I couldn't focus, couldn't return to myself. What I'd done I'd wanted to do, but I had been pushed, manipulated, and I couldn't, as Theba might have, dismiss myself from the human consequence of my actions. I was human, and I had wrought inhuman evils.

I spun about, senseless, my feet sliding on the char of what I hoped was discarded clothing. I ran, making for one of the stone openings that allowed for the artful passage of light into the opera house. It was too narrow, or was until I reached it, when the stone shrugged, crumbled, and parted for my exit. Outside I knew that I was recognized only by the gasps, the fall of bodies against other bodies, walls, the floor, anything to keep from being caught under my feet, grazed by my hands. I moved as fast as I might upon horseback or cart, feeling the fire that I had released from my body building in my lungs, a torture, but one I welcomed. I wanted to feel pain as keenly as I had dealt it. But more, I wanted this city and all of its simpering faith behind me, to leave behind me the Ambarians who would fall before me instead of fighting.

I heard something like shouting, felt it in my blood, and I knew he followed me. Gannet. I was at the gate to the city and I was alone; the guard all raced for the opera house, it seemed, since their greatest threat lay within Jhosch instead of without. I felt my heart in my ears, pounding with his call for me. I turned and stopped only long enough to see him, running without any aid of whatever immortal spirit inhabited him. I studied his lips, the warm curve that I had hoped to know better, the eyes guarded by the mask, and by extension the whole of his face. I had only one question for him then, and I didn't deign to speak it aloud.

Why didn't you stop me?

He had stopped far enough from me that I couldn't reach out to touch him, but it wasn't fear that stayed him, not like the others. I could have his reasons, could tear them from his heart as readily as his answer might have mine, but I didn't need to force him. Like all of the rest, he came willingly, he obeyed.

Would you have let me?

I was little more than the scent of ash and blood on the wind that I became, tearing out of Jhosch, aimed like an arrow for the territory beyond *Zhaeha*, the witch.

Eiren or Theba, there was no distinction for them, and no more for me.

As a girl, JILLIAN KUHLMANN preferred writing stories to admitting that there wasn't any such thing as fairies or actually mustering up the courage to talk to boys. She likes to read, a lot, and wear red lipstick. She maintains an untidy house, a husband, two baby girls, and a wicked costume collection in Cincinnati, Ohio.

Visit her on the web at **www.jilliankuhlmann.com**

If you want to follow Eiren on her journey
into the mountains, then don't miss

THE
DREAD
GODDESS

The next installment in the Book of Icons series.

Available wherever books are sold.
Pick up or download your copy today!

Printed in the USA
CPSIA information can be obtained
at www.ICGtesting.com
JSHW031704140824
68134JS00036B/3509

9 781682 307182